THE DOGS

THE DOGS

A NOVEL BY

Robert Calder

Delacorte Press/Quicksilver Books

Library of Congress Cataloging in Publication Data
Calder, Robert.
The dogs.
I. Title.
PZ4.C144Do   [PS3553.A3949]   813'.5'4   75-37568
ISBN 0-440-02050-6

FOR
MICHAEL and JOYCE PERKINS
who have never been equivocal

THE DOGS

CHAPTER 1

THE sun was vigorous and the air tangy, the leaves were new. It was a day for poignant response, but Bauer couldn't rise to it: ennui was the enemy.

Students were lunching in the shade of a big oak. The architect had saved the tree as a visual anchor. It was counterweighted on a diagonal across the quadrangle by the squat, brick Tully English Hall. Two dogs lay among the students, heads resting between paws and eyes following the movement of hands to mouths. They lunged when scraps fell. Another animal wandered aimlessly. It sniffed and stopped to paw the ground, shied away from the occasional student who tried to coax it near.

In the center of the quad a black Labrador raced beneath a Frisbee. Each time the disc was thrown too wide or too far, the dog spurted after it, leapt and snatched it from the air and landed in stride, circled away with the prize held high. Two smaller dogs followed with envious yaps.

The Labrador slowed to tease them, then bowled them over with its shoulder, or streaked away again. It returned the Frisbee to one of the players and wagged its tail, charged off on the next throw.

Several dogs frequented the campus. Some were owned, most simply wandered from apartment to rented house, staying a while, and a few were vagabonds that appeared at intervals to accept a handout or raid a garbage can, or, less frequently, stand for a little affection. Last fall a yellow cur had bitten a faculty wife and her child. A state trooper came out and shot the dog and took it into Covington to be checked for rabies. The dog was clean, but still a county health officer arrived to address a student assembly on the issue of stray and ownerless dogs, which was a heated one in Covington. His visit had no discernible effect.

Bauer crossed the quad to Tully Hall, a two-story building that vaulted over a passageway. Ivy grew up its sides. Bauer's office was on the second floor. It had a tall window through which cheerful light flooded in the late spring and the summer. In winter, the sun moved to the other side and the office was awash in dim grayness. He'd painted the walls yellow, but it hadn't warmed the winter.

He took a stack of bluebooks from the end of a bookshelf and sat down at his desk to grade them, typing out a paragraph of comment on each one and stapling it to the inside back cover. This was an open conference hour, but he didn't expect anyone to drop in. Only half a dozen students from all his classes had sought him out the last trimester, and of those, one had been seeking therapy, not academic counsel. That was a joke, Bauer as psychological adviser; he feared the boy would open himself too deeply, that it would go out of control, and he recoiled from the possibility of responsibility. In the end he'd functioned as a sympathetic friend (though that was a stance; if anything, he was put off by the boy's self-pity). He didn't know whether he'd helped or not. The kid had dropped out.

He came to Lesley Burrows' book—she was a private, intense student—and remembered that he'd promised to speak to Farrell for her. He went over to the other wing. Farrell's door was closed. He knocked.

"Yes?"

Bauer opened the door and leaned in. Farrell, in jacket and tie—he was one of the few professors who wore them—was with a student.

"Excuse me. I'd like to see you when you have a minute."

Farrell seemed to weigh this. "All right," he said. "Wait in the hall, will you?"

"Sure."

Bauer lit a cigarette. No one paid any attention to the NO SMOKING signs, not even the janitors who had to sweep up the butts. He coughed. He'd quit, with difficulty, a decade ago, picked them up again when DiGiovanni had been arrested.

He waited fifteen minutes, half of them after the student had left.

That was Farrell's style. Alone, he'd tell you he had pressing matters, be so kind as to wait. If you telephoned, he was in the middle of something, and a day or two would pass before he'd return the call.

"Come in, Alex."

Farrell ran his cuffs and filled a pipe from a tooled humidor. He tamped and lit it and puffed until it burned evenly. Then he swiveled his chair to face Bauer. Behind him, gilded old editions of the Elizabethans and Jacobeans were carefully ranked on walnut shelves. Hung on the flanking walls were framed pages from the *Wintergreen Poetry Review*, of which Farrell was editor, inscribed to him by the authors.

"What is it?"

"I have a student named Lesley Burrows who—"

"Yes. She applied for English-H next term. I turned her down."

"She's qualified," Bauer said.

"You're the only one who thinks so. She barely scraped through her other classes."

"She's been out of school a while. She's still feeling her way."

"Are you feeling her?"

Bauer ignored him. "Look, she's bright as hell."

"We are talking about an Honors course," Farrell said. "She is not an Honors student. The answer seems clear, doesn't it?"

"No. She's well read, and she can write. She wants the course, it will be good for her and she can handle it."

"I'm surprised a student would invest any confidence in you. I once suggested to Conde that your background would make a lively focus for a class. It offers certain interesting moral and ethical reticulations, don't you think?"

"Not to anyone but me."

"Oh you're wrong there. The *New York Review of Books* mentioned you in conjunction with that case in Detroit. And in Philadelphia, the government has cited your testimony as part of their argument."

"I want Lesley Burrows in that class, Farrell."

"Firmness of purpose. Resolve. Those are admirable qualities, Alex. Continue to work on them: sometimes they can lend you integrity and strength of character. Not that I don't sympathize with you—it must be hellish to weigh yourself and learn you're wanting in the balance."

To find passion, to hold conviction, God how lovely that would be. He said, "You're an asshole."

"Possibly, but at least one of principle."

Bauer dropped two manuscripts on Farrell's desk. "These qualify the girl. If you don't think so, then I'll take it up with Pritchard."

He started to leave.

Farrell said, "I ran into Ursula in town yesterday. One thing I can't fault is your taste in women. We went for a drink. Should I say hello for you next time?"

"Sure, we know each other." Bauer closed the door behind himself.

Farrell's wife Hilary had pursued Bauer with the enthusiasm of a sportful porpoise when he came to Wintergreen. It was no particular flattery since nearly everyone without breasts excited her. This happily excused Farrell his own philanderings, which were many. As cocktail chatter, Farrell explained that he was married only in a technical sense—Hilary was his housekeeper, cook, and secretary, and whatever primitive pleasures she found for her simpleminded self were of no more consequence to him than the amusements of a domestic. Farrell devoted much energy to skirting the pit of bitterness that was his core—bitterness that Cambridge had rejected him in his graduate days, that there was no chair for him at Harvard, that his little book on Herrick had been panned by his peers.

Bauer's class was lively. This term he was teaching an American Lit course. He wasn't qualified, but they were one short in the department. Pritchard, the chairman, who could have retired years ago but who was hanging on for the single purpose of keeping the chairmanship out of the hands of Farrell, whom he detested, had told Bauer not to worry about it. "You're literate, right? You're intelligent, right? So read the good criticism and you can teach them as well as anyone. This is a survey course, that's all. Don't worry about it." And Pritchard had been right, which, in a way, disappointed Bauer. His apprehension had been a bright splash of color on the landscape of his malaise.

The class was reading *Moby Dick* and most of them liked it. There was some interesting argument, growing heated toward the end. Bauer was cheered. Emerson had bombed, save for a mild response to Transcendentalism, Hawthorne had bored them, and he didn't think Poe or Crane would be much to their taste. He had some hope for Twain.

At the end of the hour a handful lingered to keep at it, but they lost momentum before long, reluctant to spend their own, free time this way. They said *Goodbye, Professor Bauer* and *So long, Alex* as they left.

Kathy Lippman was the last. She approached his desk while he was closing his briefcase.

"That was really a good class today," she said. "You got everyone going."

Bauer smiled. "Thanks. It worked out."

Kathy Lippman was pale-skinned and had fine long brown hair. Her breasts were big and she was just slightly overweight. There was an ingenuousness about her. "I like the way you teach. I never thought I could get interested in these people, but you opened them up for me and I am. And I, well, I wanted to thank you."

She seemed to mean it. "I appreciate it," he said. "You're handling the material well."

That pleased her. "I've gone ahead and finished *Moby Dick*," she said. "I couldn't wait. But actually, from the first couple of pages I thought it was going to be a dull Christian sermon."

"Dull, no. But it is a sermon if sermons are statements of personal moral vision."

"When Ahab says, 'I now know thee, thou clear spirit, and I now know that thy right worship is defiance—' "

"Yes." It was too curt. She was wounded.

"Am I holding you up? I'm sorry, I just wanted to clear some things. . . ." Her voice ended in embarrassment.

"No," he said. "That's all right."

But she wasn't to be convinced. Or else she saw some value in being aggrieved. He found the speculation ugly of himself. "We'll get to it in class," she said.

"If we don't, make an appointment and we'll talk it over."

"Okay."

It wasn't enough. He was annoyed with himself. You could fuck students up by turning them away when they were excited by something. "Which way are you going?" he asked. "I'm heading past the Science Building."

"Okay. I've got some stuff to do there. I'll walk over with you."

They went down the stairs and out. Students were sunning in the quad. A group was playing cards, a few lazed reading books. Kathy was wearing perfume, some kind of musk base. It was pleasant.

"Where did you teach before?" she said.

"I didn't."

He was suddenly sorry he'd encouraged her. He had nothing to say about himself. He appreciated Wintergreen for one reason: it imposed a structure in which he had to speak and express ideas, even if they were the ideas of others. He had little to say from within his own being.

Wintergreen was a small nongrading school, a surrogate college, a kind of halfway house for the troublesome, lazy, or slow children of the academically oriented. The school accepted flunkouts, dropouts, chemical-eaters, freaks, social cripples, and the stunned and unable. Most left after a term or two and those who did come alive intellectually tended to transfer somewhere else to take their degree.

It demanded enough of Bauer, but not too much. When he was alone he listened to music or he watched television. He slept nine and ten hours a night. Sometimes he read detective novels.

"No?" Kathy said. "Oh that's right, I heard. You used to work for a newspaper or something."

"Yes."

They walked in silence. A boy followed Kathy with his eyes. She was attractive, Bauer realized. She moved with easy fluid coordination. There was a casual and healthy femaleness about her. Bauer became self-conscious. He was tall and gangly. The sections of himself seemed in uncomfortable alliance, necessarily vigilant over his next moves, hurrying into ragged cooperation to ensure that he could get around without banging into things or falling on his face. His hair wanted to hang down his forehead so he kept it short. He hadn't lost any, but it was graying, random strands here and there. He had a long, bony, boyish face. When he was younger women had wanted to mother him, and he'd traded on that often enough. He didn't like it now; there were no longer any boyish pleasures. He was thin, and at times he'd gone on months-long caloric orgies trying to hang flesh on his frame. He wore glasses. No matter what frames he tried, the glasses, on his face, made him look intense. That raised specific expectations in others. In the past he'd sometimes tried to struggle into the jacket of those expectations, but he was never successful, and it made him feel a poseur, and people became disappointed in him.

Kathy was comfortable in the silence. He thought he heard her humming. He wondered at it.

They came abreast of the Science Building. Kathy said, "Hey, do you smoke?"

"Yes," he said, perplexed.

She took a pack of cigarettes from her pocket and

shook out a joint, and then he understood. Lord, the gulfs between people.

"Here." She passed it with little attention toward concealment. "It's very good Jamaican, very up. Thanks for being terrific. You're real. Have a good time, see you Monday." She went up the stairs of the science building.

He looked at her ass. It was firm, tense even, beneath the taut fabric of her jeans. He imagined a softness of down at the base of her spine, a sharp line of definition at the bottom of her cheeks, where the thighs began. He became partly erect, an exclusively physical response. Germ plasm drove the body, the self was only a hitch-hiker.

He walked off the campus down Wolsey Road. His home was a mile away. He'd bought a ten-speed bike when he'd moved here—good for the heart and lungs, pleasurable use of the muscles—but he walked when the weather wasn't vicious, and even in the cold and rain, because walking consumed more time. The road followed the Macamook River on his left. Between road and river lay a strip of trees and scrub brush. There was forest on the right, broken by an occasional small meadow, and two little streams passed through conduits beneath the road to enter the river. Mountains rose in the four directions. Scattered clouds were moving in from the west and the falling sun tinted their underbellies pink.

Am I real? he thought. Kathy Lippman thinks so. She gave me dope to prove it. Getting stoned is homage to the real. Is that it? This macadam, the bark of the ash trees, those are real. The hawk or whatever it is up there. Flags, love, white whales and curved space. Squirrels in rut. Time. Sit on my face, Miss Lippman, and know the enamel reality of my teeth.

He looked for a distraction. There was nothing credible. He put a blade of grass in his mouth. He chewed, concentrated on the taste, and refused questions. He spat the grass out when it went bland, and finished the distance whistling peppy Sousa marches.

The prefabricated log cabin he rented came with six acres, one acre of which had been cleared of every tree, and it was in the center of that patch of nakedness that the cabin stood. Ornamental shrubs had been planted, but they weren't hardy enough for the climate and were always ailing, piebald with rusty dead needles. The cabin logs were clumsily joined. He'd had to chink them in places and along the ill-framed windows with insulation. Mice carried off pieces of it for nests. Like many others along the Macamook, the leach field of his septic system seeped wastes into the river. The county health board warned that this section of the river would soon be unsuitable for swimming or fishing, but, because of the expense, there was little support for a corrective program. A snowmobile trail had been cut through the nearby woods and machines roared over it through the winter shattering the silence and panicking wildlife. In March, a drunk had plunged through rotting ice atop the Macamook and drowned.

He put his key in the lock. On the other side, Orph's tail banged against the floor. Bauer opened the door and Orph jumped up. His forepaws struck hard on Bauer's chest and knocked Bauer back against the jamb. Orph's tongue washed out over Bauer's face.

"Off!"

The dog hopped before him with anxious whines of pleasure, paws striking.

"Off!"

Bauer brought his knee up into Orph's chest. Someone had told him that this was the way to stop a dog from jumping. Do it hard, don't worry, you won't hurt him. But Bauer was afraid for the animal and unable to slam into it. Besides, he enjoyed the dog's exuberance at his return.

So he gave Orph only a token blow; it had nearly become a game—jump, bump—jump, bump.

"Down," Bauer commanded. He had to repeat it several times before the dog lowered itself reluctantly to the floor, more a poised crouch than a down. "Someday I'm really going to have to work with you," Bauer said.

He set his briefcase aside and went to one knee beside the dog. Orph broke his down with a swishing tail. The corners of his mouth pulled back in a grin and he laved Bauer's face and neck, burrowed his muzzle under Bauer's arm and wriggled happily. Bauer scratched the dog behind its ears and rubbed its heavy shoulders and chest.

"Good boy, that's my boy. Yes, I'm happy to see you, too. That's my good dog."

Strangely, Orph, a dog, an alien, had become the fixed point, the only sure referent—with his sons, hurtfully, his at intervals and no more—his handhold. He loved the animal. It gave him unaccustomed joy.

They had lived together more than a year now. Bauer had found Orph as a pup hanging back in the darkness around a downstate gas station. The pup had drawn away when he'd approached, but held its distance. He'd hunkered and called to it. It approached, hesitated, withdrew, neared again, circled partway around and lay down and looked at Bauer mournfully.

"It's okay," Bauer said. "No one's going to hurt you. You're a good pup, come here now."

Bauer's wrists rested on his kneecaps. He let his hands dangle and he rubbed his thumbs softly against his fingertips as he reassured the dog. The pup inched closer and finally stretched to lick Bauer's hands. He touched it. It shuddered. He spoke gently, caressed it, then moved his hand under its belly and lifted it. The pup squirmed and snapped at him. "It's all right," he said. "Calm down." He shifted it to the crook of his arm, touching and talking to it. It didn't try to bite again, but was tense, and its heart beat rapidly. Bauer walked back into the light of the arc lamps. The attendant was finishing up the windshield.

"Who's this belong to?"

The boy shrugged. "He showed up a couple of hours ago. He's been spookin' around in the shadows. Just a stray."

"He's a puppy."

"Yeah?" The boy stuffed the cleaning rag into his hip pocket. "The oil's okay. The gas is nine-sixty."

"Do you know anyone who's had a litter recently?"

"Uh-uh."

"Well." Bauer rubbed the dog's head. It looked up at him warily, but without fear. "What do I do with you, huh?"

"Take him along. You leave him here, he'll get hit by a car or someone'll shoot him."

"Shoot him?"

"This is deer country, man, and farm country. You ever see an animal that's been killed by dogs?"

"Jesus, he's just a puppy."

"Yeah, well they grow up to be dogs."

Bauer left his name and phone number—the boy said there was no point—and put the pup in the back seat. He didn't want it, but he was unwilling to leave it to be killed on the highway or shot. It curled on the seat and went comfortably to sleep. Once home, Bauer set it down on the grass. It relieved itself and he took it inside.

The cabin was a kitchen, a living room and three bedrooms. Bauer's sons slept in one of the bedrooms when they visited, he used the smallest for a den.

"What do you think?" He felt foolish addressing the animal.

The pup cocked its head up. Bauer bent and petted it. It wagged its tail and rubbed against his leg, then stepped away. It tried to lift its floppy ears, its brow furrowed comically. It sniffed the air. It walked about the living room pausing to stare at furniture, a rocking horse Bauer's son Jeff played with, a stack of books on the floor. It sniffed, pawed at a throw rug. The living room weighed, it went to the kitchen and evaluated it, then down the hall and into each of the bedrooms. Bauer followed, amused.

"Fussy little bastard, aren't you?" The pup glanced over its shoulder, and went on.

When it completed its tour and decided everything was in order, it returned to Bauer's room, picked up a slipper and carried it to the door, in which Bauer was standing, then past him and toward the living room.

"No," Bauer said. "No."

He reached for the slipper. The pup held tight.

"Come on, hand it over."

The pup braced its legs.

"Come on, I mean it. Give." Bauer pried the pup's mouth open, scratching a finger on one of the sharp milk teeth. He pointed to the slipper. "This is a no," he said. "Understand? A no. Good boy." He put the slipper atop a credenza.

The pup trotted back down the hall, appeared a moment later with his other slipper. He took that away, too. The pup resisted strenuously. Bauer went into his sons' room and got a rubber ball. He held it up for the pup to see. He said, "Okay, go get it!" and tossed it.

The pup went rigid. Its head snapped to follow the flight of the ball. The ball struck the floor. As it bounced up, the pup catapulted after it, clicked its teeth, leaped futilely in the air on the second bounce and pursued the ball headlong into the wall, careened off and went splay-legged and scrabbling across the slick plank floor. It pounced on the ball and sank its teeth deep. It tore a piece out of the soft rubber with a small growl of triumph.

"Very tough," Bauer said. "I'm impressed."

The pup ripped another piece, then stopped, seeming disappointed. It relaxed the pressure of its front paws, between which it had the ball trapped, and bunted it with its nose. The ball rolled away. The pup sprang after it, seized and dropped it, watched it bounce. The pup raced around the living room batting the ball with its paws, snarling in grandiose pretension and biting into it.

Bauer went to the kitchen and crumbled some chopped meat into a bowl, debated over a piece of cheese, then dropped it in. He filled a second bowl with water and set them on the floor. The pup was tired and resting on its side on the throw rug in front of the couch.

"Hey, pup," Bauer called. "Come here, boy. Come. Come on."

The dog lifted its head.

"Come on. Here. Come."

The pup stretched, and ambled over to the door.

"Food," Bauer said, though the animal didn't look desperate. It was outlandishly huge-footed, like a child in its father's shoes, heavy-boned and round with baby fat. Bauer rattled his fingernails against a bowl. "Dinner. Food."

The pup sniffed. It charged to the meat and began eating greedily. Bauer was amused by himself and the dog.

Later the dog tried to chew a book, then worked on a leg of the coffee table. Bauer dug through his closet for an old pair of hiking boots. He gave one to the pup, who settled down to gnaw contentedly.

He took the dog out a final time before closing the house for the night and, as it had done after eating, it promptly relieved itself. He spread a couple thicknesses of newspaper in a corner of the kitchen and brought a big bath towel in and folded it over to make a bed. The pup was asleep in the living room, its jaw resting on the boot. Bauer petted it. "Wake up, buddy." The dog opened its eyes. "Sorry, but we have to shut you in." Theoretically it was ridiculous to be explaining to the animal, but it felt natural and right. He picked up the boot and carried it to the kitchen. The dog followed. Bauer patted the towel and lay the boot beside it. The pup dropped down and gave the boot a perfunctory lick. Bauer petted the dog. "You'll be fine here. Get some sleep."

He braced a piece of plywood across the doorway with a chair. The pup watched without alarm. He turned off the kitchen light. The dog was not disturbed.

Bauer went to bed.

He woke early and lay feeling the gray burden of yet another day. He closed his eyes. He had no morning classes. He could sleep, and dream, for another few hours. He'd come to enjoy best in his life his dreams, where there was drama and intensity. Then he remembered the dog.

"Well hell." Waking seemed more attractive. He pushed back the covers.

The puppy was up. It sat in the center of the floor and wagged its tail when it saw him.

It had soiled the papers during the night, but at least had used them. "You're a smart little guy." Bauer dumped the paper and took the dog out. He didn't know how much puppies were supposed to eat, or when. He'd had a dog, briefly, when he was young, but remembered little. His parents had gotten rid of it because it had shed too much and barked a lot.

He dished out more chopped meat and cheese, and the pup devoured it all and licked the bowl. He showered and dressed. The pup investigated the house again, as if to confirm its judgments of last night, then trailed after him looking eager and anticipatory whenever he glanced at it or spoke. While he drank his coffee it circled restlessly around the table and gave him small sharp barks, as if it were expecting something.

Bauer looked through the lost-and-found column of the *Covington Freeman*. The pup wasn't listed. In the phone directory under veterinarians he found a Dr. E. V. Collier on the near side of Covington. He put the pup in the car and drove in.

The doctor was a woman, the E for Elizabeth. She was thirtyish, oval-faced, with shoulder-length dark blond hair and gray eyes. She wore a crisp white medical jacket unbuttoned over a skirt and sweater. Bauer had to wait an hour.

"You really should have called for an appointment," she said when she summoned him into the examining room. "Hi, pup," she said to the dog.

"Sorry. I didn't know."

"Well now you do." Her receptionist was out sick and she was growing irritable handling everything alone. She poised a pen over an index card. "Your name, please." She took his address and phone number. "Name and age of your dog?"

"I don't know. I found him. I just wanted to have him checked, find out what kind of shots he should have, get some feeding information."

She sighed and laid the card and pen down. "Okay. Put him up on the table."

Bauer lifted the pup to the slippery steel surface. The vet placed a hand palm down near the dog's head and let it sniff, then touched its shoulder. "Good boy," she said. She slipped her hand under its belly and raised it to a stand. She palpated its abdomen, listened to heart and lungs with a stethoscope, softly pried its mouth open and examined the teeth, took its temperature. Her touch was deft. She patted it on the head. "You're a very good boy." The dog regarded her calmly.

As she made notations on the card she said to Bauer, "What you have there is a purebred German shepherd, and a very good one. He's about four months old and probably bred from German stock. The Germans breed a heavier, more massive dog than Americans do. His conformation—that's the way he's put together, proportion, angulation, that sort of thing—is good. Something tore or bit a little piece from his ear, but it's healed fine. Hip dysplasia is the biggest physical problem with shepherds. You can't really be sure without an X ray, but these look sound to me. He's going to be a big dog. His dentition is fine, he's healthy and in good condition. A puppy needs a series of four triple-shots—that's distemper, hepatitis and leptospirosis—once every other week for two months. He's probably already had his, but personally I'd rather be sure. Double shots won't hurt him. The shots are ten dollars apiece, forty dollars for the series. It's up to you. He doesn't get his rabies inoculation until he's six months old. I can't tell about intestinal parasites, you'll have to drop a stool sample off. There's been a lot of heartworm around recently. I'd advise a blood sample. It's all up to you." Her tone was impatient.

"Look, I'm not a vivisectionist," Bauer said. "I like the dog."

She was startled. Then she gave him a smile. Professional, but still a smile. She took the curtness from her voice. "I'm sorry. I had a run of cases all this week of abuse, neglect, stupidity and outright cruelty. There are thirty million dogs in this country, and I'll turn in my license if more than five percent are owned by people who have even a remote idea of what a dog is or how to deal with one. I know a breeder who says, 'If my dogs were as dumb as half the people who come to my kennel, I'd have to put them to sleep.' It gets me down sometimes. But I am sorry for my abruptness."

Bauer had her administer the first of the DHL series and draw a blood sample. He made an appointment for the next shot. She gave him a mimeographed sheet of dietary information.

"He really is a nice little guy," she said by way of parting conciliation. "He's alert, very confident and self-assured for his age. Maybe too much. He's going to grow up bold and independent. If you stay on top of him, train him well and give him constructive outlets, he'll be impressive. But if you don't, you might have problems."

Bauer bought papers from the surrounding communities and searched the lost-and-found columns, but he was waking in the morning with growing pleasure over greeting the dog and beginning to appreciate its presence, the sense of another life in his house, and was surprised by its autonomy and minimal demands. He began checking the advertisements later each day, not wanting to find a claim of ownership, and by the end of the week, feeling he had discharged his ethical obligation, he stopped looking at all.

He decided that Orphan was as good a name as any. But that was too formal to roll easily from the tongue, and it soon shortened itself to Orph.

Bauer changed into Levi's and a sweatshirt while Orph waited with bright eyes and a tail half raised in anticipation.

"Okay."

Orph ran out of the bedroom and turned an excited circle in the living room. He went up on his hind legs, pawing at the door.

"Off. Goddamn it, Orph, stop it."

The door and framing were deeply scratched. It was beyond wood-puttying, Bauer would have to replace them when he moved.

Orph quartered across the yard with his nose down until he found a stick. He hurried back to Bauer and dropped it at Bauer's feet. Bauer threw it; the stick spun round and round to the edge of the woods. Orph raced after it, seized it as it struck and came loping back to Bauer. On the next throw the dog overshot, tore up the ground in a tight reversal and clamped the stick on the run. His teeth had made indentations in the wood. Bauer threw for a quarter hour. Orph's enthusiasm didn't falter and he still breathed without effort.

"Enough," Bauer said. "Let's go for a walk."

The forest here was mostly poplar, with some sycamore, pine and ash, an easy woods in this season. Later, nettles would spring up and choker vines would wind across the floor and around tree boles and into lower branches, like the webs of giant psychotic spiders, and it would be rougher going, but then it would offer the compensation of a sweat. They walked along a creek, whose water was cold and high with spring rains. Orph waded in and drank. He spent some time in the shallows snapping at a school of minnows that flitted about his legs nipping at the hairs. The minnows frustrated him and he barked, chopped up the surface with his teeth. Bauer smiled at him. Orph came out and nuzzled into Bauer for some petting. Satisfied, he crossed the stream to the opposite bank, shook himself.

After pacing each other a while, Orph veered abruptly and disappeared into the woods. He did that, catching a scent that intrigued him. He would course a rabbit or flush a covey of quail, tree a coon. Now and then he'd be gone for a few hours, and once he hadn't returned until the following morning, but usually he'd be back five or ten minutes after Bauer began to call.

The walk relaxed Bauer and gave him an appetite. He lit the oven and put in a big potato. He fed Orph. He poured Scotch over ice cubes and sat down to dial Ursula.

"Hello," she answered.

"Hi," he said. "It's me."

"Hello," she said, and waited.

"How's everything?"

"All right."

Depression creeped around him. Recently, she sounded as if he were stealing valuable time. "Good," he said.

There was silence.

"Are the kids there?" he asked.

"They're playing in the backyard."

He was disappointed. "Okay. Tell them I'll see them tomorrow morning then. We're still clear for tomorrow, right?"

"Yes. But they'll be next door at Janie's. I'm going away for the weekend and I have to leave early."

"You'll be back when I bring them home?"

"Yes. Sunday, five thirty."

"Would you like to have dinner some time next week, Wednesday or Thursday?"

She paused. "All right. Wednesday."

"You're on."

"But I'd like to eat in town."

When they saw each other, it was usually at his cabin. She never invited him to dinner at her house. She said it wasn't good for the children.

"Town?"

"I'd prefer it."

Reluctantly, he agreed.

He poured another Scotch after he hung up, and a little later another one. When the potato was softening, he put two pork chops in a frying pan and opened a can of corn and spilled it into a pot to heat. After dinner he poured another drink.

CHAPTER 2

A GUARD rounded the warehouse with a German shepherd at his side. The animal's leash bowed up to the guard's hand, the excess was taken up in coils and the stitched loop encircled his wrist. The warehouse was to their right, a parking lot to their left. Ahead, where the parking lot ended, woods began, separated from the warehouse by a lane of mowed grass.

They came abreast of the trees. The man stopped. The dog sat promptly, without command, and glanced up at its handler. The man reached beneath his jacket for his cigarettes. The dog looked about, unconcerned. The guard put a cigarette in his mouth and bent to a match.

A pair of men stepped from behind a truck in the parking lot. They wore bulky jackets and floppy pants and they carried clubs. The guard shook out the match. The dog sprang suddenly to its feet and whirled about rumbling deep in its chest. The guard spun. The men came rushing.

"*Fass!*" the guard said.

The dog lunged, hit the end of the leash and went up on its hind legs. Its broad leather collar dissipated the shock and restrained it without choking off its wind. The dog barked furiously; drops of spittle sprayed from its mouth. The men pulled up out of reach. The dog dropped to all fours and dragged the guard before he could brace, snapping at the intruders.

They broke to either side. The dog swung from one to the other through a ravening arc. The men feinted, but the dog was faster. The one nearest the warehouse swung his club. The dog went under it, then up for his arm. The man checked and jerked back. The dog caught his sleeve and ripped it from armpit to elbow, then released and bolted to meet the second man, who was rushing. The dog pincered him above the knee. He screamed and beat the animal's head and shoulders with his club. The dog snarled around its bite. It jerked hard and toppled the man. He shrieked and rolled into a ball covering his head with his arms. The dog let loose, slashed at his back, then reversed to attack the first man again.

The man turned and ran. The dog heaved on the leash and barked after him. The guard climbed the leash hand over hand, thumbed the release clasp and said, "*Fass!*"

The dog shot forward, flattening out. The man glanced over his shoulder, saw there was no escape, stumbled to an awkward halt and turned, pulling a handgun from his belt.

Booom! The thunderclap of a heavy caliber.

The dog didn't break stride.

The man fired twice more in quick succession. *Booom! Booom!*

The dog left the ground. Its jaws closed about the man's forearm. Its hind paws barely touched the ground and most of its ninety-five pounds hung from the studs of its teeth. It wrenched violently and brought the man crashing down. It ragged his arm, shaking its head like a hooked fish, rolling the screaming man across the grass.

The guard called: "Panzer, *aus!*"

The dog let go and backed a short step away. It remained focused on the man and emitted deep barks.

"Panzer, watch!" the guard ordered. Then he shouted to the man, "If you even blink hard, he'll climb all over you again."

He handcuffed the first man and marched him over to the dog. Panzer was growling but holding his distance. The guard retrieved the handgun and shoved it in his waistband. "Panzer. Sit, stay." He had the second man stand and put his arms behind his back. "Watch," he told the dog, and to the man, "You don't want to move."

"I'm a statue."

The guard handcuffed him and blew a whistle. An engine turned over in the parking lot. An open-topped jeep roared up and lurched to a stop. The driver wore a green windbreaker monogrammed BDI—Behavior Development Incorporated—over the heart, and a holstered sidearm. In the rider's seat was an older man with a peppery full beard, dressed in faded slim-cut corduroys and a pullover sweater. They hopped out.

The guard put Panzer in a down-stay.

One of the handcuffed men said to the bearded man, "I'm not going to work this mother without full padding anymore. He damn near broke my arm." A three-ply leather gauntlet was visible beneath his torn sleeve. It was part of a tunic whose collar extended up to armor throat and back of the neck. Beneath his pants, his legs were similarly protected, down to the tops of heavy boots.

His partner said, "He cut through to my thigh, I can feel blood there."

"Check in to the infirmary," the bearded man said. "Tell Dr. McGill to get me a report this afternoon."

The driver loaded the two men into the jeep under Panzer's watchful eye and drove them away. The dog would not have believed in the legitimacy of the exercise if the agitators had simply sauntered off.

The bearded man said, "He stayed too long on Harry's leg. Roy could have got to you if he'd been serious."

The guard shook his head. "No way. I worked him on a protest setup yesterday. He held eight guys at bay. You can check that with Dr. Tilson."

"If I'd been Roy, I'd have had you. There's no margin, none. And what about the gun? He's supposed to be retrieving them by now."

The guard shifted. "Well . . . we need a little more time on that."

"Why?" the bearded man demanded.

"He, he seems to, uh, be having some trouble with the feel of metal against his teeth."

"Is he rejecting it?"

"Not exactly."

"I'll give you three days. If he won't take it, and like a piece of steak, then I want to know. Three days."

"Christ," the guard said in frustration. "He's only twenty months. Already he's like a machine on the attack. He scores mid-nineties on obstacles and runs a maze like a computer. You can't beat him on an area search. What do you want, Superdog?"

"Exactly. Three days. Take him back to the kennel and settle him down now." The bearded man left.

The guard looked after him. Panzer read his trainer's emotions and growled. His hackles lifted. The guard dropped his hand affectionately on the dog's head. "I'd love to, boy, but we'd both be up the creek if I let you."

Dr. Chaim Mandelberg greeted them in the conference room of the stainless steel and glass building that was the installation's neural center. It was furnished with thinly cushioned Naugahyde chairs and couches, white Formica tables, and a dull coffee-colored carpet. The abstract wall lithographs were bland. The room was designed to discourage ease and minimize distraction.

There were two congressmen, the chairman of a Philadelphia behavioral institute, a pale severe woman from the Houston Space Center, a *Canidae* researcher from Johns Hopkins, an SPCA representative and two men from the Pentagon who wore civilian clothes poorly.

Mandelberg didn't know these people, wasn't interested in them, and was annoyed that he had to sacrifice time to them. Now and then some reference to Behavior Development's dog work appeared in a professional journal, piquing interest and bringing a request for consultation, which was palatable enough, but recently two silly and inaccurate articles in popular magazines had sparked accusations of animal abuse and a public outcry large enough to discomfit the increasingly image-conscious and appropriations-hungry Pentagon. A substantial amount of BDI's work was underwritten by that body, and when it felt pressured enough to pull the string, then BDI had to jump. The Pentagon had made it clear that Mandelberg himself, not a subordinate, was to give the briefing.

Mandelberg was the director of BDI's New England facility and its Canine Amplification Program. He was thirty-three years old, aloof, incisive, could concentrate to the seeming point of catatonia, and had a mind capable of intuitive quantum leaps as well as computerlike analysis. Emotions rippled him no more than a soft breeze did the surface of a pond, but he was known as a genial, open, down-to-earth man, a pose he had resentfully but painstakingly undertaken for reasons of social and professional pragmatism. Had he given any thought to the subject he would have discovered that he considered human beings little more than faulty manifestations of an interesting abstraction, gross corporeal analogs, and that discovery would have been noted and filed and left him wholly undisturbed.

A thirty-cup coffeemaker was plugged between two platters of finger sandwiches. Mandelberg poured himself a cup and smiled at the visitors. "Anyone else? Is everyone set up? Okay, fine."

He settled into a chair, crossing his legs and slouching some in the appearance of a natural casualness and said, "What I'd like to do first is give you a little background on the general nature of dogs. Every part of our amplification program derives from an understanding of that nature. The dog as we know it, *Canis familiaris*, is roughly 750,000 years old as a species, about the same age we are. There's still disagreement over his exact origins, but most likely he's either a descendant of the wolf, or of some extinct primogenitor that sired both wolf and dog. Whichever, he's a member of the genus *Canis* which also includes wolves, jackals, hyenas, coyotes and such. He is a predator —a very efficient one, I might add—and a pack animal. Like most group-hunting species, he has diverse and sophisticated relationships within his pack. It's this last quality that suits him so well for living with human beings: his human family becomes his surrogate pack.

"But forget for a moment that he's a pet. That role, in Western culture, is relatively recent—say the late eighteenth or early nineteenth century. Prior to that, through the 10,000 years he's lived with us, he was nothing but a simple tool. What small affection man felt toward the dog was the same prideful fondness he experienced over a fleet mount or a finely crafted weapon. The dog's primary function was to assist in hunting, which was the most crucial activity of the day. The animal excelled at this and was a highly prized, if not indispensable, adjunct. We see them hunting with men in Neolithic cave paintings, in medieval tapestries and Renaissance paintings, and as we sit here this afternoon there are literally several millions of them in this country and across the world who are owned solely for their utilitarian value in hunting—pointers, setters, retrievers, scent hounds, and coursing animals.

"As man became less nomadic and began to build compounds and villages, he turned the dog toward a second basic function: defense. The dog's powerful pack-loyalty, along with his predator's sense of territory, were ideal traits for this. He protected the village, he protected his owner's herds and person. From guardian, the logical extension was to warrior. War dogs are found in Egyptian hieroglyphics, and Assyrian bas-reliefs. The Persians used them, they fought under Greek handlers, and the Celts armored them in leather cuirasses set with knife blades. The Romans buried handler and dog together. Henry VIII sent them into the field and the conquistadores used them in South America. Gunpowder diminished their effectiveness in actual battle, but they continued to work as guards. Seventy thousand served in World War I, and they distinguished themselves in World War II, Korea and Vietnam. The first police dog corps was formed in St. Malo in the fourteenth century. Today there are more than 100,000 privately owned, fully trained attack dogs in the United States, and another ten million untrained 'pets' who are owned in large part for their innate protective capacities.

"Some few others work as specialists—avalanche and contraband detectors, and the like. The point is: the dog works. That's what he's been bred to do for millennia. The specific breeds we know did not evolve through accident or the whimsy of a privileged class. The dachshund isn't simply a funny-looking quirk of nature. He was bred long and low and with bold character expressly to rout vermin from their dens. Newfoundlands, at the opposite pole, were bred massive and strong, thickcoated, web-toed, and gentle, for plunging into cold seas after shipwreck victims who would cling to the animal's long coat while it towed them back to shore. Terriers were bred ever more aggressive and quick because they were used as rat killers.

"So now we have the dog as a social, pack-loyal, predacious working animal. He is also a creature of fairly high intelligence. He can conceptualize, in a rudimentary fashion, and is capable of some abstraction. He experiences emotions and can fall victim to a spectrum of neuroses and behavior disorders. Pethood has been disastrous for him. Such status is not inherently contradictory or inimical to him, but it has blinded the general population to his larger nature, to his reality. People view him as little more than a friendly, animated toy. As a direct consequence we have untold numbers of dogs whose nature is perverted, whose character is eroded, whose intelligence is confounded, who are denied constructive outlets for impulses which are very powerful, and who live in enormous frustration. Among other growing problems, both dog-bite fatalities and nonlethal assaults have increased dramatically over the last years, and can go nowhere else but up. This results from the assumption that the dog does not exist except as we desire him to, and from a rapidly degenerating gene pool. Most dogs are now being bred for those qualities usually prized in a pet, which means subservience and obsequiousness. In nature these are qualities found only in very young animals. They serve to protect the pups against aggression from older dogs. Whether through ignorance, for personal amusement, or to profit from the demand of chain stores, pet shops and puppy-palaces, the meaning is the same: Breeders are storming toward an end dog who will be infantile and regressive in mind and behavior.

"At Behavior Development, we're working to create what we consider the ideal dog. This doesn't mean a new species or even a fertile mutation. We're attempting to *maximize the native potential* of the dog. Our goal is a matter of degree. Beginning with a true comprehension of the animal, we seek to develop a strain of *utter* physical soundness, of the *highest* possible intelligence, of *thoroughly* stable temperament, of the *keenest* nose, and so on. We're approaching the problem from two directions: genetics and psychobiology. We do have a training program, but that's incidental, mostly an index of evaluation. We work exclusively with German shepherds. They're the best, most rounded, and perhaps most quintessential breed there is.

"Okay, genetics. But first—first I'd like another cup of coffee. Anyone else?"

KING'S INDIAN—KARLA VOM HANCKSCHLOSS
Alpha Litter, Age 4 Weeks
Abstract prepared by Dr. Lily Quick
Physical: Sound, conformation good, one female with overlarge head, washing of some nails to near gray, big-boned, deepchested, thicknecked, favoring classic German typology.

Vision: Good.

Hearing: Good.

Olfactory: Above average.

Sensitivity, Voice: Erratic, evaluation difficult at this point.

Sensitivity, Touch: One male, one female average; balance below average.

Intelligence: Average to medium high.

Responsiveness: Average to below average.

Alertness: Very high.

Curiosity: Average to above average.

Autonomy: Above average.

Aggression: Erratic, from average to above average.

Assertion: Above average.

Remarks: An interesting litter that warrants close monitoring. Heightened autonomy and boldness were desired from this breeding and seem to have been achieved. An unexpected bonus in apparent keenness of scent. Some minimal slippage in the high intelligence we've come to expect from Indian's progeny. Secondary goal was escalated alertness, and that is present. Sensitivity to human voice is worrisome—possibly erratic because of slow maturation, hopefully not to instability. Lowered responsiveness to handlers probably correlates with increased self-reliance. There appears also to be a greater emotional integrity than we have seen before (all but one of these pups withstood stressing procedures more easily than previous subjects, averaging 13.2% above usual maximums). Continued maintenance is indicated for the entire litter. I recommend standard socialization for four of the pups (to serve as controls and to ensure full trainability), but reduced contact (the minimum required to activate the personality and ensure later manageability) for the remaining three. I think it important with this litter to observe at least two or three maturing as undirected as possible.

Rhoda I's pups were seven days old; fat, furry caricatures of the dogs they would be, clumsy and squeaking, with blind rumpled little faces. They piled atop one another in Toby's cart. Toby talked to them cheerfully, though he knew they were too young to take real comfort from his voice.

Rhoda I had whined in her whelping pen when he'd loaded the pups. She was a skittish animal. The trainers called her a spook. She wasn't his favorite dog, but he felt sorry for her anyway. He'd reassured her and promised to bring them back right away. Toby liked all dogs—from quaking fear-biters through berserkers to the forlorn animals at the SPCA shelter. But he had preferences, and spooks were at the lower end. Rhoda I was the only dog with such a temperament at BDI. She was kept for her high intelligence and spectacular scent ability. Most of her pups were destroyed in a few months. Only one was still alive, Rhoda II, a bitch everyone was fond of, smart, a great tracker and with her father's—an imported Schutzhund III—solid, outgoing temperament.

Now and then a handler was bitten taking young pups from their mother, so sometimes they'd lock the dam away even though it was against regulations. Toby never did that; he thought it cruel. He'd never been bitten in his life, though he'd sweated it a couple times. Outside of the area guards—animals with a deep native sense of territory who had been taught to regard everyone but their trainers as enemies to be attacked on sight—he could handle any dog at BDI, and there were a couple of hardcases.

Toby wheeled the pups from the whelping area, which stood apart a little from the main bank of kennels, down a gravel path and through a break in a hedgerow into a two-story green cinderblock building; past the service elevator from which an attendant was pushing a gurney on which a drug-groggy dog with a bandaged leg was strapped, and into the first room on the left.

A rack of clipboards was mounted on one wall, a large plastic sheet marked with grease-pencil notations on another. There were a steel writing desk, two filing cabinets, and an open-topped metal drum with small containers riveted around the inner circumference of its mouth. Power cables ran to the bottom of the device, and to a simple control panel beside it.

"Hi, Bill," Toby said.

"Toby." The technician wore a hospital shirt. "Smiler's pups? Out of Rhoda I?"

"Yeah, that's what they are."

"Delta litter." Bill checked off an entry on the schedule sheet.

They removed the pups, which had been marked BDI's, notched, two days ago, and placed them in the drum containers. The pups whimpered. Toby stroked them. One tried to nurse at his finger.

"Okay," Bill said. "Two Gs for three minutes." He turned a calibrated dial and set the timer. "Here you go, gang." He depressed a stud.

The dynamo turned over with a clank, an electric whine rose, there was a *chunkk,* and the drum began to turn. Toby made himself watch. It was a penance he inflicted upon himself for participating in the work. The centrifuge brought twice the force of gravity to bear on the pups, pressing them against the outer walls of their compartments. Skeletal structures came into relief, they struggled for breath, their terrified cries were audible above the noise of the machine. Toby let his eyes go out of focus, saw the spinning tub as a shiny blur with a ribbon of black and silver. *No, no*, he thought, *you must watch.* He ticked off the seconds in his mind, tightening as the number mounted, and when he reached 180, and as the machine disengaged, and the sound of the motor faded, the drum slowing to a gradual stop, he exhaled and unclenched his hands.

The pups were crying. Most had voided their bladder and bowels. Unsteadily, some tried to stand. One was shuddering violently, another lolled drunkenly on its side. Squinting at them, Bill jotted quick notes on a clipboard. "They're all yours," he said. "Take 'em back to mama."

Toby lifted the pups gently. He crooned to them. They piled atop one another in the cart whimpering and pawing.

When Toby wheeled the cart back up to the run, Rhoda I pressed her nose through one of the diamond spaces in the chainlink and whined. The pups called to her. She barked and went up on her hind legs. Toby had trouble keeping her in when he opened the gate. She put her paws on the cart and ducked her head, began licking the pups. Toby got them out. Rhoda sniffed each carefully, as if to assure herself they were truly hers, and all there. Then she relaxed and lay down to feed them. The pups shouldered each other for her dugs. Rhoda began licking them clean of the feces and urine they'd soiled themselves with in the centrifuge. Toby wetted a rag in her water dish and helped her.

"So in the end," Mandelberg said, "there's nothing truly innovative in our genetics program. Where we differ from other breeding programs is in the number of traits we want to fix. It's substantially higher than has been undertaken before, and so the difficulties are commensurately greater, the problems more complex. I'd say we're about halfway home. We've come up with some outstanding specimens, but we're still four or five years away from breeding true with confidence.

"My personal excitement lies in what we're accomplishing in psychobiology. This work breaks down into three general categories—stress, stimulation, and forced expansion. Forced expansion is simply pushing the dog to the boundaries of its physical and mental capabilities. An athlete's regimen is a good analog—squeezing out that extra ten percent, then an additional five, then the remaining two, and so on. Limits can't be known until they are reached. For this, our obstacles are higher, our crawlpipes longer, our exercise routines and training more demanding. These programs are carefully monitored to ensure that no dog is pushed too far. They ask everything the animal can give, but no more.

"Stimulation begins as soon as the pup's sensory faculties and mental processes are functioning on more than a basic level, about ten days, and continues up to the age of eighteen months, at which point a dog may be said to be intellectually, hormonally and physiologically an adult. This includes introduction to engaging novel situations, various forms of play, and light puzzle-solving. We provide him with an interesting environment that encourages his active physical and mental involvement.

"Our stress program is the most promising and unique. It begins when the pup is one week old, is applied most heavily during the next seven weeks, and continues in an abating form to the age of six months. We've found that there's little benefit to be gained after that. With our own pups, anyway; we've worked with older inexperienced animals, up to three and in one case four years old, and gotten positive results, but not of a level to justify the effort. Stress itself is neutral. It can be either destructive or constructive, depending on the amount brought to bear. Apply too much to any organism—man or beast—and exceed its threshold, and you'll break the organism. Overuse physical stress, you cripple the subject—if you put too much weight on a bone it will snap. Overdo psychological stress, the end is psychosis—if you totally isolate a man long enough he'll go mad. But controlled stress is a strengthening factor. It's precisely what you do to your muscles when you exercise, gradually forcing development, realizing additional potential each time. Psychological stress directly parallels this, only what is being strengthened and actualized is character. That comprises mental integrity, adaptability, intelligence, and emotional texture. We use several methods: a centrifuge, exposure to temperature extremes, startling lights and noises, insoluble mazes, rooms with vibrating floors and moving walls, and so on. The results have exceeded our expectations. We have some truly phenomenal dogs here—nothing bizarre, not 'thinking' animals, or freaks, but dogs who function at peak capacity in terms of innate canine abilities, which are sufficiently impressive in themselves."

On the tunnel range a fourteen-month-old bitch stopped, dipped its head, raised it, then dipped again. Its forehead creased.

"Go on," the handler said. "Let's go, girl."

But the dog felt an expanding hollowness in its chest, a vague sense of absence. Its tongue dried.

The handler urged it a second time, and reluctantly it stepped forward, then suddenly scuttled back.

It whined and pawed.

"What is it, huh?"

The handler dropped to a knee and probed the grass. His fingers lipped a small ridge in the dirt. He worked both his hands under it and pulled. A six-foot square of ground tilted up on bearings to reveal a deep, shadowy hole. Man and dog peered down. The dog drew back.

The man hugged the dog, petted it lavishly. "Good girl, you found it! Good girl!" He fished a chunk of dried beef from his pocket and gave it to the dog, who swallowed with a pleased wriggle of its shoulders and a wagging tail.

A young male was working ten yards in front of its handler in the woods behind the warehouse. Coming up on a hanging vine loop, it sat and began to bark. The handler advanced, patted it on the head, told it it was a good dog, and to stay. He snipped the vine in two with wire cutters and pushed the ends aside. He heaped the dog with praise and gave it a piece of dried beef.

He waited until the dog finished, then pointed and ordered, "Go out."

The dog moved ahead with a long confident stride, a touch of the cavalier's attitude. It traveled a hundred yards, concentration dimming as it found everything in order and began to focus on a pleasant tingling of its skin, an inchoate anticipation of the wire-brush grooming it would receive later.

It failed to see the thin tripwire stretched through the undergrowth. Flash powder exploded with a harmless but loud *Wumph!* and a bright flare of light.

The dog yelped and dropped to the ground, ears flat against its skull. It shook.

The handler ran up. "Shame! Bad dog! Shame on you." The dog hunched its head into its shoulders and squeezed its eyes nearly shut. "Shame! If that was a real mine, you'd have been blown to bits. Shame on you!"

Two miles from BDI, on a stoney patch of land which held scent poorly, and which the corporation rented from a farmer, a handler worked an eighteen-month-old male. The leash was twelve feet long and the dog wore a tracking harness. A mile-long scent-trail had been laid twenty hours earlier, eight hours beyond the optimum limit even on ideal terrain.

The handler was bored. This was a good dog, with a superb nose. The handler knew it could handle the exercise easily, but his director had insisted he run it anyway. The handler carefully masked his boredom, concerned lest he depress and blunt the animal.

The dog followed the scent to its end, a canvas knapsack with the smell of the man who'd laid the trail, seized the sack and barked happily. The handler roughed the animal with affection, then unsnapped the leash and threw sticks for it, a game good scent dogs usually enjoyed. He decided to go over his director's head and request an exercise that would truly tax this dog and let it shine, as it deserved to do.

Entering the canteen, Cindy Falk and Ron Schlegel passed an exposure cage in which a five-week-old pup huddled in a corner, thick saliva on its jaws. Half a dozen pups were similarly caged around the room, part of the stress program. Dogs became anxious in close confinement, particularly young ones. Opaque cages mitigated this some by offering a cave sense of security, but open-wire ones, like these, made them feel not only trapped but vulnerable. Speaking to or otherwise comforting a pup in an exposure cage was prohibited. The cages were placed in high-movement areas around the installation, and sometimes taken to the parking lot of a nearby shopping center or to the high-school gym field.

Ron bought a fresh-ham sandwich and French fries, Cindy got pie and coffee. They went to a table and sat on molded plastic chairs.

"The motivation's all wrong with food reward," Cindy said, picking up the conversation again.

Cindy trained BDI's dogs for obedience and attack. Ron worked on intelligence testing. They were nearly, but not quite, lovers, and it was the little remaining gap that caused Ron, helplessly, to argue with her more than he thought tactical.

Ron used beef chunks to get his dogs to work. He was trying to persuade Cindy it was the best method.

"Hell," he said, "what more basic motivation could you have? Food is survival. Every cellular impulse he has pushes a dog toward wanting to eat."

Cindy shook her head, swirling her hair. "It's inferior.

Look, in obedience training you don't just run the animal through routines until they become habit. You want him to *think*, to *understand* what's required and concentrate on the exercises. He does this because one, it's an outlet for his intelligence and lets him strut his stuff, and two, and more important, it allows him to please his trainer, the love object, the Alpha wolf, the leader, who gives him approval and affection for doing it right. With food rewards all he thinks about is his gut, and he doesn't focus on his work. And *you* end up having to carry around a pocketful of goodies all the time, because if you can't toss him a reward after a command a couple of times, he's not going to trust you, and you're not going to be able to trust him. That's for obedience. For attack-work, forget it. The motivation there is strictly pack-defense, loyalty and love. The last thing he's interested in is a snack."

"That's a value judgment. You've got nothing but feelings to support it."

"That's a statement of fact," she said with a little anger.

"I'll tell you hard, true, and indisputably: I couldn't get more than a ten-percent effort out of my dogs without a food reward. That's bedrock biology, baby, and there's no way around it."

"If you'd look further than the door of your own little closet you'd realize you don't spend enough time with any one dog to build more of a relationship than you have with the cashier at a drugstore. And without food why else would a dog try to run a maze or differentiate between a triangle and a circle? Those are as unnatural and meaningless to him as a Rembrandt."

"You really are bullheaded, you know? Just because you're good at one end of a leash, you decide you're an expert. What do you really know about the canine nature, huh? I mean where did you put in your graduate work, or even undergraduate for that matter?"

"At one end of a leash, you donkey." She threw down her napkin and stood up. "And if you *scientists* would spend a little time at the same place, or even bother living with a dog, you could cut the budget in half and learn more in five months than you have in five years." She turned and marched off.

Ron looked after her. Unhappiness descended over him like the shadow of a swift cloud. He was supposed to take her to a movie after work. She'd still go, probably, but it was clear that tonight was not the night she would turn back the covers for him.

KING'S INDIAN—KARLA VOM HANCKSCHLOSS
Alpha Litter
Summary prepared by Leonard Atwood

Of the seven pups in this litter, one male was lost at age fifteen weeks and remains unaccounted for, one male and one female were euthanized at thirty-two weeks, one female at forty weeks, and one male at fifty-two weeks. The remaining male and female were retained for breeding and further observation, named respectively Hector and Benny's Baby.

The litter was physically sound, with a few minor conformation flaws. Sensory perception was good, with scent ability above normal. Intelligence average to somewhat above. Alertness and stress tolerance exceptionally high, curiosity above average. This was a uniformly bold and independent litter, the major goal of this breeding. However, there was disappointing instability in temperament. In the opinion of most who worked with this litter (and I concur) this instability did not derive from character flaw, but rather was the manifestation of a certain indifference to human beings, as if the handlers were simply another part of the environment instead of the focal point.

Responsiveness to humans—play and willingness to train—was inconsistent and appeared primarily determined by the mood or desires of the dogs. Handler approval and affection were not of special significance to them. Correction for misbehavior had minimal effect, food rewards were enjoyed but would not motivate them with reliability. Standard obedience work was mastered, but not enjoyed, and the animals were frequently resistant, sometimes strenuously. The dogs were strongly assertive and capable of large aggression, though they generally restrained this.

The breeding was thoroughly successful as regards desired independence. But the indifference and erratic responsiveness toward humans—possibly correlative with heightened autonomy, especially when viewed against the dogs' preference for activity and relationship with their littermates and other dogs—is an atavistic personality trait and definitely contraindicated in our program. There was some difference, but not appreciable, between the four pups who were fully socialized and the three who received diminished socialization. Both Hector and Benny's Baby are from the former group. These two dogs should be bred with an eye toward retaining their autonomy, but counterweighting it with increased responsiveness.

Playing with the pups was the part Toby liked best. They were removed from their dams to individual kennel runs at seven weeks. Seven to sixteen weeks was the critical socialization period. It was the time of greatest emotional and psychological sensitivity, in which a dog formulated the basic attitudes and mental structures that would dictate his behavior patterns through his adult life. Left alone with other dogs, he would always live more harmoniously with dogs than people. Removed from his littermates but inadequately socialized, he would never be fully compatible with either humans or dogs.

Behavior Development's canine population varied between 150 and 200 animals, and there were usually two or three litters undergoing socialization. Toby spent most his afternoons with these pups, taking them one or two at a time to a large play cage where he stroked and scratched them and rolled them over and tickled their bellies, played tug-of-war with pull-rings, tossed balls and squeak toys for them. He talked pleasantly to them, complimented them, told them who they were, spoke of his life and matters of interest to him, pointed out the shapes of clouds.

Toby was twenty years old. He was spidery, darkhaired, and had a long face with large, soft brown eyes. He was a quiet boy. People confused him, and when he mustered the courage to talk to them, his throat grew thick and words fled his mind like birds scattering at the jump of a cat. He rented a furnished room from a nice widow in town, Mrs. Harris. Her son had been killed in Vietnam and he lived in the boy's old room. He helped her with the heavy housework and kept the yard in trim, and after he'd been there a few months she told him he didn't have to pay rent anymore. He gave her some money each week for food. He had the run of the house. She cooked, and he ate with her and her daughter. The daughter was homely and overweight. She'd seduced him shortly after he rented the room and she stole into his bed once or twice a week. She was demanding and she frightened him, but it seemed to work all right, once he'd gotten used to it.

He'd always been comfortable, and happiest, with animals. Any kind. He couldn't understand why other people weren't, and so rarely knew how to deal with one. All you had to do was get close to them, look at their eyes and the way they held their bodies, and relax, and then you'd begin to feel what they were feeling, not exactly, because it was always fuzzy, like fog swirling in a forest, but enough to know what to do, and then you did it, slowly and with care, changing as you felt them change, and then they would understand you, and you could get along and do whatever it was you had to do together. It was best with dogs. Clearer than with any other kind. Often he could actually talk with them. Not in words, more like shifting weights, with his hands on them, their touch in some blackness of his mind, but talking, and they understood one another. Sometimes the understanding was simply that they wouldn't transgress upon each other's rights, but that was as good and deep as anything else.

Toby had wanted to be a veterinarian. He'd spent five years getting through high school, and even then it baffled him what the schooling had been about, and none of the veterinary schools he applied to accepted him. His counselor finally managed conditional entrance to one in New Hampshire, but he couldn't read the books and the school had dropped him after one semester. He came back home and felt lucky to get a job with BDI cleaning kennels. A supervisor spotted his talents early. They put him to working with pups, and Toby was happier than he'd ever thought he would be. In little time he came to know, at least in passing, every dog on the grounds, and they were all, in a way, his. He loved especially the big male named King's Indian. Everyone was fond of Indian, even the people who disliked dogs, and there were some at Behavior Development. Indian was big and handsome, a tough, cordial, intelligent animal with buoyant spirits. He excelled in no single way but was rock-solid through the spectrum of desirable traits, and a stud of unusual dominance. He rarely blunted a bitch's strengths in their progeny, and was highly effective in correcting her faults. He hadn't accounted for any dramatic leaps in BDI's dogs, but he'd contributed inordinately to their slow and steady improvement and was used more frequently than any other stud.

Toby spent a lot of his free time with Indian. The great

pink tongue washing over his face was the kiss of a beloved. He yearned for the animal as a young poet for an older woman of gentle beauty. He knew Indian could never be his, yet he dreamt of the dog, and his heart quickened as he approached its run. He became obsessed with Indian. He fretted, he brooded, he began to lose weight. One afternoon, working with some of Indian's pups, he was struck by the sudden revelation that Indian lived in his offspring, that while Indian himself was denied him, he could, if he were willing, possess one of Indian's sons for his own; and later in the day, while he was stroking Indian's wide head and telling him of the idea, the big dog sitting before him with eyes half closed in pleasure, Toby felt that Indian grasped and consented to this and that he would infuse his soul into one of his sons so that he could, in spirit, go off to live with Toby and be happy with him.

Karla vom Hanckschloss was the dam Toby picked. She was a hard dog, she gave people trouble. But that was because she was more given to her own life than most, less willing to compromise, and not over-awed by humans. She required a response of some complexity. Not many persons understood her, or could handle her well. But she was good, maybe even the best of the bitches, if you comprehended her as Toby did. She was a mate for Indian: They were equals. And through their son, Toby would possess them both.

Theft was necessary, though Toby did not conceive of it as such. He was not a thief or a dishonest person. It was simply the how of acquisition. Behavior Development did not sell dogs. It either maintained or euthanized its animals, there were no exceptions.

Toby picked a bigboned and independent pup, a tough little bluffer who somehow sensed the weight of its heritage but was still months from achieving that weight, and so it playacted the role in a funny blustery way. Toby loved it. He hurt when the pup and two of its littermates were marked for minimal socialization, which meant he could spend little time with it, but he endured, knowing it wouldn't be long.

He waited until the pup was nearly four months old, because he wanted it to have a leg toward maturity and because it was heavily involved in the stress program the first several weeks and he couldn't be sure someone wouldn't come at any moment to take it off somewhere. But from the time it was thirteen weeks he arrived at work each day prepared to take it and waiting for the opportunity, which wasn't long in coming. Late one afternoon everyone was occupied somewhere else and the kennel area was empty of personnel. Only loose check was kept on the movements of animals. Handlers were supposed to sign for dogs in the kiosk at the end of the runs, where, nights, an attendant read or watched television and walked the runs every couple of hours to see there were no problems, but no one paid much attention to the regulation and handlers either skipped a couple of dogs or made entries to cover their day's activities before they clocked out.

It was simple. Toby opened the pup's run, snapped a leash to its collar, swung the gate back so that it would appear closed, and walked off across a training field into the woods. He took the pup through the forest to the edge of a backcountry road, the end of BDI's property. The treeline was posted:

PRIVATE PROPERTY
Behavior Development Incorporated
No Trespassing
WARNING
Attack-Trained Dogs Present

Only a handful of dogs were actually guard-trained, and they were kept tightly controlled. But the caution did help keep people out, and since the company enjoyed good relations with the community no one took offense.

Toby replaced the leash with a length of chain so the pup couldn't chew itself free, and secured it to a sapling. He patted the pup.

"Now you wait here," he said. "It's going to be all right. You just see. You're going to have a home. I'll be back in a couple hours. You be a good boy."

The dog was unconcerned.

Toby went back to work, and two hours later, when he was driving out of the parking lot, his day over, the pup had not yet been discovered missing. Toby was perspiring. He almost hit a stanchion as he turned onto the highway. He forced himself to breathe slowly and keep even pressure on the gas pedal. His hands were shaking as he entered the woods. The pup was lying down chewing on a stick. It looked up at Toby's approach, wagged its tail once and turned back to the stick. Toby loosed the chain and picked the pup up and hugged it. Tears came to his eyes. He carried it to the car and put it on the rear seat. It investigated, jumped down to the floor and sniffed, and climbed back up. Toby started the car and turned it around. The pup didn't like the footing on the seat. It went down to the floor again and curled up, yawning.

Toby drove to the shopping center and parked. The pup lifted its head. Toby said he'd be back in a little while. The pup rested its head back down and closed its eyes. In the supermarket Toby wheeled a cart to the pet section and spent several excited minutes deciding. He bought a water dish and food bowl, a smooth-linked slip collar imported from Germany, a latigo training leash, two hard rubber balls and some chew toys. He bought two dozen cans of good dog food and a fifty-pound bag of meal. Then he hurried through the small list Mrs. Harris had asked him to bring home.

He paid at the register and bounced up and down on the balls of his feet while the clerk packed the bags. He put them in the cart and wheeled them out to the parking lot.

He'd forgotten which lane he'd left the car in. He pushed the cart up and down, searching. He grew anxious. Here, right here, this is where it should be, he was sure. But instead, there was a red station wagon. He went through the lot again, beginning to panic. A couple of people looked at him uncertainly.

The car wasn't there.

It was impossible, but he couldn't doubt it any longer. He bit his lip, he dug his nails into his palms and he pressed his fist against his cheeks. My puppy!

He left the cart and ran into the coffee shop to the pay phone. He dug in his pocket for a dime. He didn't feel his keys. He tried to remember. He'd set the handbrake, he'd turned to tell the pup he'd be right back. He'd taken the keys from the ignition. . . . No, he couldn't remember doing that, only getting out. . . . Oh goddamn!

He dialed the operator, agonizing over the delay before she answered. "Give me the police," he said. "Hurry."

Cheryl was fifteen but looked twenty, which was one of the problems; she'd been bedded first when she was twelve, and many times since. Her stepfather had caught her twice and beaten her so badly she'd had to stay home from school. He was a rotten bastard who hurt her for doing with boys what he wanted to do with her himself. He'd tried once, but when she'd told her mother, her mother had only slapped her and called her a lying slut. Her mother drank as much as her stepfather did.

Melissa was fourteen. Her parents had money and didn't drink but she hated them anyway because they never let her do anything and they were always after her to be someone else. They didn't understand her at all. Melissa and Cheryl were planning to run away, and Melissa had stolen enough money from her father's dresser to tide them over until they could find jobs. They were going to New York, the East Village, and if they didn't like it there then they'd leave for San Francisco, or maybe Los Angeles. They knew they were both pretty enough to get into the movies.

They'd been sitting in the coffee shop with a couple of good-looking boys since school had let out, and now it was after six, too late to get home in time for dinner. They were going to be yelled at anyway, so they decided to go to a movie. Walking through the parking lot, Cheryl saw the keys in the old Corvair. She stopped, nudged Melissa, and pointed. She looked around, no one was paying them any attention.

"We could be in New York before morning."

"Oh wow," Melissa said.

"Do you have the money with you?"

"Sure. But I don't know, Cheryl. I mean, what if we get caught?"

"We won't. But even if we do, things can't get any worse at home, can they? And we've never been arrested for anything, so a judge'd just let us go, put us on probation or something."

"But . . ." Melissa squirmed.

"But nothing. We decided to split, didn't we? So what are we waiting for? There won't be any better time."

Melissa hugged herself. Then she lunged for the Corvair's door, jerked it open and jumped in. "Come on! Let's move!"

Cheryl ran around to the driver's side. She started the car. "Yoweee!" She put it in gear.

After fifty miles, Cheryl's eyes were bloodshot and teary, her nose was runny and she was sneezing.

"You look like you're going to die," Melissa worried.

"Jesus, I feel like I *am*." She sneezed again, adding new pinpoint spatters to the windshield. "It's a dog, the bastard who owns this car's gotta have a dog. I'm allergic. If I even go into someone's house that's got a dog I start puffing up. Jesus, it's killin' me."

"What are we going to *do*?"

"Keep goin'," Cheryl said grimly. "It's too late now. We'll stop at a drugstore and get some Allerest. That helps sometimes."

Ten miles later, they were startled by a sleepy half-whine, half-bark. Melissa got on her knees and looked down over the back of the seat.

"Cheryl, there's a dog here!"

The pup shook itself, waking, turned its face up to Melissa and made an interrogatory sound. It was hungry.

The car was approaching a gas station, lit up by arc lights. Cheryl braked and edged to the shoulder.

"Get rid of the damn thing," she said.

"It's just a puppy."

"I don't care if it's a stuffed toy. Twenty more minutes like this and I'll need an oxygen tent." She sniffled noisily and rubbed at her wet, puffy eyes.

Melissa lifted the dog and opened her door. "I'm sorry, baby, but you'll find someone to take care of you." She pushed the dog out and closed the door.

Cheryl accelerated with a spray of gravel. The dog looked after the taillights a few moments, then it whined.

Alex Bauer stopped for gasoline that night. He took the pup into his car, and in a week he was calling it Orph.

The New York City Police recovered Toby's Corvair three weeks after it was stolen. The thief was never apprehended. The police could tell Toby nothing of his dog. He looked upon it as the punishment of God. He was too remorseful and too frightened to make further inquiries. He wondered, sadly, for years afterward what had become of the pup.

Dr. Nathan Mills, President
Behavior Development Incorporated
One Dag Hammarskjold Plaza
New York, New York

Dear Nate:
   Thanks for your letter of the 25th. Sorry I omitted the follow-up on the missing pup, but I thought it the kind of administrative detail that would just be a waste of your time. You don't miss a wrinkle, do you? I'm enclosing a Xerox herewith, though I'm afraid it's not worth much. The sign-out sheets in the kennel were incomplete (that's a problem with the dog-trainer types we have to work with, sloppiness), so we interviewed everyone who'd been in the area, but drew a blank. We scoured the grounds twice over and we advertised in the local papers for two weeks (discreetly, of course, there's a lot of horror-story rumor about what we do here). We came up with a big fat zero. I know this kind of irresponsibility is intolerable, but as best we can determine someone failed to close a latch properly and the pup simply wandered off. God knows where —we don't. We roasted our people. It won't happen

again. All I can say is, tell Accounting to write it off as a loss of matériel. I'd call it about $350.

I'm sorry this wasn't included in the quarterly report, but again, I thought it would just be bothersome stuff.

My best to Joan and the kids.

> *Yours,*
> *Dr. Chaim Mandelberg, Director*
> *Behavior Development Incorporated*
> *New England Facility*

CHAPTER 3

ONCE a month Bauer canceled a class and invited the students to an informal seminar at his home. Attendance was not compulsory, and about half would come. The gatherings were relaxed and usually productive.

There were twelve students this evening. Bauer served beer and wine, cheese and potato chips, coffee. Two kids had come stoned. Bauer had tried grass a couple of times, and it had been fun, he understood its appeal, but he was really too old—a member of the hardcore alcohol generation—and he couldn't comprehend how anyone could try to function intellectually on it.

A reporter had told him that you couldn't write while you were stoned, but you could retain insights that came to you and use them intelligently when you were straight.

Bauer didn't know. At Wintergreen there were students who'd taken their first acid trip at twelve, who couldn't reckon the amount of chemicals they'd dropped, snorted, smoked, popped and shot since then, and whose brains seemed to have been jellied beyond salvage. Others, equal veterans of the drug culture, worked with fine clarity, even if their mental processes were occasionally obtuse to him. Of the two boys stoned tonight, one sat dazed and withdrawn, while the second participated keenly, his cerebrations altered only toward a certain baroqueness, which was in itself pleasing. And Bauer could conclude nothing from that, if he'd felt any need to reach a conclusion. He didn't really care much what people did.

They sprawled in chairs around the logs burning in the fireplace, sat on the floor on pillows, and stretched out on their sides supporting their heads on their palms. It was a good session, they went deep into Melville and Bauer even managed to generate some retroactive enthusiasm for Hawthorne.

Earlier, before anyone had arrived, Orph had grown unhappy when Bauer kindled the fire. Orph didn't like fire. He'd withdraw to a far wall and lie down and stare at it warily, and if a charred log collapsed or sparks showered, he'd rumble and come half to his feet with his hackles lifting. He refused to leave the room when one was burning, as if it were an adversary that would become dangerous free of his watchful eye. Bauer, who liked fires, didn't build as many as he might have.

When the first students rang the bell Orph rushed the door barking. Later, he growled at a girl who laughed loudly, then at a boy arguing a point. Bauer thought it prudent to close him into a bedroom.

Orph liked an infrequent person well enough to allow himself to be petted, and on rare occasion he invited such attention, but he wasn't fond of human beings in general, seemed to tolerate them by exercise of will.

Ursula didn't like the dog. She was disdainful, nearly contemptuous of his affection for it, and reluctant to place the children in its presence. She'd asked Bauer to get rid of it. Orph accepted Bauer's sons when they visited, but his spirits always brightened as soon as they left and he had his home, his cave, to himself again.

Bauer had consulted the vet when Orph, seven months old, had first showed his teeth at someone. She said, "Well, he has a home now. It's his territory and he's getting possessive about it. The other thing is his hormones. They begin changing at six months and they don't stabilize until eighteen months, which is when he reaches maturity. In males this means, among other things, increasing aggression. He'll get progressively tougher until his metabolism levels, and then that's where he'll stay. You can control it with training, of course, but you can't diminish it."

Orph was nineteen months now, and Bauer was relieved. He figured he could control the dog at this level.

The seminar ended well. A few students lingered over coffee or wine. Kathy Lippman was the last to leave. She held a cardigan sweater hung over her shoulder by one finger.

"Thanks a lot," she said, "it was terrific. I hate to stick you with this mess, though."

"That's okay, it won't take long."

"You want a hand?"

Bauer smiled and shook his head.

"Oh, let me give you one anyway." She tossed her sweater on a chair. "It's a drag cleaning up after other people."

"Thanks, but it's really not necessary, Kathy."

"I know," she said, beginning to round up ashtrays, "but I don't mind, and it'd make me feel guilty to walk out and leave it all for you. And you don't want me to feel that way, do you? Guilt is very destructive."

"Okay, okay." He turned his palms toward her. "You win."

"That's nice, I like doing that."

They collected the plates and glasses and cups into the kitchen.

Kathy turned on the water. "Sit down and have a brandy or something while I wash these."

"Come on, I just put 'em in to soak and whip through them in the morning."

"Sit down and be quiet or I'll clean your stove too."

Bauer poured himself a brandy.

"How long have you been living here?" Kathy asked as she soaped the dishes.

"A little more than a year."

"And you were a reporter before you became a professor."

"No. I worked in public relations a while in between, not long."

"Yecch."

"That's what I decided too."

"Why did you get out of the newspapers, because of that testimony thing?"

"More or less," Bauer said quietly.

"That must have been rough, I looked it up in the library last week."

Suddenly Bauer felt at bay. He tried to sound casual. "Why?"

She shrugged, her back to him. "I was curious. The guy was an ape. It's a good thing he's in jail."

Bauer didn't say anything.

"Why Wintergreen instead of someplace else?"

Bauer was unused to being asked such direct questions, and Kathy's ingenuousness made him uneasy.

"It was Covington I wanted, Wintergreen was the means."

"Personal reasons?"

"Uh-huh."

"A woman?" Kathy looked over her shoulder. "Am I getting too personal?"

"My wife."

"Oh. Ex or still?"

"Estranged. Leaning toward ex, I guess."

"I'm sorry."

"It happens."

"It does. There you go." She put the last cup in the rack and dried her hands. "Can I have one of whatever you're sipping? For the road?"

She sat with him.

"That's nice, what is it?"

"Metaxa, it's Greek."

"I like it." She hooked her hair with her thumbs and flipped it back over her shoulders, a poignant, thoroughly female gesture. "Did you smoke that joint I gave you?"

"Not yet."

"It's really good stuff. Would you like to do it now?"

Bauer hesitated, then said, "I'll take a raincheck, okay?"

"Sure." If Kathy was disappointed, Bauer didn't see.

She went on as brightly as before, but he noticed that she shifted to neutral subjects. She finished her brandy. "Time to split," she said.

At the door, he said, "Thanks for the help, Kathy."

"No sweat. What's your wife's name?"

"Ursula," he said, taken back.

"Bet you five-to-one you're going to see her in the next couple of days."

"Tomorrow night."

"Guilt," she said. "It's destructive." She took his hand and pressed it to her cheek. She released it and grinned. "Night, Professor Bauer."

Bauer waited until she turned her headlights on. Then

he closed the door and let Orph out of the bedroom. The dog brushed past him. It went through the house sniffing, looked reproachfully at him.

"Yeah. Well, if it makes you feel any better, I'm probably an asshole."

Pointedly, Orph went to the other side of the room and lay down with his back to Bauer.

Bauer stretched out on the couch and put his hands behind his head. But he didn't want to think about Kathy Lippman and he got up after a couple of minutes. He worked to draw Orph out of his sulk. This wasn't easily done. When the dog got mad, it stayed mad. But the animal relented in a while and they went for a walk. The air was brisk, it cleared Bauer's head.

He went to bed. Orph pressed up to get his head patted, then left. Orph slept in the living room, near the door. He slept lightly, in short naps, and awakened frequently to prowl the house. He wandered into Bauer's room two or three times a night to check on him.

Bauer had bought one of the training books the vet had recommended and he'd done a little work with Orph —some heeling, the down and the sit—but he had neither the taste nor the personality to become involved with training, and he'd let it go before long. He was guilty about this. Orph was more or less civilized around human beings, but he was a hard dog. He needed controls and constructive outlets.

Bauer enjoyed his company. While he'd never anthropomorphized the animal, he did look upon it as a friend. Part of the value of that friendship was the dog's alienness. It pleasured him to look over the chasm into the animal's serious brown eyes, to feel the sea of their difference, the small islands that were the overlapping of their beings and the grounds of their understanding. He loved Orph, and learned from him. Orph was content with his singularity, complete within himself. Bauer on the other hand felt himself an amorphous creature ill-equipped to live alone. Though he still fell into sloughs of despondency, was blanketed by anomie, taking the dog as a kind of model he'd rallied his will (despite thinking it an exercise in delusion) to emulate the dog's wholeness and make it his own. He hadn't metamorphosed, but at least he felt moments of solidity, and the attempt lent him a sense of positive occupation.

When Orph was nine or ten months he had returned from an afternoon forage with a rabbit in his jaws and displayed it proudly. Bauer had little knowledge of such things, but he thought healthy rabbits too quick to be caught by any but coursing dogs. He took the carcass away to examine it. Orph waited with a wagging tail. The rabbit appeared normal, but Bauer was afraid to chance disease. So he took it outside and put it in the garbage can, snapped the lid down. Orph looked from the can to Bauer, back to the can, and whined.

"Sorry," Bauer said, "but we can't risk it. Inside. Let's go."

Orph jumped and knocked the garbage can over. The lid popped, the rabbit spilled out and Orph picked it up. "No!" Bauer righted the can, dropped the carcass in again and put the cover on. Orph wouldn't leave, so Bauer gripped his collar and marched him into the house. The dog sat by the door and whined. Later, when Bauer went for a book he'd left in the car, Orph lunged past as he opened the door, ran to the garbage can and tipped it over. Bauer locked the rabbit in the trunk of the car. The dog stationed itself at the rear bumper and wouldn't move. It barked at Bauer.

Orph never brought game home again, but sometimes he returned with dried flecks of blood on his muzzle and wasn't interested in his dinner.

When Orph was a year old, he'd torn Bauer loose from the rational world. It was winter, with the skeletons of deciduous trees frozen in ice and the ground deep beneath the snow. Bauer woke in blackness, his scrotum shriveling. sweat suddening on his palms. The wail filled his head and clawed down his spine, the moan of a hero unburied, the lament of a wandering shade.

He sat up with a tripping heart.

His mind engaged in quick defense, and he thought: Orph, it's Orph. And the fear began to recede, but slowly, like water from a flooded basement. The wail attenuated, there was a moment of silence, then it went soaring upward again.

Bauer eased out of bed and padded down the hall, stopped at the edge of the living room.

Washed in the thin cold light of the full moon, the dog sat on its haunches before the bay window with its head arched back, eyes narrowed to slits and ears flat against its skull, jaws agape and throat pulsing out a wavering howl.

Bauer was frozen. The wild ululation pulled at his guts like a tide, summoning him from his body. The sound peaked, then spiraled down through long moments into a haunted stillness. The dog stared up through the window, contemplating the moon. Bauer hardly breathed. The animal turned its head. It looked into Bauer's eyes and regarded him calmly. Bauer grew disjointed and apprehensive. He was dislodged from the habitat of his own being and drawn into a foreign realm, where he could find neither landmark nor handhold. He felt himself rolling in some murky river, attacked by vertigo, fear burgeoning, while the dog, concrete and certain in this universe, remarked him with indifferent sufferance. It became unbearable, but Bauer couldn't pull away. Orph released him finally, turning back to the moon. The animal was alone once more, though Bauer still stood by the door, and it lifted its head and issued forth its call, its testament of vassalage and barony, its acknowledgment, assertion, and integration, its clear cry of dominion across the emptiness.

Bauer returned to his room. He lay with his arms at his sides and his eyes open, listening to Orph. The dog's communion ended soon, and Bauer heard nothing more from the animal that night, not a creak of board beneath its weight, a scratch of nail against the floor.

The Country Inn was a beef and seafood place with barn-siding walls, captain's chairs and gingham tablecloths. Bauer took a table and ordered a double Scotch. Ursula still hadn't arrived when he finished, so he ordered another, and midway through it she appeared in the broad arch that demarcated the bar from the dining room. She wore heels, and a skirt and jacket of pale green. She was a tall woman, but had always been comfortable with her height and she liked the way heels turned the line of her calves. She was handsome, with green eyes, clear skin and fine bones; and high-breasted and willowy, had a tight round bottom and superb legs. She was supple, strong, like a swimmer, sure in her movements, and quick to judge. Men either disliked her or desired her passionately, sometimes both. Bauer had always desired her, still did; the inaccessibility of her self, which he had discovered—or rather eventually had to accept as intrinsic rather than a deliberate, protective mode, which could have been relaxed or even discarded in time—only after they'd been married some years, had disappointed him but not diminished his love of her.

They greeted. He held a chair for her, an unpopular convention he couldn't break.

He saw that she'd dyed the gray out of her hair; it

was the first personal uncertainty he'd ever seen in her. He felt compassion; he was also angered a little—she had taxed him sorely for his own confusions, though his had not been physical.

Her new hair stripped a few years from her, which mattered nothing to him, but he supposed it was why she'd done it.

"I like your hair," he said.

"Thank you." She was careful, examining the compliment for obligation.

Watching her, he knew it wasn't just another man, which had been responsible for her last period of coolness toward him, but that she wanted to finish it. Ordinarily when they dined together he cooked at his house and she stayed over the night.

She didn't seem in a hurry. Over appetizers, they talked about Michael and Jeff, and about each other's work—briefly, since he was no more interested in what new lines she was buying for the department store, to whose executive stratum she belonged, than she was in his late adolescents—and then social topics. They were both intelligent and they liked each other's minds. Together, they'd been given more to intellection than emotion. People of intimacy, of personal revelation and inquiry, had unsettled them, especially Ursula. She detested publicness, and thought candor a weakness.

They were easy enough through dinner, in the molds of habit, and Bauer actually enjoyed it.

Over coffee she said, "I want to talk to you seriously, Alex."

"Okay. About us?"

"Yes. Bluntly, I think it's time we get divorced."

"You don't see any possibility of making it work?"

"No."

"I don't think it's likely either, but I'd be willing to try, just on the chance. It'd make a better ending if we were both sure it was dead."

Not unkindly, she said, "Alex, please, give it up. It's possible we could get along—we like each other, at least I like you, underneath all this melancholy and existential malaise you've been indulging in—but what for, what would be the point? Being friends hardly justifies the daily work of living together."

He smiled. "Well, you fuck good."

"So do you when you're not questing the meaning of life, but then so do a sufficient number of other people, and one hardly needs to be married to fuck, so that's quite irrelevant, isn't it?"

"The formality of a divorce would seem irrelevant too, unless one of us wanted to marry again."

"I find marriage a useful concept in hunting societies and on frontiers, but a senseless gauntlet otherwise. You, of course, are entitled to your own views, but since you agree that the formality or lack of it is of no special importance, then you shouldn't have any objection. I'm bothered by the ambiguity and I'd like to resolve it."

"That's the problem with ambiguities, they can bother your soul to pieces. Unfortunately we live in a sea of them, and part of the quality of an ambiguity is its impossibility of resolution."

"Well, here's one you can resolve, and presto, your burden becomes lighter by one. Come on Alex, don't go clever. Will you be pleasant, or do we have to send lawyers into the arena?"

Bauer signaled the waitress and ordered two brandies. "Sure enough," he said to Ursula. "Let's get divorced."

She was suspicious.

"I mean it," he said. "It's okay."

She nodded. "Thank you, Alex."

"Jesus, you're polite—you're welcome."

The brandies came. Bauer lifted his. "To a long happy divorce."

"On the surface you appear to be dealing with this well. But I wonder whether you're really dealing with it at all."

"I am," he said soberly. "What reaction did you have in mind for me?"

She shrugged.

He lit another cigarette from the stub of the one in the ashtray. He inhaled and coughed.

"You should stop that," she said. "It'll kill you."

"Maybe. I'll quit someday. We don't have to hassle over the kids or money or anything, do we?"

"Not unless you want to change the way things are now."

"I'd like them to live with me."

She shook her head. "It's better for them to be with me."

"Probably, for them anyway."

"But as they grow, if they ever want to go and live with you, I won't fight it."

"Fair enough." He was quiet several moments. "Ursula, don't cut yourself off. Love or whatever, some kind of union, it's a context in which people can transcend themselves and become larger, more multiple than they could be alone."

"Your experiences would hardly seem to lead to a theory of such rapture."

"We didn't find the way, that's all."

"Oh for God's sake. That's romantic claptrap, Alex. Do you know what's real? Stone is real. That's all. You're burying yourself in intellectual quicksand, Alex, you're destroying yourself inside your skull. Don't do it." She put a hand over his. "The kind of love we were taught to believe in doesn't exist," she said softly. "And that hurt us both. It wasn't either of our faults. I am fond of you, Alex, even if you can't understand the simplicity of that."

Bauer placed his other hand atop Ursula's. "Then, in the spirit of camaraderie, why don't you come and spend a friendly night with me."

Ursula pulled away. "You can be detestable."

"It was a joke. My brave smile into the face of horror. Inside, is a man who weeps." He said it with self-mockery, the only way Ursula would tolerate it, but it was fairly true.

He listened to music and drank too much, he smoked his lungs raw and wondered at his lack of reaction. He went to bed and fell asleep.

In the morning he was profoundly depressed. The sense-lessness of life collapsed upon him like a wall and buried him beneath its rubble. He clung to the image of his sons; they required no raison d'être, he refused to break them upon the rack of enquiry.

He could not accept Ursula's vision. It demanded a lobotomy of the spirit, something to which he'd have submitted in many moments of his life, and with joy, if he'd known how. Maybe, he thought, I am insane.

They'd married young, and had both been happy in the early years. They were people of activity and decision, little reflection. Bauer had some ruminative capacity. He'd never exercised it much, having occupied himself with immediacies, but he'd preserved it, thinking that someday, like a hobby, he'd have time for it. He thought it would be a part of his life with Ursula, but she equated it with daydreaming, a childish pursuit, and he discovered that she'd armored her inner being so strongly that she could no longer perceive its existence, and he resigned himself with sadness, but only a little, because their life was full and busy and they did enjoy each other and he found her a good and strong person, and he was reasonable enough to love her reality rather than turn from her because she couldn't measure to his fancy. They had the children late and it was in them, particularly Jeff, the youngest, that Bauer experienced his deepest gratification. It was more intense than he'd ever imagined anything could be; he immersed himself with neither reservation nor apprehension into another human being. The rivulet of his contemplation began to flow. Simultaneously, he was reaching an age in which he was accomplishing much of what he'd strived for through his youth, and was beginning to see the limits of his life, could fairly well predict its progression to the end. As he moved through his early thirties he underwent, with surprise and initial incomprehension, the spiritual climacteric that grips most men to some degree at that time, and it took him strongly. It became increasingly a need to explain his existence, to position himself in the puzzle of the cosmos, to say something more than that he'd been born, had bred, and would die, and he and Ursula began to drift apart. It was barely perceptible at first, but painfully evident as the months accumulated. She could not or would not join with him in this thing. His old diversions became hollow, the hurrah of his work, which had consumed him before, meaningless; he and Ursula had come to know as much about the other as each was capable of knowing; a certain listlessness settled over them; and Ursula was deciding that the earth did not shake nor the heavens tremble, there were no rhapsodies, that those were lies handed down through generations simply to facilitate the continuance of the species, and she felt betrayed, and resented it.

The DiGiovanni case exploded in this period. Bauer had been preparing a series on paramilitary groups. He'd built trust and had been privy to volatile and dangerous information. He'd been pressured by Federal and state agencies to turn over that information, and had refused. Then, after a week of racial fighting in Newark high schools, two black teenagers were shoved into a car at gunpoint, taken out of town to a salt marsh and shot to death. Anthony DiGiovanni, a construction contractor and founder of the American Defenders, was arrested with two of his men. But their alibis were strong, and though the district attorney succeeded in getting an indictment, his evidence was circumstantial and conviction was in doubt. Bauer had written at length on the Defenders. He was subpoenaed to testify.

He dropped into a private hell. He'd been questioned about the Defenders before—once in an arson case, once when a militant headquarters had been shot up and a black man wounded. He'd known the Defenders were guilty, but he'd learned that in confidence, and both times he'd kept his silence, though jail was threatened. Because of this, DiGiovanni and the Defenders considered him trustworthy and one of their own at heart. In the week between the murders and the arrests, Bauer had been in DiGiovanni's paneled basement with some of the Defenders. DiGiovanni was expansive and slurry-tongued after half a case of beer. "Well shit, friend," he said. "Just who do you think put them blackaboos under? No one else had the balls to stop 'em from burnin' the schools the goddamn bleeding hearts built for 'em to learn how to tear the country apart."

"Tony!" someone warned.

But DiGiovanni was too full of himself and didn't care. "That was me and Martha, friend, with a little help from Carl and Bill." Tony's favorite gun was an unregistered Army .45 he'd brought home from Korea. He liked to refer to himself and the gun as Me and Martha. "You just look up the police report if you don't believe me. Those bucks were downed with dum-dums. But they didn't run that in the papers, so how else would I know, huh? I ask you that."

It was a conundrum of moral responsibility. Law and government were the fabrications of men, valuative judgments that mutated, doubled back, reversed and even contradicted themselves through the continuum of history. Yesterday's heroes were today's monsters, tomorrow's dullards; nothing was fixed; he had given his word, the only absolute he could cleave to; alone, he was being asked to render moral conclusion and consequently dictate the future of three human beings. What did he owe the dead, the living, the law, himself? The prosecutor swore jail for silence. The paper pledged support. Anonymous letters threatened death either way. Ursula was infuriated by his anguished vacillation, she said it was insane, an infliction of self-torment. He could not find solution, and didn't know what to do, even to the moment he was called to the witness stand. Sweating, he stepped forward, took the oath, and heard himself in the voice of a stranger answer the questions put to him, repeat DiGiovanni's words and name the location of the arms cache, which the Defenders had not been aware that he knew. DiGiovanni's Martha was in court the next day, his fingerprints on it, the rifling matched to one of the recovered slugs. Santo DiGiovanni, Anthony's elderly father, a frail man in a pressed inexpensive suit who had attended the trial in expressionless silence, turned and looked into Bauer's face. A tear ran down the old man's cheek. He rose and walked from the room with stiff, arthritic steps, his head bowed. And the impulse of Bauer's—for it wasn't a decision but a conditioned response to social obligation, a synaptic cultural agreement that murder should be punished—became an act of physical effect, it was done.

But Bauer had answered no question, his will and spirit

remained paralyzed, entrapment waited behind every turn. He was damned by all, had satisfied none. The external world was scarcely real anymore. The division between him and Ursula widened. In a little while she asked for a trial separation. He tried to dissuade her. He couldn't, and what remained of his vitality went from him. She wanted to take the children away from the metastasizing cancer of the city. She went back to Covington, where she had been raised, where there were relatives and old friends, and a decent job for her.

He followed a few months later. Ursula and the children were all he knew to be true.

Harry Wilson sat before a mike in WCVS's taping room, watching the second hand on a big clock sweep up toward the 12. Harry Wilson owned the radio station, and 51 percent of the *Covington Freeman* as well, a legacy from his parents. They'd died within a year of each other while he was in graduate school, eight years ago. Harry was a fiery man who espoused many causes, often unpopular, but always controversial, which was the point. Once upon a time Harry had had personal convictions, and he still assured himself he would find some if he sat down to think about it, but such process was a luxury of the fat and satisfied, and Harry was neither. He wanted to go to the state legislature, he wanted to be governor someday. There was Washington. Time and tides don't wait.

The second hand hit the 12, a red light winked on, the engineer in the control room jabbed a finger at him.

Harry looked down at the first typesheet. The lead—*WCVS, Your Voice in the Valley, presents an Editorial on the Air by Station Manager and President Harry Wilson!* with a little fanfare—would be spliced in before broadcast.

"Last night at the intersection of Prince and Fair streets,

an elderly woman was viciously attacked and savagely bitten by a large stray dog," Harry said. "This is the sixth such incident in Covington this year. We have addressed ourselves before to the dog problem. Now we believe it is time to take the gloves off and go at it with bare knuckles. Something *must* be done. I'm going to give you some hard facts, and like 'em or not, they *are* the facts.

"**Item:** There are 6000 dogs in this city alone. Each day they release 4800 quarts of urine and drop 3000 pounds of excrement into our living space.

"**Item:** This waste material can lead not only to garden varieties of infection, but also to a host of serious diseases like toxacara canis, visceral larval migrans and leptospirosis, which can cause blindness, gross neural damage, meningitis and brain impairment. These diseases are frequently misdiagnosed, and some authorities believe they are moving to epidemic stage in this country.

"**Item:** Two hundred seventy-four Covingtonians were bitten seriously enough last year to seek medical attention.

"**Item:** The Covington SPCA had to put to sleep nearly 2000 ownerless or unwanted dogs last year. Across the nation, the number topped fifteen million, at a cost of $60 million.

"**Item:** There is a dog population explosion in the United States, and the animals are increasing their number by 36 percent every twelve months.

"**Item:** According to the Pet Food Institute, dogs devoured six billion pounds of dog food last year, their owners shelling out a hefty $1 billion. This in a time of economic recession, and this forcing non–pet owners into economic competition with dogs for red-meat products.

"**Item:** Across our nation, there are hundreds of thousands of dogs gone wild, and perhaps as many as 10,000 in this state alone. In Georgia last year wild dogs killed an estimated 5000 head of cattle. In our own state, they tore apart more than 12,000 deer and countless numbers of sheep, goats, chickens, small game, and nesting birds. Several leading naturalists have called dogs the largest predatory menace this country has ever faced, and wild dogs are vastly more ferocious and dangerous than wolves ever were.

"Dog owners refuse to accept their responsibilities, and authorities apparently do not intend to fulfill their legal obligations. All right. If that's the way they want it, then that's the way we'll give it to 'em. We feel we have no choice but to put the following proposals, Draconian though they may be, before the city council and *demand* their enactment. First, raise dog licenses to $50. Second, fine dog owners $100 for failure to keep their dog leashed, chained, or secured behind a fence the first time, $250 for the second offense, and next time confiscate the animal. Third, confiscate and euthanize any dog who bites a human being unless it can be proved that the victim directly provoked the bite. Fourth, specially license all female dogs owned for breeding purposes, and mandate spaying of all females not so licensed by the age of twelve months. Fifth, conservation officers and other law-enforcement personnel will be required to shoot any dog found roaming in forest or meadowland, and any private citizen will be legally entitled to do likewise.

"There you have it. We are no longer worried about a problem, we are struggling with a crisis. And I assure you that no matter how harsh the measures we must take, we *will* take them. We are not—and this is no pun—going to let this city, this state, or this nation go to the dogs.

"This is Harry Wilson, concluding a WCVS 'Editorial on the Air.' "

The red light went out. The engineer raised his thumb.

His voice came through the speaker over the control-room panel. "That was nice, Mr. Wilson. You want a playback?"

"Yes."

Wilson listened. He was pleased with his delivery. He ordered an extra girl on the switchboard through the day tomorrow, when the tape would be broadcast every hour on the hour, to handle the calls.

Homer McPhee dumped the baled hay in the pasture and pushed the wheelbarrow back up the slope to the cinderblock barn. They didn't use the barn anymore, let the cattle winter over in the pasture. It was Homer's idea. His father had said they'd lose half a dozen to winter-kill. Homer said if they did, he'd meet the cost out of his own pocket. John McPhee had agreed on that basis. They'd been running a small herd of black Angus for six years, a bull and eighteen cows, and had lost one or two and sometimes three to respiratory infections each winter. Homer had argued that the humidity was too high in the barn, the cows would be healthier in the elements. He'd been right, and his father was happy to admit it.

John McPhee had been raised an urban boy, but had loved the country from the day his father had bought a summer house and the family began to vacation there. After graduation from the State Teachers' College he took a job in Covington and married. When his father died, his finance-baffled mother turned the insurance money over to him and he bought a large tract that had been decent farmland a couple of generations back—mostly first-growth timber now, with good contours, streams and two spring-fed ponds—and he built a house big enough for him, his wife, his mother and a couple of children. McPhee taught mathematics in Covington, and was good

at it, but he loved the land more than anything else. Week-
ends and summers he built, cleared, excavated, reclaimed,
and fenced. He grew vegetables, raised poultry, sheep, and
later cattle. He felt in harmony with the land and knew,
with pride, that if civilization went to hell, he and his
family could make do just fine.

His oldest son, Homer, was a great satisfaction to him.
Homer was big, strong, and able, and saw the land as a
medieval baron must his fiefdom; it was Homer's birth-
right and heritage; it was as much a part of him as his
heart. John would have been happier if Homer had gone
to agricultural college, but Homer was impatient, and he
was taking correspondence courses from the college, which
in the end would probably be good enough. John marked
a hundred acres for the boy and told him he'd deed it
over as soon as Homer had a house standing and some
acres ready to cultivate and graze. John was forty-five
and hardy; his old age was only a flicker in the dim
future, but it pleased him to think he would spend it with a
son like Homer, who, like his tough forebears, could provide through his own skills everything he and his required.

Homer put the wheelbarrow away and went into the
house, to his room, and got the syringe and bottle of hor-
mone he kept hidden there. In the pasture, he pierced
the stopper and drew the liquid into the cartridge, injected
the hormones into a calf, which, eating, did nothing more
than grunt and step to the side. He reloaded the syringe
and went to the next calf. His father would have been
furious. Homer loved him, but John McPhee was a man
who lived in the past. He wouldn't use chemical fertiliz-
ers, and thus harvested only a small portion of what he
could have otherwise. He wouldn't modernize his chicken
coop—"It's not natural for a creature to live in a wire
cage from birth to death and never even touch the ground"
—or automate the feeding. He refused to force the growth

of his cattle. Homer had clandestinely injected all of last year's calves, and they averaged 200 to 300 pounds more at sale time, profits up substantially, which was all the reason Homer needed. John marveled and praised the soundness of his stock. Homer smiled and kept his silence. There were many things his father wouldn't do, almost as many as Homer would.

Bauer picked up his children from Janie, Ursula's neighbor, early Saturday morning. Janie had trouble meeting his eyes. She was always that way when Ursula had gone off with a man.

Bauer took the boys shopping and bought them sneakers and shortsleeve shirts. At the hardware store, he picked up some things he'd put off buying until today. Both boys loved to wander up and down the aisles and neither of them was greedy, they were happy with an occasional inexpensive item that caught their fancy. Jeff was green-eyed like his mother, features as fine as a steel engraving, and had lustrous chestnut hair. He held his father's hand and chattered on. He was four years old, verbal and animated. Michael was seven, subdued and concerned with dignity, a boy of restraint who had been hurt more by the separation than his brother and still resented Bauer for it. He needed a few hours to warm up to his father. Bauer knew that and was patient.

They lunched at McDonald's, which the boys considered a special treat, and Bauer took them to a movie. They emerged in high spirits.

Orph made a fuss over Bauer when they got home. He gave Michael a lick, then stood unhappily, but stood because Bauer held him with his eyes, for hugging and petting from Jeff. Orph wasn't fond of children. He put up with Bauer's sons because he had to. He favored Michael, who usually left him alone. Jeff was enamored of the dog and would have been all over it if Bauer had allowed him.

In the afternoon Bauer hauled the grill from the garage, filled it with charcoal and got a fire going. He brought out a card table and chairs and started ferrying the meat, rolls, soda and plates from the house. The boys were playing in the front yard, Orph was lounging nearby.

In the kitchen Bauer put the condiments on a tray, cracked open ice and began dropping cubes in glasses.

Jeff shrieked. Michael screamed. Bauer ran outside.

Jeff was on his knees shaking violently, hands raised as if to push something back. He keened in terror. The left side of his face was awash in scarlet. His cheekbone was visible. A flap of flesh that had been his cheek hung from his jaw like a long bloody jowl.

Michael stood between Jeff and Orph gripping a branch. He was chalky-faced. The crotch of his pants was wet.

Orph's hackles were raised. His teeth showed.

"Orph!" Bauer shouted.

The dog swung its head, but remained braced.

"Goddamn you!" Bauer roared. "Get inside!"

The dog took a step toward Bauer, tail sinking in supplication. Bauer swept Jeff up in one arm and gathered in Michael with the other. The dog stared at them, hackles fluttering up and down, like ferns in a gusting wind. It backed away. Bauer cursed at it.

Orph was caught by countering surges. He moved toward the house, stopped, drew away, looked at Bauer and dropped to his belly. He trembled and came to his feet. His ears clicked forward, he shook himself mightily, as if trying to throw something off, or wrench free, then he turned and ran toward the woods.

Jeff moaned.

Michael buried his face in Bauer's side. "He bit him," he sobbed. "Orph bit his face." He clawed at Bauer. "He's going to kill us! Don't let him, Daddy! No!"

Jeff went limp. His head fell back, his mouth slacked open. His eyes were dull. He breathed shallowly. The blood had soaked his clothes and stained down Bauer's shirt.

"Michael." Bauer dug his fingers into Michael's shoulder and shook him. "Michael!" Michael raised his hands to his mouth. He turned an ashen face up. "Listen carefully," Bauer said. "Can you understand me?" The boy nodded. "All right. Now I want you to go into the kitchen. Take four clean dish towels. Fill one with ice and fold the corners to make a bag out of it. Bring them to the car. I'll be waiting there with Jeff. Everything's going to be all right. Do you understand?"

"Yes," Michael whispered.

Bauer drove with one hand and held the icepack against Jeff's face with the other. Jeff's head rested in Bauer's lap, his legs were elevated across Michael's. Michael changed the towels as the blood and melting ice soaked them. Bauer held his speed at an even 65. He talked calmly to Michael, and tried to reawaken Jeff's numbed mind.

CHAPTER 4

KATHY LIPPMAN parked her Volkswagen at the end of the dirt road, next to an old Chevy van. A multihued evening sky was painted on the side of the van, an orange sun sinking behind the jut of a mountain, and a cute little aardvark on the driver's door. Kathy didn't bother locking her car. The overgrown road was still rutted from wheels of years ago, when there'd been some logging in here, and maybe even farther back—there were old foundations in the woods and long stone fences, from a time no one alive remembered.

Kathy took her sandals off and put them in her tote bag. She started up the trail, swinging the bag from its drawstring. The soles of her feet were tender and she hopped and said "Ouch" to herself and stopped to balance on one leg and examine her foot for blood (there wasn't any). She stayed barefoot, wanting to toughen the skin again after a long winter in shoes.

She picked some wildflowers along the way and twined them in her hair. She wore a light summery dress which swirled about her legs in the breeze. The straps were low on her shoulders. The breeze slipped between her breasts, just a little too deliciously cold, teasing her nipples to hardness. She turned her face up to the sunlight, closed her eyes, and poked her tongue between her lips to taste the spring. She shook her head, shimmering her hair. Heaven, Heaven—oh what a day!

She was wincing at the end of the trail, a quarter mile up from the car, but pleased with herself. She put her sandals back on and stepped into the clearing. She felt a pang. School seemed suddenly vulgar and stupid. She should have dropped out last term when Josie had and come to live here. Well, not really. She liked plumbing too much for one thing, and all that implied. But sometimes she was wistful.

Josie and Harriet and Billy were digging over the garden behind the chicken-wire fence. Ed was on the roof nailing tarpaper down. Ellen was sitting naked in the sun with Ananda, her baby, and Hero, Harriet's little boy. Hero was three. He wore one of the guys' old tie-dye T-shirts, the bottom flopping about his ankles, the sleeves down to his elbows. He was bouncing a handmade puppet that hung from a stick by a string. A bearded guy Kathy didn't know sat next to Ellen playing a flute.

"Hi!"

Kathy got some smiles, some waves. "Hi," Ellen said. "You're late. I figured we'd see you with the thaw if you were still around."

"Work, work," Kathy said. "First it was days, then before I knew it, it was weeks." She grabbed Hero and hugged him, kissed him. "You miss me?" He squirmed loose and hurried around Ellen and pretended Kathy wasn't there.

"He's gone shy," Ellen said. "It'll take him a couple of days."

"Aw, Hero." Kathy had lived at the Treehouse last summer and she'd grown fond of him. He ignored her.

"Bookwork?" Ellen said.

"Yeah, I'm kind of into it, I guess. For awhile anyway."

Ellen shrugged. "Multiple are the paths."

"Ananda's huge," Kathy said.

Ellen picked Ananda up. "Isn't she? Nine months last week. Twenty pounds already." Ananda rooted for a breast. "Uh-uh, you ate already." Ellen twirled a twig to distract her. The baby took it and put an end in her mouth. "Kathy, this is Pancho. Pancho, Kathy."

Pancho took the flute from his mouth. He looked at Kathy several moments and said, "Hey."

"Right," Kathy said.

He fished a joint from his pocket. "Smoke?"

"Later."

Pancho went back to his flute.

"You going to be here this summer?" Ellen said.

"I think so, if there's room."

"Good. But you better tell Bill—we got two already, we can only handle one or two more."

"Okay."

Ananda began to fret. Ellen lay back on the grass and held her aloft, sang her a nonsense song and bounced her up and down. Ananda's dangling feet grazed the wild expanse of pubic hair that grew up Ellen's belly to lap with tendrils at her navel. Ed thrust the hammer into his belt and came down from the roof. He gave Kathy a big squeeze, lifting her from her feet, and kissed her. "How's it going, babe?" Ed had been Kathy's old man through most of last summer. Then Ed and Josie had got together, and Kathy paired off with a thin, speedy kid from California.

"Pretty good. Did you get through the winter all right?"

"Not bad." Ed walked her over to the goat pen. "We got snowed in a couple of times and the vegetables ran pretty low, but we had a better time of it than we've had before. Things are coming together."

Three of the does had given birth, one to twins. Everyone was pleased with the bonanza and they'd changed the billy goat's name from Jerk to James Bond. The kids were cute. One tried to suckle on Kathy's fingers and it tickled.

Ed took her into the house. Billy Harris and Ed and another guy who hadn't stayed long had built the big high-ceilinged structure around a huge live oak. The trunk rose up from the center of the floor, disappeared through the ceiling, and the broad branches sheltered the roof from the summer sun. The joists and rafters were split logs, the walls roughcut planking from a local mill. Windows and odds and ends had been scavenged from dumps and appropriated from construction sites. They drew water from a handpump. This winter they'd built sleeping balconies, which cut down the wood they had to burn for heat. There was an outhouse around back, a tool and equipment shed, and a dugout storage cellar. They raised chickens, goats and rabbits and shot a deer or two in the winter. The permanent population varied between eight and ten, there was always a transient or two, and a few more would come to stay while the good weather lasted. When necessary, one of the men would hire out as a carpenter or housepainter a few weeks, or a girl would go to work waitressing. It was a good place and a good way to live.

Billy Harris said sure, she was welcome for the summer if she wanted, just let him know definitely sometime in the next week or two.

Kathy found Spirit chewing on a bone. He was a black and white dog of medium size with long silky fur and a feathery tail. Unlike Hero, he hadn't gone shy. He remembered Kathy—at least she thought he did; you could never tell, he was an indiscriminately affectionate slob—and he pounded his tail on the ground and licked her face. Spirit was around more often than not, but came and went as he pleased. He was fed table scraps, but not much, because there was little wastage at the Treehouse, but more because everyone was expected to pull his own weight. So he foraged in the woods for most of what he ate, gone for a day or a week.

At sunset some of them went to a nearby bluff that overlooked the valley and sat crosslegged with the backs of their wrists atop their knees and their thumbs touching their forefingers, and meditated until the light failed. They went back to the house, where the kerosene lamps were lit and Josie was cooking dinner, and passed around a little Lebanese red in a pipe, and Kathy sighed, as she sometimes did when all the naggling vicissitudes of life slipped away from her and she went floating up into peace and happiness, telling herself it should be this way for ever and ever and ever.

Ursula told him to come after the children were in bed, she didn't want him to see them. Despising himself, he almost agreed. But then anger welled up and he said, "No, I want to put my sons to sleep."

"You've done enough already," she said.

"I'll be there at seven, after dinner."

"You'll find the door locked."

"Don't fuck around, Ursula. I *am* going to see my children."

She greeted him icily. Pulled into a bun, her hair lay flat against her temples and brought the sharp planes of her face into even greater relief. Her mouth was thin, like a cutting edge. She let him in, then absented herself to the kitchen while he talked with the children and put them to bed. Jeff was still badly shaken. His face was swathed in bandaging and, five days later, he was still under sedation. He didn't want to play any games. Bauer read to him. Jeff was usually bouncy and garrulous before bed, but he sat quietly, hunched in a corner hugging his pillow and watching Bauer intently, as if he feared some violence from him, and Bauer's heart broke.

Ursula was paging through a magazine in the living room.

"We should talk," Bauer said.

"In the kitchen. I don't want them to hear us and get upset."

She poured herself a cup of coffee. Bauer had to ask for one for himself.

"You really did it this time," she said. "You let that beast tear your son's face apart. My baby's face. He wakes up screaming. I hold him, I rock him, and he doesn't know where he is. He screams 'Mommy, don't let him! Stop him, Mommy!' I could kill you, Alex."

"Cut it out. We both love him."

"Don't use plurals—you've lost your right."

"First, *Orph* bit Jeff, *I* didn't. Second, he's the one in pain, not you or me, so stop getting off on your maternal number. You didn't do either of them a damn bit of good with that scene you pulled in the hospital."

"Jesus, you're incredible. Your dog nearly kills my child, and somehow I'm responsible."

"The dog didn't 'nearly kill' him. He bit him, Ursula. Once. If he'd really attacked it would have been a lot worse."

She curled her lip with ugliness. "Somehow, I fail to feel appreciative."

"Jeff was trying to get Orph to play with a stick. The dog was trying to get away. Jeff hit him in the eye. It

was an accident. The dog responded instinctively. It did
not follow with an attack."

He didn't tell her how precarious it had been, how close
—he'd known it in his guts—the dog had come to a full
assault. Against Jeff, against Michael, even him. He'd
wakened from nightmares himself.

"Now it's Jeff's fault. No, Alex. It's not mine, it's not
Jeff's, it's not even primarily that monster's. It's *yours*.
Because you harbored a creature like that—a dangerous
wild thing that should have been destroyed or at least
locked in a cage where it couldn't hurt anyone. But you kept
it, against my wishes, against my desires, and you made
no effort to control it, you let it run free, you wouldn't
even put it away when your own children visited. It's
your fault, Alex. *You* did this. I have an appointment
with a lawyer next week. I can no longer entrust you
with the children's welfare. I won't stop you from seeing
them—not yet, anyway—but you're going to do it here, in
this house, under my supervision."

Bauer looked down to his coffee. He waited until he had
control. "No. The one thing, and maybe the only thing,
that I will not surrender or compromise on, is my children."

"At least there's one thing. It may be a first. But you
don't have any choice anymore."

Bauer stood. "Ursula," he said carefully. "If your lawyer's any good, he'll tell you you don't have a case. But if
you want to fight it, then go to court. Maybe it *is* better
to have this kind of thing on paper. But I'm going to get
them summers, and alternate holidays, and every weekend
if I can, at least twice a month if I can't, and I'll have it
written in to the order that you can't move more than
fifty miles from here. That's for openers, Ursula. Don't
ever threaten me with my children again. If for any reason you succeed in getting me barred from them, then

I'll take them to Europe, Ursula, and you won't see them until you're a toothless old woman. I *can* do it, and you know that I would. So think very carefully before you act."

She gave him a disdainful smile.

"Good night," he said.

She followed him to the door and stood there as he went down the porch steps. "When that dog comes home," she said, "I want it killed. I'll get a court order on that too if I have to. But I want it dead, so I can tell Jeff that it can't ever hurt him again, so he can sleep at night."

Bauer continued to his car without looking back.

Orph had been painfully hungry the first two days. The ground squirrels were too quick, the field mice vanished the instant he moved, and the crippled bird he'd stalked exploded into the air, not crippled at all, and by that time he'd been led too far and couldn't find the nest-scent again. He spent an afternoon digging up a long tunnel for nothing but a mouthful of dirt. The third day, he did not draw deeper into the woods when he encountered a human scent, as he had done before, but instead turned and moved slowly into its expanding intensity. He followed it to the edge of the trees, where it was powerful enough to overwhelm all the cracks and gabbles, weights and sinuous threads that were the various other odors and washed them back against a shallow reef of his awareness, and he stopped there and lay down in the shadows to stare at the unfamiliar house. He swallowed against the saliva that rose to the multicolored stratum of food winding in and out of the human scent. He didn't see any movement, but he knew they were there; their odor came to him on waves, a living presence, not a mark of passage. He waited until nightfall. Humans were creatures of the light.

He rose in the deep blackness and padded wide around the back of the house toward the food. The sounds from within indicated their own containment; the humans were oblivious to him. The food was in a metal can, as He had kept it. Orph nudged the top with his nose. The can rocked slightly on the stone, making a noise. Orph stood still and listened to the house. Nothing had changed. He bumped the top again. It stayed tight. He looked to the house. He sniffed the air, turned his ears. The night was unruffled. He knocked the can over. The top popped off with a clatter, junk and food spilled out. Pieces of meat, fat, bones. He swallowed greedily. A light went on over the back porch. Orph looked up, jaws still working, crushing small bones. The door opened, a man stepped out, raised his hand to his eyes and craned his head.

"Hey! Get out of there."

Orph backed up, ripped open a paper bag, snatched fat from it.

"Go on, damn it! Get out!" The man grabbed a piece of firewood and hurled it. It sailed over Orph's head. The man picked up another one and started down the stairs.

Orph swallowed, seized a big jointed bone with ragged pieces of gristle and turned and ran. A piece of firewood crashed against a branch as he plunged into the woods. The man didn't follow. Orph trotted until he found a place he liked, beneath a rock overhang, then settled down with the bone. After he'd ripped and gnawed off the tissue, he cracked the bone in the powerful vise of his jaws and licked the splinters clean of marrow.

Over a week, he learned. He began to anticipate the routes and movements of prey, he developed patience. He stood before mouse holes and runs, inching forward, stiffening, then the high pounce and snap of jaws. He began to catch a few, but was still hungry. He came out of the woods one night to another house and knocked the can over. There was an abundance in it. He ate for several minutes, then a light flashed from a darkened window and caught him at the food. A man's and a woman's voice. A metallic sound. And suddenly an alarming resonance in the muscles of his chest; harshness, anger from the house. Orph sniffed deeply. A powerful exudation, thick with savagery and killing; twined within it, the scent of oil, metal, and an unfamiliar pungency. Flat thunder clapped, flame stabbed from the window. Pain seared across Orph's back. He sprang into the darkness and raced to the trees. The light swept after him but didn't touch him again.

Orph licked the hurt through the night. It scabbed over by the next evening, and itched some after that, but wasn't very painful.

When he crossed human scent, he withdrew, unhurried, but carefully. Once he came upon one acrid with the killing odor and overlaid with the oil, metal and black pungency he'd smelled the night he'd been hurt, and he moved quickly then, putting half a mountain behind him before he felt easy again.

His cells swelled outward, he was received by the stone and wood. The tight, thin compression he'd lived with all his life abated, then was gone. There was clarity. He celebrated, he exulted.

At moments, though, was an uneasiness, an imbalance, a discordancy, which was Orph's nearest approximation to unhappiness. He had no literal memory, the recollection of vignette, but in a sensory consortium could see the image of Him, taste His scent, hear the timbre of His voice. There were throbs of emotion: colors, warmths, hungers that could not be stifled with food, sweet touches that penetrated past the skin to thrilled organs.

These brought him back one night. He emerged from the trees in darkness to stand looking at the lighted cabin.

He could smell Him, he heard the music He played. The comfort of His closeness, their bonded roaming, the gentleness and playfulness of His hands. The strange thing that made him want to be near.

Orph stepped toward the cabin.

The woods behind him pulled. The imminence of Him drew softly. Orph shuddered.

A stale blood scent. The roar of his own throat. Teeth. The shock of His anger. Shame and confusion. The pulsation of kill tremors from Him. The moon cold and powerful on his back. The rustling of the woods. Home: Home. Orph was palsied. He salivated. A riot in his mind, madness, unbearable pain, weakening legs, a drop of urine leaking his penis. He began to pant, he whimpered. He took a step backward, then another, and he whirled and went running into the woods.

The chain tore through the last of the spruce bole, spitting out a spray of resiny sawdust, and the tree began to lean, creaking, and Buddy Stokes hit the oil button, lubricating the hot saw, the screaming whine shrill in his ears even beneath the earplugs, but it was a part of the condition of his life, it was the music of his days, and he loved it.

The tree angled sharply and the few centimeters of bole wood left began to snap and tear in stringy fibers, and Stokes narrowed his eyes and curled his lips under in concentration and anticipation and pressed the singing chain hard against the wood to beat the rupturing, to finish it himself, and then the saw burst through, the spruce was severed, and it crashed down to the earth.

Stokes released the trigger and let the saw wind down and cough itself dead. He pulled his earplugs out. He wiped an arm across his forehead. The spruce had fallen well, where he wanted it. He was working a small rise, the land dropping at a soft decline beneath him, mostly denuded now, the limb-stripped trunks scattered like the bodies of brave, mindless soldiers after a massacre. Tomorrow morning he'd cut the limbs from the trees he'd felled today, by midafternoon he could start skidding the trunks out.

He sat on the new stump he'd made and lit a cigarette. He felt terrific. Buddy Stokes liked bringing trees to earth. He liked the awkward weight of his 3½-horsepower 20-inch saw. He liked things that were big, things that were heavy, things that were tough. He liked roaring through woods on his trail bike and snowmobile, pushing his car until it began to shake itself apart, big guns, the Ruger .41 Magnum single-action revolver he hunted deer with, the .338 Magnum Browning autoloader he took bear with. He liked fucking his wife in the ass and brawling in bars. He didn't mind broken teeth. Tattooed on his muscled forearm was a hammer and anvil.

He finished his cigarette and stomped the butt under his heel. He stood, wrenched his arms back, stretching, and went "*Waugh!*" Like a grizzly bear, a stag in rut. He made his way out of the ravaged woods to his jeep, tossed the saw in the back, and chewed up dirt when he turned the jeep around. He drove to the Granite Bar and Grill.

"Hey, hey—Buddy's here!" he boomed.

He greeted a couple of men. They slapped each other on the back, punched each other's arms.

"What was the double at Green Mountain?" Buddy said. "Anyone know?"

"Five and two."

"Goddamn. I had five and three."

"Paid nine hundred and eighty-seven."

"Goddamn," Buddy said again.

Charlie, the bartender, brought Buddy a shot of Seagram's and a mug of beer. Buddy dumped the whiskey into the beer and chugalugged it.

"Willis Quigley called about an hour ago," Charlie said. "He wants you to call back."

"Whooo-eee! That's the one I been waitin' for," Buddy said. "Gimme some phone change, Charlie."

"How big you think he's going to go?"

"Big as I can make 'im. Mama wants the money."

"Did you get that hundred down for me?"

"Can't get any local action, nobody wants to go against me. Are you comin'?"

"I don't know if I can get away."

"Well, if you can't, let me know. There'll be a bunch of out-of-town sports. I'll get someone to lay it there for you."

Charlie nodded.

Buddy went into the phone booth and closed the door. He dialed. "I want to talk to Willis Quigley," he said to the woman who answered. He waited.

"Hello?"

"Quigley? This is Buddy Stokes."

"Hi, Stokes," Quigley said amiably. "I hear you're putting a piece of stock up Sunday."

"That's right."

"Digger?"

"Uh-huh."

"Two and oh, right? Both kills."

"Yeah, that's right. Against the Red Dragon. Gene Murphy's from down by Cambridge. Same record. Even money. So what'd you have in mind?"

"Somewhere in the neighborhood of $500."

Stokes snorted. "Hell, that don't hardly pay for gas or stitches."

"Make it a thousand."

"Make it fifteen hundred."

"You got a bet, Stokes."

"I got a winner, Quigley."

"See you Sunday," Quigley said.

"Right." Stokes hung up. He stepped out of the booth. "Made 'im come, boy!" he said to Charlie.

"How much?"

"One five."

"Jesus, Buddy. That puts you three, three-and-a-half all together, doesn't it?"

"Four, but that's all money in the bank, friend, money in the bank."

Orph had come across another dog's scent line his first week in the woods. Respecting the animal's rights, he'd trotted along parallel to the scent and passed over its territory on the high side.

He encountered another territory the second week, staked off by more than one dog. He sniffed deeply, grasping for something elusive that wound through the claim. His mouth moistened. A tremor rippled his loins. He sniffed rapidly, then lifted his head.

He stepped over the boundary.

Nose up, he unraveled the thread from the others. He concentrated. He became certain. His blood rose.

He moved slowly through the proscribed territory, uneasy in his violation, tensing as the sense of the others' presence grew. His ears pricked forward to sound the crackles and rustlings of the woods. His eyes saw a static colorless backdrop, all shades of gray, the natural sway of vegetation unremarkably harmonious, the sudden sharp movement of animal life clashing across this quiet stage, quick to bring attention to itself. He sniffed rhythmically as he went, and at intervals he stopped to stand motionless and read, feel, and listen to the woods.

As he neared, he moved more recklessly, preparing for challenge, ready to take the blood-bitch.

They saw him first, as he came through a stand of black alders. He heard a deep growl and he froze. There were three of them, as he'd known from the moment he crossed into their territory.

They were resting in shade. One was a big black shaggy male, a little taller and heavier in the chest than Orph. At its side was the blood-bitch, a dun-colored dog of sixty pounds or so. The other male was the size of the bitch, a spotted dog with a curled tail. It was lying several yards from the black and the bitch.

Orph had come from downwind and startled them. The black jumped to its feet, hair lifting from its skull to the root of its tail. It pulled its lips back from long teeth and snarled. The bitch barked, but a coy sound, not a threat. The spotted dog rose and growled. The black gave it an angry bark and it slunk back with its tail between its legs. If the bitch had not been in blood and the black asserting primacy over the spotted, all three would have attacked Orph and driven him off.

The black laid its ears flat against its head. Its upper lip curled high above the gum to expose the full length of its teeth. Its eyes bored into Orph's.

Orph returned the stare. He advanced on stiff legs, threatening, his tail rising. He and the black circled, presenting each other with three-quarter's profile, drawing closer, maintaining eye contact, brinking the point of commitment.

The bitch yipped excitedly and raced around them. The spotted dog whined.

The black roared. Orph answered. They rushed together.

Their jaws met, they jerked their heads. Orph's muzzle was furrowed, the black's tongue ripped. The black went for Orph's shoulder. Orph sank his teeth into the side of its neck and tore flesh. The black pierced his ear, a tooth scraped the bone of Orph's skull. They went up on hind legs, snapping. The black slipped Orph across its shoulder and opened Orph's flank. Orph got on top and slashed the black's back. The black bit into Orph's hip and threw him. They rolled across the ground slashing at each other. Their coats splotched with blood and spittle, dirt caked the hairs. The black was up before Orph and went for Orph's leg. Orph lunged under its chest, flipped it over on its back and drove for the throat. He pierced the skin and bunched up the flesh between his jaws, but stayed the enormously powerful flexion of muscle that would have ripped most of the throat away, to the spinal column. He poised tensely. He rumbled deep in his chest.

The black sprinkled urine and splayed its legs, exposing its vitals. Its tail curled up to lie across its lower belly. It turned its head, offering its throat fully.

Orph released it and stepped back a little, watched closely.

The black avoided Orph's eyes. It rolled in the opposite direction and got to its feet. It hung its head and walked away, lay down without looking at Orph, and began to lick at its wounds. The spotted dog barked at it. The black sprang up, knocked it down and hung over it snarling insanely. The spotted dog gave it instant, terrified submission. The black allowed it to rise, and it hurried away.

The blood-bitch was looking at Orph with her tail high and wagging, eyes bright. Orph trotted over to her. They stood side by side. He raised his tail for her to know him, felt the touch of her nose. She lifted her tail. He licked her blood and swollenness. His legs trembled with excitement. He put a paw on her back.

She spun out from under and faced him. They touched the ends of their muzzles. Their tails wagged. She batted his face with a paw. He reciprocated. They stood on their hind legs and swatted each other. He raced around her, then rushed headlong toward her and pounced, landing a few feet in front of her. She whirled and slammed her rump into his side, went speeding off. He pursued her. They ran with great sweeping strides. He bumped her repeatedly with his shoulder, herding her. She reversed on him and plunged into the brush.

They ran for an hour, teasing each other. She stopped with her tongue out, panting. His muscles coiled and he seemed to grow bulkier. He put his front paws on her back and she bowed under his weight, but braced and supported it. He pumped against her side. She didn't move. He shifted his hind feet in a series of clumsy steps. His organ was half emergent. He shoved it against her hindquarters, against the blockage of her tail. She stood several minutes, then jumped out from beneath him and went running off again.

They courted two days, the taste and smell of her swollenness unfolded an increasing heaviness in Orph. They ate and drank little. They ran and wrestled and mock-fought each other into weariness. When she squatted to urinate, Orph lapped at the liquid with saliva foaming his jaws. When she was done, he paused to squirt his own urine on the patch of ground, marking it and her as his.

The black and the spotted dog followed at a desultory half mile. The black approached once when Orph and the bitch were resting, but Orph snarled and rushed it, and it retreated hastily and didn't try again.

On the morning of the third day, Orph licked the blood-bitch and his legs went weak. His throat thickened. His loins trembled. He hurled his weight on her. She ran him. He herded her roughly, biting at her ruff and slicking it with saliva. Finally she stopped. She lowered her head and flagged her tail high and to the side, exposing herself. He went up on his hind legs immediately, clasping her tightly around her loins with his forelegs. Humped over her, his eyes glassed and saliva dripped from his mouth in strings and he battered against her. In a minute he penetrated, and she yelped, and he drove frenziedly for some time. One of her back legs buckled, both of them staggered as she worked to regain her footing, but he didn't stop, and it went on that way several minutes, and then panting he slowed, and then didn't move, he was huge and deep within her, knobbed, unable to separate, and he slid off her back at an angle to her, still tied, and slowly he worked his left rear leg up and over her back and down to ground, and they stood rump to rump facing in opposite directions.

A quarter of an hour passed, and then all his strength shot into her. He shrank, slipping out, and walked away unsteadily. He stopped. The spasms began. His abdomen tightened, toward his backbone, the clenching moved forward to his diaphragm, started from the rear again, rolled that way several moments. He made choking sounds. His stomach emptied in a rush. He retched for several moments, than sank down in exhaustion. His eyelids lowered flutteringly.

A little later the spotted dog came creeping toward the bitch, who had rested only a short while and was now up and ambling about. Its scent drifted into Orph's sleeping mind, and jarred him awake. He lunged up with a roar. The spotted dog ran. Orph overtook it and bit it twice, hard, on the rump. The spotted dog shrieked. Orph stopped the pursuit and stood long enough to be sure the spotted dog was gone, then he returned to the bitch.

Orph mounted her twice again in the next two days. The other dogs lingered not far away. Orph permitted them to approach on the following day. The bitch was no longer in blood, and he was unconcerned. She sported and teased them and they responded eagerly, but when they tried to climb her she snapped and drove them back, would not stand, her season past.

Orph was ravenous. The other three dogs milled listlessly. Orph walked about, head high, tasting the air. Faintly, in the direction of the sinking sun, came the scent of a food animal.

Orph set out in that direction. The bitch and the spotted and the black fell in behind him.

CHAPTER 5

ELIZABETH COLLIER washed her hair and brushed it until it hung lustrous and silky about her shoulders. She put on a red blouse with long collar tips and puffy sleeves, snug black ski pants. She looked good, provocative. Ordinarily she wasn't very concerned with her appearance. But the Covington American Legion chapter had invited her as a veterinarian and canine-behavior authority to debate Harry Wilson before an audience. She wanted to discomfit him. It was a petty tactic, but she didn't care. She didn't like Wilson. He was a pompous opportunist, with limitless ego. He was married to a bewildered child of a woman, whom he made the butt of hurtful jokes. He'd asked Elizabeth out, and once when he cornered and groped her at a party, she'd said she'd turn celibate first and figure she had the best of the deal.

Wilson was late. They waited, the audience grew restive.

Half an hour after the debate was to have begun, Wilson's office phoned with his regrets, he was tied up with something else. So Elizabeth spoke alone.

They weren't happy. The antidog people didn't want to hear anything but that the animals were a menace and a plague, which they were not, and the dog owners refused to accept any responsibility at all.

Elizabeth left in anger and depression. She wasn't impressed much by the human race and wouldn't have given more than 50–50 on its ability to survive itself. She wasn't sure whether that mattered. The planet would probably be a nicer place without them.

Bauer walked down the stairs of Tully Hall with Kathy Lippman after class. He'd hurried to gather his material into his briefcase and he felt foolish and obvious. She'd scribbled some final notes, then rummaged through her purse before she got up, one of the last students to leave, so maybe she'd waited for him. He didn't know. He'd never been very good at recognizing female approaches.

She'd been friendly and bright since the night of the seminar, perfectly easy, but that could mean anything. Maybe it was a closed issue for her. How could he tell? He was flustered and clumsy.

"Going to take the summer term off?" he asked.

"Uh-huh. That's one thing I can't do, study during the nice weather. It's all I can manage to finish up this term."

"Are you going home, or working in Covington?"

She laughed. "Not home, except for a long weekend. My parents can't communicate without shouting at each other. We get on fine if I limit it to a couple of visits a year. There's a kind of commune up around Sproul's Mountain. I'll do the summer there."

They emerged from the building onto the quad,

moments from going their separate ways. Bauer was tight. How? Christ, each time was like the first, as if he'd never done it before. Kathy looked at him curiously. Well shit, he thought. If she said no, he wasn't a dead man. It was what he'd done to her, after all.

"I thought I'd smoke that joint tonight. I . . . was wondering . . . which end to light."

Their pace slowed.

"Usually," she said, without expression, "one end will be thinner and tighter than the other. That's the one you put in your mouth. Light the fat end."

"Oh," he said. She wasn't buying. Fuck it.

She continued to look at him.

"I thought," he forced himself to say, "that you might like to smoke it with me."

"Sure."

Bauer was relieved, and happy. "Well, why didn't you say so in the first place?"

"I did. Before. Remember? You turned me down. I figured you should do the asking this time, not just leave me an opening."

"Fair enough."

"And see, *I* didn't turn *you* down."

He was feeling pleased with himself. "Maybe I'm irresistible."

"No, not at all. But you're attractive."

"Knock me down, build me up."

"That's part of the fun, isn't it? Besides, we know where we're going in the end."

Bauer was cheered by Kathy's presence on the walk home, and charged with anticipation of her, calmed and deeply gratified by the certainty. It was good, then, to luxuriate in delay. They exchanged small personal notes, they made some jokes. She was funny, in an intuitive, whacky way. He relaxed. They appraised each other's body frankly, in anticipation, with little smiles.

The western horizon was a brilliant, bloody wound when they reached the cabin. Kathy looked about and said, "Where's your dog?"

"I don't know. He . . . took off into the woods one afternoon. He's been gone two weeks."

"Does he do that?"

"Now and then, but never this long."

"Will he come back?"

"I don't know."

"I'm sorry. But I do feel a little looser, you know? He didn't seem to like people, I was nervous around him."

Bauer had placed an ad in the paper, inquired at the houses around him and hiked hours in the woods calling the dog's name. At first he'd felt rage at the animal, and still had some anger, but, miserably, was of the growing conviction that he had failed both it and his sons. Recrimination had led to self-revulsion.

He didn't know what he would do when Orph returned, *if* Orph returned. Not destroy him, certainly. The dog, he finally understood, was truly dangerous, but—and here he questioned himself to determine, hideous to contemplate, if he loved and needed the animal so much that he'd excuse it the mutilation of his own son—not morally culpable; it simply was what it was, a natural creature that had acted out of nucleic demand. There was fault, but it was Bauer's. He owed his sons for the pain and brain-stunning terror. He owed Orph, for not having given him the training and discipline that would have precluded an attack.

Ursula's lawyer had served him with divorce papers, including sole custodial rights to the children (the attorney was staunchly in her corner, but did indicate that he

thought her position extreme and would try to talk her
into reasonableness) and was petitioning the court for an
order mandating the dog's destruction. Whether she succeeded or not, Bauer couldn't keep Orph. Jeff would never
come within sight of the dog again, nor would Bauer let
him. There were alternatives. Orph was a superb German
shepherd. He was a stray, but there were procedures for
obtaining conditional registration papers. Bauer could give
him to an exhibitor. Or to a police canine unit, the mili-
tary, a guard dog school. Someone experienced with a dog
of Orph's nature. Any of these, though it saddened him.
The loss would be his; Orph would probably find fulfill-
ment. Though he wanted to see Orph and know he'd be
properly cared for, part of him hoped the dog would make
his home in the wilds and never return. In retrospect, he
saw that Orph hadn't been a pet, that his soul had always
been in the mountains, alien to the works of men, and that
he'd blossom in freedom and become the creature of his
blood.

Bauer smoked the joint with Kathy. The grass got
beneath him and carried him up; his tactile awareness
soared, he thought with clarity, he relaxed and became
easy and comfortable with Kathy. Histories weren't important. They talked of their immediacies, tiny and large, and
it was a lubricated exchange. He put the Mass in B Minor
on. They lay on the couch. He stroked her hair, he unbuttoned her shirt and caressed her breasts. She told him to
roll onto his stomach. She forked him and leaned on her
hands and massaged his back. At the end of the "Gloria"
she said, "If you go to sleep on me, I'll murder you."

"Not a chance," he murmured.

She got another joint from her purse. It hit him fast.
He voluptuated. They touched each other. He explored
her mouth with his tongue. Then her tongue was atop his,
beneath it, around his cheeks, into the pockets between his

lips and teeth. She shrugged out of her shirt and took her
jeans and panties off, removed his shirt and trailed her
hair and nipples across his chest. She undid his pants. She
rolled his shorts down slowly, freeing the swollen hardness
of his shaft by degrees, then when it bucked unfettered
she slipped her lips over its head, lowered her mouth to
its base, then drew back with equal care, and released
him. They went into the bedroom. Kathy opened herself
and they joined, as key pieces in a puzzle, and found a
synchronous rhythm immediately, and they touched each
other in different places as they moved and, in a while,
their deep rocking ceased to be a means toward an end
and became its own significance, he banded her with his
arms and they pressed their cheeks together and breathed
hypnotically, nearly whole, expanding to a total melding,
which was not possible, and gradually drew back into
themselves, assenting, and drove steadily deeper, and sens-
ing his tentative imminence she slid from herself to him,
assisted, encouraged, accelerated and finally compelled him
to hammer into her and he arched his torso up, driving
to the limit, and threw his head back and emptied with
spasms rippling his body and harshness tearing from his
throat. He remained still several moments after it had
passed, and then began to move again, pulling her up from
the stasis into which she had frozen herself to do for
him, catching it before it could fade, and releasing her
back to herself, becoming her acolyte, the instrument and
partner of her will, and she moved greedily, mindlessly to
it, and the ascent was steep, but not far, and as she
poised and gathered in, shuddering, on the edge, he
wrenched control from her for an instant and pushed her
into the resolution over which she hesitated, then subju-
gated himself again, and her pelvis rose, her eyes opened
and widened without focus, and a great elongated
"Aaaaaaaaaaahhhhhhhhhhh!" issued from her, and as it

fell he pounded once, twice, and she soared up again, and he waited until she began to spiral down, then ground into her, and saliva appeared at the corners of her mouth, her head lolling spastically, and he kept her there until she was convulsing and his receding strength deserted him at last and then he lowered his chest to her pillowy breasts and his head sank over her shoulder, and she went limp beneath him.

After silence, she whispered, "Oh my motherfucking God."

Later they did other things.

Bauer woke with the sunrise and the bird chorus. He was lying on his back, Kathy was sleeping on her side, nestled against him. It was a strange sensation. He liked her warmth. He recalled the night with amazement, scarcely able to credit that it had been him. He dissected it and tried to place it in a context. Malaise seeped in around his edges. He made himself stop, but feared he was evading an obligation, defaulting to something he could not name. He shunted the feeling aside. Now, at this moment, he felt good, and he was weary of not feeling good. He intended to let the pleasure live as long as it could. He wondered briefly if he might still be high and decided that if he was, he didn't care. He rolled over and bowed against Kathy, put a hand over her breast. She pressed in without waking. He closed his eyes and went back to sleep, happy.

Orph led, the others followed. The black was more experienced, and better at killing, but Orph was stronger and bolder. Orph ate first, snarling the others away. After a few days he allowed the bitch to eat with him. When he was done and had stepped away, the black and spotted would tear in hungrily.

The pack had killed a few deer in winter, when the animals were foundered in snowdrifts, but the deer were too swift and large otherwise, a larger pack was needed to bring them down, and so they didn't try often, settling for the luck of a very young fawn or an occasional sick or crippled animal.

In his ignorance, Orph ran them after deer, which startled them. They pursued single file, strung out over a fifth of a mile, with the spotted dog, who was the fastest, soon taking the lead. As the quarry cut and angled, the dog with the best possibility of interception would veer off and the other three would swing in behind it. Once, on level ground along a stream course, the spotted dog boxed a doe against a high deadfall, between two rock walls. The doe tried to scramble up, but fell back. The spotted dog seized a rear leg. She kicked him off and whirled. He jumped, snapping for her lips. She reared, flailed at him with hard, sharp hooves. One thudded painfully into his shoulder, the other split the skin of his muzzle and broke off a tooth. He rolled over, momentarily dazed. The doe leapt across him and bounded out of the box and was gone. After half a dozen futile coursings, Orph didn't try again.

They spent most of their time seeking food, like every other creature in the woods. They ate squirrels and frogs, nesting animals and fledgling birds. Orph learned: He stalked his first porcupine alone, while the others circled nervously, harrying it with barks but holding back; the animal flared its quills, which doubled its size, but Orph kept after it in dancing lunges, suppressing the sense of wrongness that prevented him from a solid bite and made him want to draw away, and then the porcupine's tail flicked against his foreleg and set it afire. Quills bobbed from the leg, hurting him fiercely. He retreated. The other three dogs followed with relief. He dropped down and chewed at the quills with small hard bites. The porcupine watched the dogs several minutes, backed away, waited, then turned and waddled off. Orph had to chew into the meat of his leg before he could pull the last of the barbs out. He was sick for two days.

They ate groundhog when they could cut one off from its burrow. Orph took the animals head-on while the black went for their backs, the belly if Orph flipped them over, and the bitch and the spotted dog tried for legs or the rump.

Their territory shifted as they ranged out of it, abandoned old runs and marked new boundaries. They were most active in the early morning and evening hours. In midday they rested in shade and groomed themselves, or each other, and sometimes they would wrestle or chase each other in play. Nights, they turned, pressing down grass for a bed, and slept close to one another, waking at intervals to lift their heads and listen and take the air. Orph slept restlessly, rising to pad about and probe for menace, and at first the other dogs sprang up in alarm when he stood, but they accustomed themselves to his movements before long and didn't pay them much attention.

When they ran across human scent they turned away from it, unless there were strong traces of food; then, if they were hungry, they would follow it and eat at a camp if they found it empty, or nose out buried or abandoned scraps at an old one.

CHAPTER 6

THEY met in a dilapidated barn on a farm thirty miles outside Covington. The barn leaned, and was braced against collapse with a couple of whole tree trunks, to which bark still adhered and from which the long stubs of old branches projected. A section of the high roof had fallen in. The barn hadn't sheltered animals in years, there were car parts and rusted appliances around, confused heaps of junk. It smelled dry and dusty.

They'd trickled in starting at seven A.M. in panel trucks, station wagons, pickups, sports cars and sedans, avoiding a single large convergence of vehicles, which would have been noticed and might have drawn attention from the law. The license plates were largely local, but New York was represented, Rhode Island and Massachusetts. One guy had come from Ohio. A carload of sports had driven up from Virginia. The dogs had been brought in the panel trucks and station wagons, locked in wire cages. There were upwards of a hundred men.

A single electrical cord ran the length of the barn, tacked to a central beam. There were simple porcelain fixtures and bare bulbs. A 200-watt floodlight was mounted in the center, above an area of freshly raked dirt. One of the farmer's sons, in peaked hat and coveralls, sold beer out of ice-filled tubs for a dollar a can. His mother stood behind a plank table selling sandwiches from platters covered with waxed paper for a dollar and a half. It was only coming on nine, but three cases of beer had been finished already, and a few men were swigging from pint bottles. Tobacco smoke hung beneath the harsh lights.

Buddy Stokes arrived swaggering and loudmouthed. He *knew* Digger would take Murphy's Dragon, and he'd decided this was the make or break and borrowed another $3000 from the bank on a fraudulent Home Improvement loan. He wanted to rile the gentry, piss the good old boys enough to put up the salad. And he did, got it matched by the time the pit was up.

The pit was twelve feet square, its walls waist-high panels of plywood hinged for easy setup and knockdown, stained with old brownish blood. It belonged to a guy from Mount Vernon. They put it together over the raked dirt, directly beneath the floodlight.

Stokes had a total of $7000 riding. If he went bust—but he wouldn't, he knew he wouldn't—it'd be back to the bush league until he could build the roll up again, two or three years. But if Digger topped, there was $14,000 in the kit. That would be enough to finance him to Florida in November, and Texas in December, the big time, the highrollers' run. Figure $4000 for expenses, which left ten. Play it safe in Florida. Pit Digger for five. If he lost, still five left for Texas. But if he won, $15,000 in the pocket, and Texans, grab your asses. Between today and the Florida match, he figured Digger'd pretty much have it. Retire him with honor, keep him around a year or two for stud, then out to the rosebush. Some guys sold their old dogs to grubbers for a few hundred bucks. Stokes respected his animals too much. When they got old or crippled, he put them down himself, with one clean shot, and gave them to the rosebush. The rosebush was Stokes' prize, a great, sprawling mountain of summer fire, one of the wonders of the neighborhood. It had thrived on the numberless kittens and the few dogs he'd fed it.

If he got to Texas, he was going to fight Buddy's Bad Boy and back him with the whole $15,000. Boy was Digger's son, out of a good bitch from Syracuse, the toughest, meanest, sonofabitchin' bonecracker of a dog Stokes had ever seen. Stokes suspected early on that he had a genuine all-time champion on his hands and he'd put everything he had into the dog's training. He wasn't disappointed. He'd fought Boy only once, over in Concord, at a small meet, wanting to test him without attracting much attention. God Almighty, Stokes had never even *heard* of anything like he'd seen that day. Boy was a goddamn meatgrinder, just spit the pieces of that other dog all over the pit then looked around for something else to destroy. Got a lot of play in the sportin' magazines, which Stokes hadn't wanted (no sense letting the opposition know what they'd be up against), but the reports were mostly hearsay and Stokes didn't pit him again, ignored the inquiries he received. Let the speculation build. Unless Boy went against a boar grizzly in Texas, he'd mop up anything they threw at him and Stokes would come out with $30,000; more if he could get odds, which might be possible, since hardly anyone had seen Boy's stuff. He'd be on the way then.

The referee hadn't shown up and men were grumbling and growing surly. There were arguments, some shouting. Various people volunteered to referee, but were accused of having bet too much to judge fairly. Willis Quigley, slight, with a thin moustache and a large diamond on the ring finger of each hand, proposed that a coin toss between the men who were pitting animals in the second match determine the referee of the first, a toss between the owners in match three to determine the referee of match two, a man from the fourth to judge the third, and a man from the first to judge the fourth. This was agreed to be a fine solution and the selections were made quickly.

Stokes was to referee the first match. "All right," he said to the handlers, "bring your dogs and let's get it on."

He stepped over the plywood wall into the pit and scratched his belly, surreptitiously shifting the flat Mauser .380 Autopistol under his waistband to a more comfortable lay. Pit fighting used to be a small, gentleman's sport, but it was growing bigger, and the money heavier, and undesirable elements were moving in. Last year in Georgia two rip-off artists had shot a guy and knocked over a match for $20,000. Stokes had spotted half a dozen men in the barn with concealed guns. The .380 was a dinky little caliber, but easy to hide, fast-firing, and accurate, and Stokes used handloaded, jacketed hollow-point slugs which would blow up a pretty good hunk of meat. At short ranges, the load had the impact of a .38 Special, a decent man-killer.

The dogs were brought in. Stokes was disgusted. This was a slop match. One of the animals was a huge Great Dane–Doberman cross that snarled and showed its teeth at everyone. It was charged with amphetamine. Drugs were rarely used on real dogs; it burned them out too quickly and left them weak and vulnerable. The crossbreed was more than twice the size of its opponent, a nice-looking black-and-white Staff. A handful of amateurs shouted out bets on the cross. The smart money picked them up right away. A couple of pros bet a little on the cross at five-to-one, trying the long shot just for kicks. The dummies grew uneasy, suspecting they'd been suckered, which they had.

The dogs were pitted under Stokes' instruction. The cross attacked the Staff crazily, slashing all over its back and side. Silently, the Staff seized one of the cross's forelegs and crushed it. The cross fought like a maddened bird of prey, the Staff like an imperturbable juggernaut. The fight lasted less than ten minutes. Bones broken, deep gaping wounds in its chest and sides, the cross tucked its tail, screamed and tried to flee.

"Cur! He's gone cur!"

Stokes turned to the cross's owner, who'd bought the dog from a junkyard dealer for a hundred dollars. "Your dog has curred, Mr. Andrews. That's the match."

Andrews stuffed his hands in his pocket and looked unhappily into the pit, where the Staff had the cross down and was on its neck. "Aw shit, let Scanlan's dog finish him."

The cross was dead a few minutes later. Someone helped Andrews lift its corpse out of the pit. Scanlan removed his dog and began cleansing its wounds. Only one needed suturing. The dog licked Scanlan's face.

The winners collected their money, the farmer raked over the dirt and worked in some sawdust to dry up the blood. A ten-minute break was called. Men got new beers and chewed down sandwiches. There were brags, tales of other fights, speculation on impending ones, a lot of jibing.

"Hey, Charlie. How you going to write up that abortion?" The man who asked had his shirt unbuttoned to the navel. A tattoo of two dogs twisted in combat spanned his chest.

Charlie Daws published an underground news magazine

for the fight audience. Its subscription list was closely guarded and expansion was cautious. He looked disgusted. "Garbage match," he said. "Scanlan's Iron Bite killed a big mongrel in a quarter hour, period."

Stokes brought Digger in, a four-year-old fawn Staff with a white chest. The Staffordshire terrier had been evolved down through the centuries from the best stock of what had once been the broadly popular sport of pit fighting. Their primogenitor, far back in history, was the early English mastiff, a terrible brute the hairy tribes had sent against the Romans in barbarous Britain. The Romans were sufficiently impressed with the beasts to name them *Canis pugnaces*, warrior dogs, and they imported and bred them by the thousands to fight in the arenas against men and bears and wild bulls, and incorporated them into the army where their ferocity and power were used to break infantry attacks and rout cavalry.

The Staff was a shade smaller than a Labrador retriever, but there comparison ended. The Staff's head and muzzle were deep, the skull broad and domed. The cheek muscles bulged like swollen bladders. Its chest was massive and hard. The wide shoulder blades were sheathed in muscle. The ribs were well sprung and prominent and the back and hindquarters were muscled in cables. Occasionally, other breeds were fought and someone was always experimenting with crossbreeding and pitting the results, but the Staffordshire terrier was the favorite, and the finest fighting dog on earth. The whole of its being tightened into a knot of fighting frenzy at the sight of another dog, it was grossly powerful, a creature of raw courage, and it considered pain beneath its attention. With human beings, it was affectionate and gentle, particularly responsive to and protective of children.

Some guys said it was all in the blood and training didn't make any difference, you couldn't build heart in a loser. Well, the blood part was true, but the rest was bullshit. You bred for a monster, a wildass gut-eater who'd keep coming after he'd been quartered with an axe, but it was training and careful management that made the final difference between glory and a fortune, and a sack of ripped meat that was a dead dog. Stokes started a pup when it was three months old. He used a thick piece of leather as a pull toy, tugging hard against the pup, strengthening its bite and developing its musculature. When the pup was six months, Stokes began bringing home kittens, and a little later, cats. He nipped off the claws with a wire cutter and hung the felines in a loose mesh bag from a spring-fixed rope that had bounce and give, over a small pit he had in a shed. He restrained his pup to let its eagerness and frustration mount as the cat thrashed and moaned, then he said, "Go get 'im!" and released it, and urged it on excitedly while it worked the kitten over. If the kitten survived, Stokes kept it overnight and tossed it into the pit the next day for the pup to finish. He used up to fifty kittens and cats on the average dog, burying the carcasses in the bed of his rosebush. After the cats came the suspension leather, a thick piece on a rope. Once the dog locked its teeth in, Stokes hauled the rope up, lifting the animal into the air. Then he squatted next to it saying, "Hang in, hang in, that's the boy, that's my killer, keep it up, you're iron, baby, you can do it, hang sweetheart, hang, all the way, baby. . . ." In time, a good dog could twist there half an hour, forty-five minutes. It built jaws with the bite of a hydraulic vise, a front assembly with the power of a locomotive. He maintained the hang work through all of a dog's fighting life, and he never stopped working them on the treadmill, walking in confinement atop an uptilted belt whose speed could be varied; muscles turned into stone. It was one thing to have a hardbiting dog with heart, but another to have one with experience to boot. The best training for combat was combat. So Stokes and a couple of friends would pit their younger animals in controlled matches, careful not to let it go to the point of grievous damage, getting the dogs used to pain, pairing them with animals just a hair more rugged, to force them to greater effort. In a real match, for blood and money, people usually pitted equals. Some liked bitches—they fought faster and more viciously—but Stokes preferred males, who had more guts, were more brutal and willing to take greater punishment. A guy in Chicago was supposed to have a seventeen-fight winner —Podowski's Gutbuster—but Stokes didn't believe it. A dog needed at least three months to recover from a decent fight—frequently as long as a year—and Stokes had never seen a veteran of six or seven fights that didn't look and move like he'd been put together by Dr. Frankenstein.

Digger weighed in at 43 pounds even, a good catch-weight. At chain-weight, pet status, he'd have gone another 10 to 12 pounds. Stokes stood by while Gene Murphy, the Red Dragon's owner, and the referee washed Digger with clear water from a big bucket—to remove any poison, tranquilizer or caustic that might have been applied to the dog's coat to enter its opponent's mouth. Dragon turned the scale at 43 pounds, 8 ounces. He was a brindle Staff. The cartilage of one ear had been ravaged in a previous fight and the ear lay aslant across his head. Stokes and the referee washed him with the same water used on Digger.

Stokes took Digger into the pit. Murphy and Dragon entered from the other side. The dogs fixed each other with steady eyes and strained forward in silence, ears pricked, brows furrowed.

Murphy nodded. Stokes nodded. "Pit 'em!" the referee said.

Digger and Dragon lunged across the pit and met with

an audible clacking of teeth, going for muzzle holds. They locked and stood stifflegged, used their necks and shoulders to try to throw each other down. They wavered tensely, like arm wrestlers.

Stokes was down on one knee by Digger's shoulders. "Pull," he said, "pull, baby. Take him to the side. You got him. That's the way. Good boy. Twist it, baby. Get him, get him."

Murphy was close to Dragon giving encouragement.

The spectators jammed shoulder to shoulder and egged on their favorites.

The dogs hauled and jerked at each other several minutes, shifting their footing to balance or to throw sudden leverage into the struggle. Blood welled around their jaws. Dragon bowed low, forelegs extended nearly parallel to the ground, pulling Digger's head down, and used his powerful thighs to plow backward, trying to drag Digger to his belly.

Stokes and Murphy moved with the animals, voices urgent.

Digger missed a step and stumbled forward. Dragon jerked. Digger released suddenly, twisted free of the brindle's hold and came in over it to seize an ear. Dragon couldn't find a hold of his own and Digger forced him down and over on his side. Dragon writhed there, then heaved up, but couldn't break the ear-clamp. Digger bulled the brindle around the pit.

Dragon tried for a leg hold, ripped flesh but didn't lock. He threw his shoulder into Digger's chest, and simultaneously pulled his head in the opposite direction. His ear was shredded and partly ripped from the base, leaving a bloody stump from which an edge of white gristle showed. He spun in a circle and came in low, his favorite direction, while Digger came high again. Dragon went solidly into Digger's chest. Digger caught Dragon's flank, and a piece of thigh meat too. Bent into a rough circle, the dogs turned, seeking leverage with which to dump each other.

Stokes and Murphy turned with them, crouched, whispering into their ears. The audience grew louder. The fight was getting serious now.

Digger yanked Dragon's thigh up, unbalancing him, and threw him over. Dragon's teeth were spiked into Digger's chest. He dragged the fawn down with him. They lay twisted awkwardly around each other, straining without sound. Muscles corded, blood flowed around their jaws. They chewed each other long minutes. The crowd leaned to see precisely what damage was being done. Then there was a sudden flurry of paws, quick contortions and savage jerks of the head, and both dogs were up, free, and they went muzzle to muzzle again.

The crowd cheered.

Digger had the top hold. He worked Dragon's nose and bone. Dragon came down on Digger's tongue and up through the bottom of his jaw. Their sides heaved. Carefully, they stepped round and around.

Digger's chest had an area of raw red meat the size of a man's hand. Blood ran down to his belly. Dragon's thigh was bloody and he favored that leg, but only slightly. The dogs sprang apart and Dragon whirled, slamming his hard rump into Digger's shoulder, staggering him to the side.

"That's a turn!" the referee yelled. "Hold your dogs!"

Murphy and Stokes grabbed their animals in both arms before they could engage again. A turn was a bid for respite, like a boxer wrapping an opponent up or pushing him away. The referee brought a bucket with a single sponge. Murphy and Stokes washed their animals' wounds, cleansed the thick saliva and blood from their mouths.

The bucket was removed, the dogs were set against each other again.

Digger got into Dragon's side and chewed a rib apart. Dragon worked Digger's foreleg. He broke it above the dewclaw. Digger's foot flopped. He maneuvered on a bone stump. They went back to muzzles and drew cheers and whistles from the crowd: the nose was the most sensitive target, an animal badly ripped there often curred, and most were careful about their snouts. They punished each other's muzzles without flinching, then Digger trapped Dragon's nose with a side bite, between the rear molars, and ground away. Dragon had trouble pulling loose. When he did, his nose was split and mashed and he was exhaling blood through it in bubbles. But he didn't turn. He ripped a fist-sized piece of meat from Digger's shoulder. Digger wrecked muscle on Dragon's hip, hobbling him and felling his tail. It was an hour into the fight. The crowd was high. The dogs were tiring, sides heaving and breathing hoarsely, Dragon sucking air mostly through his mouth, with difficulty when he was on a bite, losing his holds more quickly than Digger. The pace slowed. Both dogs became more cautious and deliberate, but their quiet brutality didn't waver. Stokes and Murphy hung near them, sweating, voices rough with strain. Dragon was weakening. There was a ripple of new betting, with Digger's people offering three-to-two odds. Then Dragon threw Digger and straddled him with teeth sunk into his withers. Digger couldn't find a bite. He couldn't break loose. The brindle bored in, and his money cheered. Digger bellied backward, at the expense of ripping flesh. He pulled himself and Dragon up against the wall, then squirmed along it until Dragon was partly caught in the corner. He worked to tear loose from Dragon's teeth. Dragon's bite pulled away from muscle and meat, finally held only skin. Slowly, he peeled the skin up over Digger's shoulders, exposing raw beef-flesh and overlays of quivering gray muscle. Digger went into shock. He lay with his legs splayed out, shuddering. Dragon skinned him halfway up his skull, then the hide split apart. Dragon shook the big bloodied piece. He spat it out and went back to Digger. Stokes was shouting at his dog. Digger sighed. Dragon's teeth pierced him, going deep to some nerve. Digger spasmed. He exploded up, throwing Dragon over backward.

"Go baby! Get him, get him!" Stokes screamed.

Digger went to the belly. Dragon curled and locked onto the naked flesh of Digger's neck. When they broke, they went head to head, and a rope of intestine bulged from a hole in Dragon's abdomen, a flap of meat hung down Digger's neck exposing a trembling half-severed tendon. They chewed at each other's faces. One of Dragon's eyes was ruptured. Digger went deep into Dragon's throat and ground his jaws. Dragon lay on his side. His bleeding tongue lolled out. He lifted his head feebly, scratched at the dirt. Digger stood over him, chewing. Dark blood swelled. Dragon convulsed.

The referee said, "Mr. Murphy?"

Murphy looked down at the dogs without answering.

"Tear him up," Stokes urged Digger. "Good boy, good boy. Finish him!"

Dragon's spurting blood soddened the earth. His eyes were closed, his paws twitched. He trembled, then lay still. Digger went on chewing. He released Dragon in a few minutes and sat back to lick at the stump of his own foreleg. He returned to Dragon's throat, stopped to lick himself again.

The referee said, "Hold your dog, Mr. Stokes." He knelt beside Dragon, wetted his palm and held it before the dog's mouth and ruined nose feeling for breath. He plugged a stethoscope into his ears and presssed the bell to Dragon's chest. He got up an announced, "Mr. Murphy's

Red Dragon is dead. The match goes to Mr. Stokes' Digger."

The crowd applauded. A couple of men jumped the pit to slap Stokes on the back. Stokes was elated—he was on his way. He went down on his knees and took Digger's head gently in his hands, careful not to touch the raw flesh. Tears rose in his eyes. He kissed the dog. "That's my baby, that's my love." Digger swished his tail and licked Stokes' face. Stokes lifted him out of the pit and turned him over to a friend, who began flooding the animal's wounds with hydrogen peroxide.

Stokes went to Murphy and shook his hand. "He was some kind of dog, Gene. All heart. Guts right to the end. I'm sorry you had to lose him."

"It goes that way," Murphy said. "You got a real animal there. You think he'll make it?"

"I don't know. I never saw a skinning like that. The leg don't look good either. I'm going to get him over to Worcester. We'll give him the best we can."

The crowd was garrulous and happy, only the heavy losers were subdued. It had been a hell of a match. Charlie Daws had snapped a roll of film. His camera hung from his neck and he was scribbling notes in a pad. He looked up as Stokes passed. "Congratulations," he said. "One hour and sixteen minutes of top-of-the-line action. I'm giving feature coverage to this one."

Stokes collected his winnings. He carried Digger out to the truck and made a bed of an old blanket on the cab floor. He started for Worcester, sixty miles away, where there was a vet who'd treat pit dogs without filing a report. "Hang on, old friend," Stokes said tenderly. "We're going to get you taken care of."

Most of the bandaging was off. Jeff's left cheek was taped with gauze from the bottom of his eye down past his jaw to the top of his throat. Bauer had changed the dressing at noon. It was the first time he'd seen the wound since the attack and his stomach had lurched. There was a great swollen semicircle of ravaged flesh crossed with ugly, knotted black sutures. The infection was under control but the wound still oozed a viscous yellow fluid and the dressing had to be changed frequently, ointment applied. Bauer suppressed an impulse to crush his son to his chest and weep over him.

"It's coming along pretty well," he said, trying for an easy tone.

"It doesn't hurt a lot anymore, only a little." Jeff was beginning to regain his weight and color.

Ursula had taken him down to New York to a plastic surgeon. He was going to need four or five operations over the next few years, and Bauer ached for him, but the surgeon was optimistic.

Ursula was still determined to win sole custody, and Bauer's lawyer was in consultation with hers, but at least her attorney had convinced her that it was to her benefit not to interfere with Bauer's visitation privileges until the case went before a judge.

She wouldn't forgo making a point of her anger, though. She left the house before Bauer arrived and had Janie turn the children over to him. She refused to speak to him on the phone, Bauer was furious with her; it was making the children withdrawn and wary. He'd written to her in reasonable words, but she hadn't acknowledged the letter.

The boys had agreed to spend the Saturday with him, but neither was willing to stay the night at his cabin, they wanted to go home at the end of the day. He took them to Lake Kilmer and rented a boat and cane poles. They fished the shoreline and weedbeds and filled a stringer with panfish. Jeff liked being on the water and got excited when he caught a fish, beamed as Bauer unhooked it and put it on the stringer. While Bauer threaded a worm onto his hook Jeff said, "I can't do that yet. I'd stick myself with the point. But in a couple years, when I'm as old as Michael I'll be able to, won't I?" Jeff was resilient and irrepressible, a relentless positivist. He was no longer much more impressed by his mauling than he would have been by a skinned knee. Bauer marveled at him, and marveled that the boy was his son. They played rhyming games while they fished, and improvised dialogues for imaginary characters. Words were delightful toys to Jeff, his imagination a playground.

Pleasuring in Jeff, Bauer worried about Mike. He was tense, wouldn't smile, and responded with short, polite answers. Bauer tried to draw him out, but didn't push. Mike walled himself in when he felt pressured, and no threat, bribe, or amount of love would persuade him to remove the barricades. Though he didn't have the necessary coordination, he wouldn't let Bauer hook his worms or secure his fish to the stringer. He jabbed himself with the hook a couple of times, bringing a bright pearl of blood to his fingertip.

Late in the afternoon he landed a bluegill the size of a cake plate, far the biggest they'd caught. He jumped up from his seat and nearly fell out of the boat. "Look at that, look at that! I bet he's the biggest bluegill in the whole entire lake!" He pulled the stringer in and unhooked the fish with nervous fingers. Trying to work the stringer clip into the mouth, his hand slipped, he squeezed down on the fish in panic, and the bluegill popped over the side into the water. He wailed. Bauer grabbed the net and plunged it down, where the fish, dazed, was just beginning a slow glide to the bottom. He scooped it up and back into the boat again.

"Got 'im. And he *is* the biggest in the lake, no question. Here you go." He passed the net to Mike. "Do you want me to put him on the stringer for you?"

Mike hesitated, then nodded.

The boat was quiet the next quarter hour. Mike stole glances at his father. Bauer smiled when their eyes met.

"Hey," Mike said. "Do you, uh, do you want to hear a new one Billy told me?" Mike collected jokes, laboriously printed them into notebooks, which he kept on a shelf over his bed.

"Sure," Bauer said.

Mike told the joke. Bauer laughed. Jeff did too, though he didn't understand it.

Bauer told Mike a joke. Mike liked it and had Bauer repeat it so he could remember it. They swapped another set, then Mike began telling Bauer stories about school and his friends. He was happy when they rowed the boat in. Bauer displayed their catch to a couple of fishermen on the dock and pointed out his son's giant bluegill. An old man said it was the biggest he'd ever seen come out of this lake. Mike was thrilled.

Bauer put the fish atop an old newspaper in the trunk. They were going to stop at his place for sandwiches and to clean the fish and wrap them for Ursula's freezer.

Suddenly Mike spun back against the car lashing his foot out. "No! No! No!"

A Dalmatian had come sniffing up to him. The dog backed away and cocked its head bewilderedly. Its tail gave a tentative wag.

"Get away!" Mike screamed. He grabbed a handful of gravel and flung it at the dog.

Jeff reached for Bauer's hand, but was otherwise calm.

"Mike!" Bauer put his hand on Mike's shoulder and interposed himself between his son and the dog. "It's all right, he's not going to hurt you."

Mike covered his face with his hands and cried.

Jeff's mouth trembled.

A man came running from the public boat landing and took hold of the Dalmatian's collar. The dog snapped its head around in surprise, then wagged its tail and licked the man's hand.

Bauer had an arm around each of his children. "They were attacked by a dog," he said.

The man was embarrassed. "He's really very friendly, he wouldn't hurt anyone. I'm sorry he—he's deaf and he wanders away sometimes, that's a problem with Dalmatians, deafness, it comes from inbreeding—I'm really sorry, I. . . ."

"Well damn it," Bauer said in frustration, "you ought to keep an eye on him."

The man bobbed his head, apologized, and led his dog away.

"He's gone," Bauer said. "He was just a friendly dog, he didn't mean any harm."

Mike was shaking.

"He's deaf," Jeff offered. "That means he can't hear. He wasn't going to bite. He just wanted to play, Mike."

They were five. The new one was a female with coarse hair, mostly gray, with a wash of russet. She was the size of the dun bitch. Her face was boxy and she had a small beard. She was young. A Boston couple had got her through a "What's for Free" ad in the *Freeman* for their children, at their summer home, when she was three months old. The pup had a glorious summer. She slept outside, since the woman didn't want to bother with the effort of housebreaking, and could wander about at will but usually didn't go far or stay away long because she was well fed each morning and night, and during the day the children played with her and slipped her treats, and sometimes they sneaked her into the house at night to sleep on their beds.

In the late summer the family drove off one afternoon, as they occasionally did, and the dog wasn't unhappy since they were never gone more than a few hours and they always gave her something especially good to eat when they returned, but they didn't return, and not the next morning either, or the day after, or the day after. The dog remained near the boarded-up house foraging in the nearby woods as best she could, losing weight, sleeping on the porch and whining and scratching at the door. She grew lonely and despondent as the empty days passed, gradually losing the sense of what she was waiting for, and then after two weeks, she turned away from the house into the woods to seek her own way.

The family had known, of course, that she was with them only for the summer. In Boston, their lease prohibited dogs, and anyway, neither the husband nor the wife felt it was fair to an animal to live with the restrictions of an urban environment. But they were dog lovers, and they'd thought it a positive and healthy experience for their children to live with a pet awhile and meet the responsibility of feeding and caring for it, and they had put forth effort to find her a new home at the end of the summer. But people with dogs didn't want another, and everyone else wanted to start with a pup, which was cute and lovable, and not an unhousebroken half-grown animal. The family knew that dogs turned into animal shelters had a life expectancy of three or four days and was unanimous in voting against depositing her there. They decided that when their pet realized they weren't coming back, she'd strike off on her own, and since she was a nice dog they were sure someone would take her in. If by some chance she couldn't find a new home, then she'd learn to fend for herself and at least she'd be free and alive. The family was sensitive; they were not the callous kind of people who would use an animal for their pleasure, then consign it to execution in a shelter.

The dog was clumsy in its youth and not much of a hunter. It grew gaunt and was endlessly hungry and unhappy. Something happened to its eyes. Its vision was unimpaired, but an irritating liquid oozed from them and formed crusts that had to be pawed away several times a day. It found another dog in the woods, a better hunter, a dog who always knew where there was water, who found good places to sleep. He avoided human beings, radiating a powerful fear and anger whenever he came across human scent. While she'd been alone she'd gotten food from people sometimes, and occasionally some play and affection, but his response quickly obliterated the thin linkage she'd felt with them.

They bred in the early winter, and she bore three pups in the dead of a blizzard and ate the sacs they were born in and licked them clean, and warmed them in the small burrow with her body, and ate what the dog regurgitated to her after a day's hunting, but the snows were deep and there was little food and the whining creatures sucked at nipples that were often empty and they died before their eyes were open. She nearly died too and he became weak hunting for them both, but they got through, and there weren't many days to pass before she went out to hunt with him, and she followed him down from the mountain, sharing his nervousness around the human scent.

They fled a chicken coop, bloody-mouthed, when they heard a noise from the place where the humans lived and a quick crunching of feet in the crusted snow. But not soon enough and her mate was knocked over by thunder before they could reach the trees. He dragged himself to safety, untouched by the second thunderclap, but he could travel neither fast nor far, and he died in the woods, and she stayed next to his cold body for a day before she left it, reluctantly, and turned back up the mountain.

She found the pack in the early summer. The males charged when she stepped nervously into the clearing, but they left her alone once they'd read her scent. One, a smaller spotted animal, batted her playfully. A dun bitch snapped and challenged her. She answered and they went at each other while the males circled in agitation. The dun was older and stronger and had the edge. The gray offered submission, and with the order settled the dun left her alone and the pack accepted her. She felt fullness, she was happy. She learned their ways quickly and fit to them well. She was bolder than the dun bitch, and faster. The dun flared into jealousy on occasion and forced her into submission or drove her off with savage nips, but usually she could coax one of the others into wandering with her a little, or involve him in grooming, or curl up to sleep with her side pressing against his, and the dun would cool off in a while and everything would be all right again.

After a week of poor hunting and a morning's trek some distance out of their customary range, Orph led them through thinning woods along a current of scent so heavy and rich with meat that saliva rose in their mouths and dripped from their tongues and they grew anxious and taut with purpose, heads high and ears pricked forward. Orph stopped at a fence line. The dark warmth of the meat overwhelmed their nostrils.

Bulky black forms milled in an open field. Orph tasted the air, weighing the human odor woven through the dense meat scent. He paced back and forth along the fence. The pack waited poised and alert, watching him. Orph stopped and stared at the meat animals. He listened, and heard nothing but the rustle of wind over grass. The pack moved up beside him. He swung his vision slowly across the field and saw only the movement of the animals.

He dropped to his belly and wriggled beneath the bottom wire, into the field. The four other dogs followed him under, lunged up to their feet, and broke into run behind him. He swept toward the calves with his head stretched forward, tail flowing back.

A calf jerked up its head and bawled in alarm. It whirled and went running off. The rest of the herd followed in panic.

Two crashed up against another fence and cracked a cedar pole, tore their hides on the barbwire. The herd wheeled behind them and pounded off in another direction.

The dogs closed fast. The spotted stripped past Orph, gained the last calf and began slashing at its hocks. The calf bawled in terror and the herd took up its cry. The spotted dog went up in the air and seized the calf's tail, hung twisting from it, banging against the beast's flanks, taking a blow from a hoof when the creature humped up and kicked.

Orph came abreast of the animal and went high for the throat. His teeth bit and ripped loose. Running, he leapt again and locked into the thick neck. The big calf faltered and tried to heave him off. Orph was whipped about. The black hit the calf on the other side. He ripped open its shoulder, attacked again and bit deep into the snout. The calf twisted its powerful neck and tossed its head. The black was flung through the air. He struck the ground, rolled, and sprang at the calf again. The dun bitch was working the hind legs and the gray was darting in to slash at the belly. The black was on again and his writhing weight, with Orph's, stumbled the calf to its knees. The spotted dog hit the flank, the dun joined the gray on the belly. The calf staggered to its feet. Its eyes rolled and it screamed, threw its head about. The rest of the calves huddled several hundred yards away in a corner of the fencing and struggled to climb upon each other, raising a great din. The calf planted its legs and braced against the dogs, swinging its head, trembling. Its shaggy black hair was matted with blood. It frothed at the mouth and the froth turned pink with blood from its ripped tongue. Orph got into its throat and jerked to bring the beast down. The black was on the snout, dragging the calf forward. The dun bitch ripped the belly open and the calf fell heavily on its side. Orph scrambled out before he could be crushed, then flung himself back on the throat, tearing. Both bitches were into the belly. They pulled out dripping mouthfuls of flesh and gut. The spotted dog joined them. Blood fountained from the calf's throat. Orph and the black went to the belly with the others. They shoved their snouts deep and fed greedily. The black and gray came out holding opposite ends of the same bloody chunk. They tore it in half and gulped down, went in again. Massive convulsions wracked the calf, its legs beat weakly.

Homer McPhee was applying a poultice to an abscess on a cow in the main pasture when the uproar reached him. He'd never heard anything like it before, but he knew it was the sound of mortal dread. He ran up the small hill between the two pastures. The calves were 400, 450 pounds now and he'd separated them from the cows to wean them last week.

He topped the hill and looked down with shock to see one of them bloodied and standing on wobbling legs under attack by a pack of dogs. His mouth gaped. The calf went down. The dogs swarmed over it.

Homer balled his hands into fists and raised them over his head and bellowed. The dogs were tearing bloody pieces from the calf and gobbling them down. Homer grabbed a fist-sized rock from the ground, kicked another one free of the soil and picked it up, ran down the side of the hill screaming, "I'll kill you, you bastards, I'll kill you!" A length of thick branch lay in his path. He dropped a rock and snatched up the branch. He reached the fence, threw himself on his stomach and rolled under it.

He was two hundred yards to the slaughter. He ran it blindly, furiously. The dogs didn't see him. He skidded to a stop and hurled the rock. It thudded off the side of the dead calf. Orph and the black went still. The dun bitch and the spotted dog backed from the carcass. The gray dipped down to feed again.

"You fuckin' bastards!" Homer roared. He rushed them. The bitches and the spotted dog ran off a few feet. Orph and the black took a slow step backward. Homer swung the club in a looping blow and caught the black in the side. Ribs cracked and the black toppled over. "Yaahhh!" Homer screamed in violent, mad triumph. He raised the club again.

Orph hit him, teeth plunging into Homer's forearm. The sudden, crushing pain staggered the boy. He screamed. The branch fell. He couldn't free his arm. The massive German shepherd bore down, digging his feet into the ground and moving backward with a muffled snarl, dragging the boy with him. Homer was in agony. He sucked breath noisily, the color drained from his face, sweat popped out over his body. He saw the black on its feet, lips skinned back from its teeth. The black growled, then shot forward. Homer shrieked. The black bit into his knee and threw him down. Homer's mind gibbered. He tried to pull his knees up to his stomach and he hunched his head into his shoulders. He kicked at the black, beat at the

German shepherd with his free fist. The black was tearing at his legs. The German shepherd released his arm, and Homer saw the great jaws yawning toward his face. He flung his hands up and the teeth crunched down on them.

Homer fainted.

He was unconscious only a few moments, and when he woke, his eyes snapping open, his bowels and bladder emptying into his underwear, the German shepherd was standing a few feet from him, its teeth showing, a deep rumbling sounding, and the others were tearing meat from the calf.

Homer squeezed his eyes shut and sobbed. His body shook. The German shepherd snarled. The sound of the feeding stopped. It was quiet several moments. Homer's lids lifted slowly, despite his will. The German shepherd was trotting off toward the fence bordering the trees. The other dogs were following in a file.

They disappeared into the woods.

Homer lay still, afire with pain, his mind incapable of thought. He was crying. He performed the impossible task of sitting up. His hands were bloody and raw. Jagged ends of tiny white bones showed in the ruin of the right one. His index finger was missing. Dumbly, he tried to stand. His bloody legs shook so violently that he couldn't. He began to crawl in the direction of the house, openmouthed and spasm-wracked, moaning.

CHAPTER 7

SPIRIT had been roaming. For a while he'd paired
with a collie who belonged to a mail carrier (he
slept two nights with the collie under the woman's
porch, and she fed him) and for a while by himself. He
was on the south face of Sproul's Mountain, four or five
hours from the Treehouse if he went over the top, seven
or eight if he circled around the base. He was tired and
he took the longer, easier way.

He grew hungry trotting along the potholed road, so he
turned off on a dirt driveway and went up toward a small
house with a raw plywood extension. Sensibly, Spirit never
put himself to the effort of hunting when there were
alternatives. He was facile with garbage cans. He could
look endearingly forlorn. A child was playing in a sandbox
in front of the house. Spirit stopped discreetly fifty feet
away and waited to be noticed. Some humans were definitely not friendly. They chucked rocks at him when he

came begging. He'd be off in a flash at the first aggressive move: if he got a smile or a call, he'd rush and roll over and whack his tail on the ground, making himself lovable, and invariably food would follow.

The child glanced up, made a noise and climbed out of the sandbox and ran into the house.

Spirit looked after him in perplexity, but still with hope.

Eileen Bernholz was taping and spackling the new sheetrock John had nailed up in the addition last night. One more wall to sheetrock, then the framing around the windows, sheet vinyl over the subflooring, and it would be done. The larger of the two new rooms would be for the baby, which was due in three months, the smaller would be a laundry room—she could finally get the washer and dryer out of the cramped kitchen.

Mark ran in. "Mommy there's a dog outside!"

Eileen set the spackling knife aside and wiped her hands on her jeans. "Where, honey?" Mark was four and overly excitable. She didn't want to send him into hysterics.

She and John had warned him about dogs last week, after that terrible incident with the McPhee boy in Marbleville, which wasn't far. For two days after, he'd refused to go outside without one of them with him.

John was a town constable. He'd seen animals killed by dogs and he'd shot two wild ones last winter that were tearing apart a crippled deer. He'd instructed Eileen clearly and unequivocally, and she, who had been raised in the mountains, was not a vacillating woman.

She went into the kitchen and looked out the window. She'd never seen this dog. It wore no collar. Its coat was matted and dirty, there were burrs in it. It was not a groomed animal, not a pet.

"Mark, honey," she said. "Go into the living room and turn on the television. Mommy's going outside for a couple of minutes. I'll be right back."

Mark's parents regulated his television time strictly. He was thrilled with this windfall. He dashed into the living room. The set came on, loud.

Eileen took down a double-barreled 20-gauge shotgun from pegs over the door, broke open the breech and dropped two highbrass Number Four shells into the chambers. She snapped the gun closed and thumbed the safety off.

A woman came out of the house. Spirit stared at her, searching for a sign. She pointed something at him. Spirit became confused and anxious; she'd given him no tone of voice to interpret. Her quiet focus unsettled him and he took a step backward.

Eileen squeezed the first trigger. *Boooom!* The butt punched into her shoulder. An ounce of lead shot exploded bone fragments and brain tissue out from Spirit's head in a crimson aureole. The impact flipped him over backward. The second, and superfluous, charge bounced his body off the ground.

The *Freeman* and WCVS came out swinging. Harry Wilson attacked dogs, crucified their owners, and screamed for the passage of his proposals. Media in neighboring communities were only slightly less vivid. The *National Enquirer* bannered WILD KILLER DOGS BIGGEST THREAT IN U.S. across its front page and ran a picture of Homer

McPhee being lifted bloodied and stunned from a state police car onto a stretcher, and another of the mutilated calf. AP and UPI carried the story on their wire services. Covington polarized, and dogs and their supporters got the nastiest end. A woman from the Purebred Dog Association was shouted down and spit upon at a public meeting. Police rounded up strays and unconfined pets and issued in excess of a hundred summonses. A few dozen dogs were put to death at the humane shelter—including a fair number brought in by owners who said they didn't want them anymore—and an attendant was beaten by two men who thought their missing pets were locked up there. Mayor Thomas Josephson appointed an emergency committee to investigate and make recommendations.

Dr. Chaim Mandelberg set down his morning copy of the *New York Times*. He braced his elbow on the desktop and rested his chin lightly upon the tip of his raised index finger. He tapped the eraser of a pencil on the story, two small, vertical furrows appearing in the center space between his eyebrows. He signaled his secretary on the intercom.

"Yes, Dr. Mandelberg."

"Sheila, how far is Covington from here, do you know?"

"Oh . . . about a hundred, a hundred and twenty miles. Should I check for an exact figure?"

"No, no, that's all right, thanks. Ring Bill Hazlett's extension for me, will you please."

Ursula reported the attack on Jeff, and Bauer was called to give an account. He arrived at the County Office Building late in the afternoon. Four people waited ahead of him. The workday had ended and most of the offices were vacated by the time he was ushered in.

The committee comprised a Covington police sergeant, a

woman from the mayor's office, a conservation department representative, Elizabeth Collier and Harry Wilson. A man named Bill Hazlett, from a downstate scientific organization that worked with dogs, was also present, as an observer. Wilson wore a checked sport jacket over a white turtleneck sweater. He took notes with a silverplated pen.

Bauer told his story in a few minutes. "That's all there was to it," he ended. "My son will need plastic surgery, but he's recovering well."

Councilman Thomas, who was chairing the proceedings, looked embarrassed, as if he'd inadvertently stumbled into a private and personal matter. "Thank you, Mr. Bauer. I'm glad to hear the boy wasn't more seriously injured." He looked to see if any of the others had questions.

Only Harry Wilson did. "You haven't seen the dog at all since that day?"

"No."

"Did you read the description of the animal that led the attack on the McPhee farm?"

"Yes, I did."

"Do you think they're one and the same?"

"The description could fit Orphan."

"But do you think it *was* him?" Wilson pressed.

"The report could fit any of fifteen or twenty German shepherds I've seen at my office," Elizabeth Collier said, "and at least thirty or forty more in the general area. I'd also like to state, for the record, that people inexperienced with the breed are prone to call any dog remotely resembling the shepherd conformation—and that's a classic canine conformation—a German shepherd. I think you want to be careful to avoid setting off a pogrom here."

"The point is well taken," Thomas said.

"But what do *you* think?" Wilson said to Bauer. "He was your dog. Did he ever display unusual aggression toward people before, do you think he *is* the one?"

Bauer hesitated, hoping he wouldn't have to answer. But even Thomas was interested now, as if identification would somehow represent a step toward solution.

"He might have been hit by a car," Bauer said. "Someone else might have taken him into their home, he might be living in the woods by himself, or, yes, he might be leading that pack. I don't see how we can even speculate, and I don't know what good it would do anyway—it's not like a criminal case where you learn the man's name and go to his house and arrest him. Whether it's Orph or Spot or Rover or some dog born and raised in the wild, he's still out there somewhere and knowing his name isn't going to help anyone find him."

Elizabeth Collier nodded agreement.

Thomas was disappointed. "Unfortunately I suppose that's true."

"Yes," said Hazlett, "it is." He looked around somewhat apologetically. "I know I have no official part in these proceedings, but if I could add something?"

"Certainly," Thomas said.

"It's a long shot, but if you could identify the animal, it might be a little easier to extrapolate its actions and movements. Was there anything distinctive about your dog, anything at all, Mr. Bauer, that would help single it out?"

Bauer shook his head. "*I'd* know him, but he was mine. I don't think anyone else could tell him apart." He paused. "Orph had a little nick out of his ear. The right one, near the base, but you probably wouldn't notice it unless you were patting his head. Other than that, nothing."

Thomas adjourned the meeting. Wilson put his note pad in an attaché case and snapped it shut. He stopped behind Elizabeth's chair and laid a hand casually on her shoulder. "You free?" he asked.

She turned her head up and smiled. "Completely. And I

intend to stay that way." She shrugged off his hand, stood and turned away.

The County Office Building was three stories, stainless steel and black glass. They rode down from the top in a silent elevator and signed out, since it was after hours, in the security guard's book. They dispersed their separate ways on the street. Elizabeth was parked down the street in the same lot with Bauer.

She fell into step with him. "You handled Wilson well," she said. "I enjoyed that. I'm sorry about your dog and your son."

"Thanks," Bauer said. "You don't seem to have any trouble with Wilson yourself."

"I've had experience. He's an ass." She rubbed the back of her neck.

"Hard day?"

"Depressing."

"Could you use a drink?"

She hesitated. "Sure, that would be nice."

They went past the parking lot and across the street to the Jury Box. There were simulated beams of styrofoam, woodgrained Formica tables, and chairs with vinyl cushions that were supposed to look like leather. Ersatz junk, but the place was clean and quiet and friendly.

They took a table. Elizabeth tied her hair back with a scarf. She wore a beige skirt and sweater, a thin gold chain around her neck. Her coloring was that of patinaed ivory, her eyes light brown. She had slim, strong hands.

The waitress brought their drinks. Bauer looked at his a moment before he took a swallow and set it down. "I think," he said, "that it is Orph leading that pack."

"Why?"

"We lived pretty close together. I got to know him— well, not know him probably—but I developed a kind of emotional familiarity with him. He couldn't really be

known, that was one of the things I realized in retrospect."
He told her about Orph, with some sadness in his voice.
"So it's mostly intuition. Still, I'm nearly certain it's Orph."

"I thought you felt that way. You were trying to protect him." She reflected. "It could be him."

"It is," he said soberly.

"Maybe, maybe not. At this point, no one can know
what's out there. I wasn't lying when I said there were
three or four dozen animals in the area who fit the
description."

"You're being politic. If it is Orph, then it's my responsibility. You told me in the beginning, when he was a pup,
that I should be working with him. I didn't. Now this has
happened."

"Oh, I'm angry," she said. "That pack isn't at fault, nor
is any other wild dog. Under the circumstances, they're
behaving quite naturally. The owners bear the moral guilt
—only the animals have to do the suffering. But I'm not
outraged at you. It is your fault—the attack on your son if
nothing else—but you're not trying to sluff the blame onto
the dog and excuse yourself. Everyone else does."

"I'd like to, I'll tell you that."

"Why? We're all responsible for our own actions. How
society judges us doesn't mean anything, except in terms
of crude pragmatism. How else are you going to forge
your being except through internal confrontation? You
don't find that in many people, and that's why most people
aren't worth even having a drink with."

"You're a nice person," Bauer said.

"No, I'm not," she said. "I'm hard, I'm intolerant, I'm
selfish and I'm grim. My husband called me a bloodless
cunt. He tended to confuse beer-sweat with blood. Luckily
we weren't married long enough for things to become hellish between us, only ugly. On the other hand, he was just
the first to call me names. I seem to provoke that. But I

respect my 'self' too much to live meanly or blindly, or to evade pain simply because it is pain."

Bauer laughed. "Christ, you *are* tough."

She'd worked herself up, features constricting defiantly, gaze finally losing Bauer and seeing past him to some shadowy incorporation she despised and that had cost her pain. She blinked, startled by her sudden return.

"I'm not a nice person," she said, "but I think I'm a decent person." Then she laughed at her seriousness. "And I can't resist betting on horses, and I'm a movie addict—I don't care how bad it is, as long as it's on a screen and moves I love it—and I giggle uncontrollably when I'm tickled." She caught herself. "Strike that last, it's not an invitation."

"Who's your bookie?"

"Do you bet?"

"No, I was just striking your last. Have another drink, and I'm hungry and I'd like to order something, and it would be nice if you'd have dinner with me, and that's not an invitation, it's a statement."

"Fine. Get some menus."

They told each other a few things about themselves—nothing revealing or intensely personal, but sufficiently biographical to mark the broad contours of themselves for each other.

In the parking lot, at the side of her car, Bauer said, "Those were a good couple of hours. I'm glad you spent them with me."

She took his hand, in the clasp of a possible friend. "It was nice, Alex. You lifted me up."

"Well . . . Good night," he said.

"Good night. Thank you."

He drove home, alternately happy and depressed.

The sun had been up an hour. The pack had made a kill at sunrise, three young raccoons and their mother. The mother had bitten Orph on the shoulder and the spotted dog on the paw, but neither wound was serious. The black dog's ribs were knitting, lumpishly, but the pain was lessening and he could eat again. Their bellies were full, they were fresh and playful. The gray bitch was running tag with the spotted dog. The dun, in whelp, her belly lowering, nipped sassily at Orph. He consented to dance with her. They batted each other.

Orph heard it first. He stopped nibbling on the dun bitch's whiskers. He stood up and pricked his ears. His posture triggered the others to their feet. They listened, snuffed the air and looked about. A buzzing noise, coming nearer.

Orph found the direction but couldn't catch a scent. He looked up. A dark blur was moving against the sky. He had seen others on occasion, but they'd been very high and their sound faint in his ears. This one was wrong. It didn't belong. He turned and led the pack trotting into a crowded stand of saplings, into the dark shade beneath the leaves.

Trooper George McHale followed the contour of the mountain, maintaining a steady altitude of 400 feet, banked slightly to the right to give a better field of vision to Attilio. Attilio had a pair of 8 $\times$ 32 binoculars pressed to his eyes.

"Anything?" McHale said over the drone of the single engine.

"Nothing, not a damn thing." Attilio knuckled his eyes a moment and pressed the binoculars back again. "I'm going blind," he said. "This'll drive you crazy. We got any aspirins?"

"In the ditty bag."

"I'll wait til we turn. Jesus, you could hide a fucking army down there. You can't see anything through the leaves. If it was fall, we'd have 'em."

"Or out west. I flew the Rockies once. You can spot an animal a mile away."

McHale took them over the hump, made a wide, looping turn above High Falls Road, and started back. He unhooked the mike and depressed the stud. Attilio rummaged for the aspirins.

"One-One-Foxtrot to Base. Come in, Base," McHale said.

"Base to One-One-Foxtrot," the radio replied. "We read you. Over."

"One-One-Foxtrot to Base. We've done Solomon's Point, Hanover, Little Cap Mountain, and Sector Bravo-Two-Six. Turning at High Falls Road now. We'll be making a run over Sector Bravo-Two-Seven."

"Did you spot anything?"

"The volunteer line on Hanover, our people on Little Cap. A couple of cowboys with rifles moving up the west side of Hanover—you better inform our people so they can watch shots. But that's all. Oh yeah, Vic says to tell he saw a good flock of wild turkeys on Little Cap. He says you're a turkey hunter. Over."

"Acknowledged. The sheriff's department shot a dog on Balsam Cap half an hour ago. Definitely feral, but not one of the pack. Thought you'd like to know. Thank Vic for the turkey spot. Over and out."

Attilio had the binoculars up again. "I'm going blind, I tell you. I really am."

"Hold out til tonight. We're giving up then."

"It'll be too late," Attilio said.

"He's ours," Hazlett said to Mandelberg. "I know it in my bones."

Mandelberg watched a line of smoke curl up from his ashtray. "Would you know it in a court of law?"

"Well, ear notching isn't all that uncommon."

Mandelberg nodded. "But I agree, I think we *have* found our missing pup." He got out of his chair and walked to the window. A handler was taking a dog over a series of hurdles. Mandelberg watched. "What would happen if we publicly owned to that dog?"

"They'd want our heads on platters."

Mandelberg turned back to Hazlett. "Yes. If it got bad enough, we might even have to suspend operations here."

"Christ, it's only a dog, not a science-fiction monster."

"Tell that to the public."

"There are a million 'pets' who'd respond exactly the same way in similar circumstances."

"That's one of my points. You've read the file, haven't you—alpha litter, King's Indian out of Karla vom Hanckschloss?"

"Yes."

"This is a tough dog, and intelligent and independent. But is it a freak, a savage, bizarre in any way?"

"No."

"Actually, it's a pretty damn good dog. Maybe even the kind of animal dogs used to be ten thousand years ago— five thousand, hell, a hundred years ago."

"And maybe not."

"Maybe," Mandelberg said curtly. "But the fact remains that we bred a dog. A dog, nothing more, nothing less." His eyes focused on a patch of empty wall. "Just a dog." Carefully, he opened a new pack of cigarettes, removed one, and lit it. "So first, we have no moral responsibility here. Now, is there anything we could do, or tell these people, that would help them find the animal?"

Hazlett shook his head. "No. It's a matter of predator's habits, and hunting. The conservation department knows more about that than we do."

"So, two, there is no assistance we can render. Three, when the dog is found, *if* it's found, nothing can be proved, even to our own certainty, that would indicate origin from BDI. Given all this, I can't see anything but serious, unnecessary, and undeserved damage to us if we were to claim it as ours. Therefore, I think this should stay strictly between us."

"What if someone else is attacked?"

"No one will be, unless they box the dog in. The same thing would be true of any of those million 'pets' of yours too. Hope that it doesn't happen. But if it does, nothing changes."

"I guess," Hazlett said. "You know what I feel worst about? The dog himself. He didn't ask for any of this."

"Maybe he has the best of it," Mandelberg said. "If he can get free. Men are the only real problem dogs ever had."

Orph stayed to the shadows, scraped low under brush, skirted clearings and open plateaus. The pack followed him with the same silent caution.

He stood patiently at the edge of cover to survey new terrain for half an hour, an hour if he felt uneasy, before he would commit them to it. Prey could freeze and become so much a part of the landscape that a predator could pass by in total ignorance if the wind was wrong. Some human predators could imitate prey in that respect. Orph had learned this the first day the humans had come into the woods, heavy, beneath the odors of metal and oil and pungency they brought, with the scent of killing purpose.

He'd winded one, stiffening instantly, that was close enough to see or hear, yet he could do neither and it disturbed him deeply. He remained absolutely still—as time passed, as his muscles began to cramp—and listened, scented, and looked, with all the concentration he was capable of, which was formidable, until at last he found the man. The man was far up the side of the ridge, seated at the bole of a big tree, dressed in clothes that melted into the background. He'd shifted to relieve the strain of his careful wait, the smallest adjustment of posture, but it was enough. Satisfied, Orph drew back into the brush and led them away in a wide circle. In the following days he located and circled two more humans in the same fashion. There were not many who behaved like this. The rest, the ones who came tramping with clumsy feet, who shouted to one another, whose acrid tobacco reek was borne far ahead of them on breezes, who coughed and spat, gathered together and lit fires at night, even fired their guns out of boredom and frustration, were easy to keep clear of.

Orph brought his pack far out of its range, to the mountains to the north, where the human predators were sparse and infrequent. In a little time the humans quit the woods, Orph probed back, found the territory untroubled once more, and the pack returned. Now and then some men would invade, but the pack had no difficulty moving around them, and their stay was brief.

It was a hot day. They sweated. The slickness of their skin lent an exoticism to their caresses. Afterward, Kathy went into the bathroom. When she returned she brought a face towel she'd soaked in cold water and squeezed out. She swabbed his body with it. It jarred at first, then refreshed. He reciprocated. Then they napped atop the sheet with a breeze from the window blowing over them, not long, and awakened feeling good.

He kissed her breasts. He took a large part of one into his mouth. It seemed if he could suck hard enough, he could pull her whole breast into his mouth, down, deeper, and contain all of her in time, become full with her. She pushed her fingers into his hair and rubbed his scalp.

"Oh that feels good," she said, free of the urgency of desire, with lazy pleasure.

He released her and ministered to her other breast.

She closed her eyes and sighed.

He pillowed his head on her breasts and looked up at her.

"Your body is very important to you, isn't it?" he said.

"Isn't everyone's?"

"Not in the same way."

"How sad for them."

"You fuck with every piece."

"Sure. If I'm not lucky enough to die young, it'll be all dried up and falling apart some day. It would be terrible not to have memories at least."

"I like the way you use it, but I'm not so sure about the motivation."

"That's a killer word. Reasons are pasts and futures. That makes 'Now' impossible, and anything that does that is evil."

"Evil is the impossibility of now?" he asked incredulously.

"What else? You, you fuck like you were going to be shot tomorrow. That focuses you, which is good, as far as it goes, but it must be an awful drag."

"No."

"There's never any reason to be desperate, you know."

"You don't know much about me," he said, with a touch of sarcasm.

She stretched, contented. "Of course not. No one can ever know themselves, so how can they know anyone else? We're butterflies. I mean that's what we can be. But almost no one understands that, so they just stay caterpillars all their lives."

"What do butterflies do?"

"They fly around in the sun in the summer. But it's not so much what they do as what they are. They're very beautiful creatures—who are content just to be beautiful. They don't try to understand anything, they're too busy *being*. Every moment is pleasure, and every moment is all that ever was and all that ever will be."

"But there are lepidopterists at large. They pin butterflies to boards."

"There are always people who want to kill beauty. When you see them, you fly away from them, and if you can't. . . ." She shrugged. "Tomorrow the earth could fall into the sun, and anyway we'll all get caught by something sooner or later, even the catchers and that's a joke on them. So there's no point in doing anything at all that doesn't feel good and make you happy."

"This doesn't sound like the same person who was pursuing Melville with such determination last term."

"That was then, love, and I was playing student. The butterfly always plays whatever it wants to. Now it's summer and I'm playing at the Treehouse."

"Kathy, your soul is a glass snowflake."

"That's pretty."

"But easily shattered."

She shrugged. "You have bars of lead in yours, and you just can't fly very far that way."

"Tell Icarus it's a bad idea."

"That's a very puritanical myth. It says too much rapture will kill you. People are afraid of pleasure."

"What are you afraid of?"

"Nothing. What happens, happens. I have a good time until it does."

"Mundane as they might be, there are necessities. The brow must sweat sometimes."

"Work is only a surface process, and knowledge is just a tool to get it done faster and more efficiently with. That's the trouble with people, they don't understand the purpose of knowledge. They think it's an end all in itself and they spend their lives accumulating it and think it's wisdom. But if there is such a thing as wisdom, then it's nothing more than simply *being*, like I said. You don't have to have a single scrap of knowledge or an intelligent thought in your head to be wise. The butterfly doesn't, but it's wise—because it's happy and that's what being wise is."

"Owls will be distressed to learn that."

"Owls are not wise, they think too much. Thinking is deadly. It's abstractions, and abstractions are unnatural. Can you imagine animals killing other animals over a religion or a flag? Only humans do that. You know, we slaughtered a goat yesterday. Some people tell you that meat is bad, that the killing hurts your spirit and the meat messes up your body systems and gives you diseases. But it's really not the meat that hurts, it's what the meat becomes when you don't kill the animal right. We took the goat out of its pen and we all sat in a circle, and we touched it and gave it our love, and then Billy had a long talk with it. He explained how all living creatures have to eat, and how in the end everything feeds everything else, and the rabbit isn't evil for eating a carrot even though the carrot doesn't exist as a carrot anymore, or an antelope when a lion eats it, but the *essence* of the carrot joins with the rabbit and the essence of the antelope with the lion, and he told the goat it was going to join with us, and explained how we'd fed it and cared for it, and that now it was going to do the same thing for us, and it was all natural and good, and in time we'd die too, at least our bodies would, but our essences would go back to the soil and that would be the food for growing things, and the growing things would be the food for things like goats and other animals and so it was all the same—goats, butterflies, and people—and it was good. We helped the goat to understand. That's all that ever has to be done. Then the meat becomes healthy and it isn't bad for you."

Bauer raised himself and supported his head with his hand. He looked at her.

"What are you doing?" she said.

"I'm thinking about you."

"No," she said. "No, you're not. You're just obfuscating the truth—see, I can use the jargon too, when I feel like it."

"What am I obfuscating?"

"The simple and only fact: that I turn you on. You can't just accept that, you have to build a whole rational construction around it. It's silly to hassle yourself. Pleasure is the only truth."

"That's a pernicious philosophy."

She lifted a leg and placed her foot against his wrist. "*Shee-it*." She shoved, knocking away his support arm.

He dropped and she sprang upon him and rolled him onto his back, ducking her head, drawing his organ into her mouth. He began to tumesce. She loosed him, held him in her hand, smiled triumphantly and said, "Pleasure, Alex. Your body doesn't lie." Imperiously, she sucked him, forcing him swollen and hard.

And it was pleasure, but beneath it he felt fraudulent and afraid.

CHAPTER 8

ONCE Eddie Meisler had had a summer cabin on Loon Lake. It wasn't a big lake, less than two miles long and one wide. There were two rough resorts that rented small cottages, and eight or nine other private cabins like Meisler's. The kids had been six, five, and three when he'd bought it. They'd handtamed chipmunks and coaxed raccoons to eat scraps on the porch. The kids loved it, and Meisler's wife was happy there. Dawns, he fished in pleasurable, regenerative solitude. Midday he'd play with the kids or lie in a hammock reading, putter with the house, or go for a walk. He and Dot went to bed early, tired in a pleasant way, and the temperature often dipped into the fifties at night, snug sleeping beneath a light blanket or two, and their lovemaking was frequent and deeply satisfying at the lake. He'd had to scrimp and work a lot of overtime to buy the place, but it was altogether the best thing he'd ever done for his family and himself, and he never regretted it.

It was a past time now, but the memories still warmed him. Each year, as the kids had grown, another cabin or two had gone up on the lake, and then a new resort with a big rustic lodge where they served dinners and kept the bar open til the early morning hours, and you could hear the jukebox music thumping across the water at night, and then in the closing 50s and early 60s the process escalated, with most everyone having time and money to spare, and the big natural lakefront holdings were broken into one-acre and even half-acre lots, and the whines and poundings of construction sounded spring through fall, and the fishing-boat motors grew bigger and bigger, and then the power boats and water skiers appeared, a couple hydroplanes, and canopied pontoon boats that wallowed beneath floating cocktail parties, until at last it was ugly and noisily crowded, like a rough bar or a deep-city bowling alley, and Meisler was mortally stricken. It hurt him in his heart, it turned his blood bitter.

The kids were all grown and had children of their own. They were busy with their lives and the cabin was a thing of their childhood, they hardly went to the lake anymore. Meisler sold it, a thing of joy whose degradation he had been forced to watch, helpless to stop. He sat home and brooded the next two years, refusing to consider alternatives: he'd had what he wanted and it could not be replaced. Dot, who was sensitive and patient, and loved him, succored him gently, and the next year, his spirits restored, he bought them a camper. It was tough and could handle terrain too rugged for most vacationers, and, mobile, he would not be anchored to any single place; when the marauders came to begin their destruction, he would simply go somewhere else.

The first years of his retirement, he and Dot lived in

the camper as much as they did in their own home and it was great fun. He grew eccentric. He tonguelashed campers who despoiled the countryside with garbage, people who abused the woods and streams, and if he came upon an empty site littered with someone's detritus, he'd police it scrupulously, muttering curses. Men, he'd come to believe, were descendants of the criminals and defectives of some stellar race who had dumped them on earth, a galactic asylum or penal colony. He had little love and less respect for them. He made a point of not reading papers or listening to newscasts.

They were traveling New England this summer. Eddie had bulled the camper a quarter of the way up a mountainside over the brushy remnant of an old homesteading trail. He parked and chocked the wheels on grassy plateau next to a clear stream in which there were German browns. He took the browns with a handwound bamboo rod and dry flies he tied himself. It was the middle of the afternoon and Meisler was napping inside. Dot was sunning.

He woke to Dot's shout. "Shoo! Get out of here! Shoo! Go away!"

He rubbed his eyes and swung his legs down and went to the door. Dot was waving a stick at a bunch of dogs who'd knocked over the aluminum cans at the back of the camper. Meisler buried his vegetable scraps, and put everything else in the cans, whose tops clipped snug to foil raccoons and skunks. The big dogs had bowled the cans over and popped the lids. They'd strewn the garbage about and were snapping meat bones and licking grease, glancing up at Dot between bites. One, a wide-chested German shepherd, was chewing slowly and watching Dot with unwavering eyes.

"Get out, go home! Now!" Meisler yelled from the door. Four of the animals backed away a little. The shepherd stood its ground, and swung its hard stare to Meisler.

"Scat!" Dot raised the stick high and advanced.

The shepherd snarled. A black dog growled.

"Don't push, honey," Meisler cautioned. "Those two don't look friendly."

Dot lowered the stick. "I don't know where they came from. I woke up when they knocked the cans over."

"Just stay where you are and don't threaten them."

He turned back inside and opened the storage drawer beneath his bed. A Colt Woodsman target pistol lay in the corner. Beside it, a loaded eight-round magazine. He slid the magazine into the pistol, flicked off the safety, pulled the slide back and let it snap forward, throwing a cartridge into the chamber. Meisler wasn't fond of guns but he knew how to use them, and he carried the .22 automatic whenever he camped. To dispatch sick or wounded animals he found, to shoot a varmint when necessary, and as protection. It was tiny caliber, but he used hollow-point slugs, and eight rounds gave him enough firepower.

Dot saw the gun and said, "Oh Eddie, don't *hurt* them."

"I won't." He pointed the muzzle in the air, bellowed at the dogs, and touched off three quick rounds. The dogs whirled and were into the woods by the third report.

Meisler and his wife righted the cans and picked up the garbage.

"It's outrageous," Meisler said, tossing a porkchop bone into a can. "Now we have to put up with dogs too. I don't care who wants what for a pet, but if they're going to own dogs, then they have a responsibility, don't they?"

"Yes, dear," Dot said.

"I mean a dog isn't something you just fool around with to amuse yourself and then ignore when you get interested in something else, is it?"

"No, dear."

"Right," he said. "People like that shouldn't be allowed to own dogs."

Bauer was confounded by the quality of Kathy's intimacy. There was nothing she wouldn't say, nothing she wouldn't do. There were no guarded rooms within her. She told him willingly about her life, but it was clear that histories meant little to her, at best offered mild anecdotal material to fill silences that had become boring. Courteously, but without much interest, she asked a few questions about his life. He was largely tempted to allow himself to be seduced into her sense of present, with its vitality and lucid focus. Certainly it was pleasurable, and she was right, the hour past was dead, the one to come unborn. But his old self mocked. And though that self had served him poorly, it was of some power nonetheless, and not easily discarded. But most telling—while she withheld nothing, she could not be touched. He could find no core in her, she was a single plane, and nothing, he suspected, meant more to her than anything else. Hers was an indifferent intimacy, a candor without consequence. They had fun together, but always, around the periphery, Bauer sensed a lifeless chill. It unsettled him, intimating, as it did, the quality of his own malaise.

He telephoned Elizabeth Collier. She was busy, she said, and he was disappointed, but she ended the brief exchange by saying, "Please call me again, though. I'd like to see you." The following week he did. They had an early dinner then drove fifty miles to Hammertown, where a theater showed art films on Wednesdays and Thursdays, and saw a German piece. It was uncompromising and starkly stylized, but had the weight to back up its mad risks. It was a good film.

Elizabeth lived in a trim white-sided house set back from her office and kennel, on the outskirts of Covington. He walked her to her door. He put his hand on her hair, which was very soft, cupping her head, and kissed her lightly. He drew back to say goodnight, because while she'd been animated and seemed to have a good time, she'd markedly given no indication that anything beyond pleasant companionship was possible, but he paused with the word in his mouth, possibly through intuition but more likely, he thought, in the flicker of the suspension, because of wish.

She pursed her mouth. "Why don't you come in and have a drink," she said.

Inside, she poured him a brandy and excused herself. She returned in a long satiny nightdress cinched at the waist with a braided cord, Grecian and beautiful.

She was a long woman. There was pliant grace in her. Subtly, but with firmness, she kept their lovemaking formal and calm. His orgasm was sweet. He didn't know whether or not she counterfeited her own. She wore reins, but they were firmly in her own hands.

In the soporism that followed, she fit herself in against him and said gently, though the words were blunt, "Let's nap, but please, my house is my own, and that's important to me. I don't want anyone to stay over the night."

Later when he was driving home, beneath a rind of moon and stars that glittered in configurations he'd never been able to read, he wondered if it was not Ursula who hadn't wanted him, but he who had not wanted her; not Kathy who was without core, but he who lacked dimension; not Elizabeth armored with a hard carapace, but he who barricaded himself. Or was he an aberrant hive insect in a race of solipsists? If he'd been an adolescent, he might have thought that he loved Elizabeth Collier.

Buddy Stokes knew where there was a pack of dogs. Maybe they were the ones that had attacked the McPhee kid, maybe not. But there were five of them and they were wild.

He was lumbering a parcel up at the narrow end of Watson Hollow, which notched between the flanks of Heerman's Mountain and Claypipe. A New York doctor owned the whole valley, more than 400 acres. There was a lot of good maple in the high 50. The doctor had sold the maple, standing, to a baseball bat manufacturer and jobbed the felling and skidding to Stokes. The first morning, Stokes walked the land familiarizing himself with the growth and formulating a program. He was done by noon. He sat on a log, opened his six-pack and ate the sandwiches in his bag. He crushed the empty cans in one hand as he finished them and tossed them back over his shoulder. He lit a cigar afterward, thinking about nothing. He wasn't much for thinking. What happened in his mind was more a series of pictures, like random slides projected on a screen, in soft, almost blurred focus. Sometimes he had emotions about the pictures—especially the sexual ones—other times he didn't. He had no trouble sleeping, and liked his dreams. Smoking, he pictured Digger. The stitches were out, the cast gone, the bandaging removed. The dog walked a little gimpy and was hairless horny scar tissue from its withers halfway up its skull. Ugly as sin, but by God he'd come through—worth every fucking penny to the vet—and he'd be able to fight in Florida. That was a dog with *two* pair of balls.

Stokes put the cigar out and set up the side of Claypipe chewing the butt. He hadn't been up the mountain in two or three years. He wanted to look for deer sign, see if it was worth a stop this fall. He found rich droppings and well traveled runs, many buck rubbings.

And he found the remnants of a slaughtered fawn, too.

The carcass was eight or nine days old, there were maggots in the jellied eyes and the few remaining bits of meat. He spent half an hour sorting out the sign around it. The ground had been wet when it happened, and for a day or two after, and had hardened into a pretty good record. Dogs running a doe and a fawn. The fawn lagging here. The dogs on it, paw print over paw print. The doe went on another hundred yards, then spun back. She made a fight of it. Gutsy. She was lucky they were hard on the fawn and didn't pay her much mind except to defend themselves. She stayed until it was all over for the fawn. And was probably ripped bad herself. Then she fled, and the dogs settled down to feed. Coons and skunks after the dogs. Crows. Maggots and bugs finishing up now. The hide would rot into the soil in a year or two.

He quartered a half mile up the mountain. A few tracks, where the ground would take them. Some droppings partially scratched over. A place in the lee of a boulder, alongside an inch-deep rivulet of water, where they'd bedded down, the grass matted in ovoids.

There was no point trying to track them. For every small stretch that would hold their sign, there were acres, miles that wouldn't. Even with a clear trail, he could have tracked them weeks, months, around and up and down the mountains and never seen the tip of a tail. Not a dog gone wild. There wasn't anything smarter in the woods. That was a joke, those state cops and sheriff's deputies who'd gone after them. A woods dog knew when it was being hunted, and unless you had it in a dead panic it could slip right by you fifty yards away while you were picking your nose to hell and back wondering if you were on the wrong mountain.

Stokes didn't like pets, mutts or fancy show animals. A dog was a working animal, like a man. Trackers, guard dogs, pit fighters, those were animals to respect. So was a woods dog. A man could be proud of himself for taking one down. Stokes wouldn't hunt anything he didn't respect, just as he wouldn't fight anyone but big truckers and bar brawlers; you couldn't slap yourself on the back for whipping on some simpy faggot.

Buddy Stokes was going to get himself a wild dog. Drag it right into Harry Wilson and get his picture in the paper. Then he'd lead the assholes in and show 'em where, sit back and see if they could stumble on the others, or make fools of themselves the way they did last time.

The next two mornings he arrived at the hollow an hour before dawn and took up a stand as the woods were coming awake. He held it, cradling his .338 Browning, until noon, when he gave it up and went to do a little cutting. He was back on stand at four thirty, and he remained until the light was too poor to shoot by. It was big odds against. He didn't see anything, but it had been worth a try.

He showered carefully that night and rinsed himself under clear water a long time. He had his wife run a set of clothes twice through the washing machine while he boiled leg traps in a couple of roasting pans. He picked the traps out with tongs and when they were dry he pulled on rubber gloves and dropped them into plastic bags, twisted the ends closed. In the morning he dabbed himself with doe tallow. It stank, but it would mask any of his own, human odor that lingered. On Claypipe, he put on the gloves again and set and staked the traps burying them under a thin layer of loose soil and leaves. He wired bait alongside them, mostly hunks of beef, but three live chickens too.

Over the next week he caught some raccoons and skunks, and one badger. A foraging squirrel had stepped on a pan and been cut in half by the jaws. He didn't see anything else.

Trudging up the hollow with his chain saw one morning in the second week, he stopped and cocked his head. The usual racket of the woods (and it was a racket if you knew how to listen to it) was greatly muted. He listened, and the absence grew as loud in his ears as a diesel taching up, and the hairs on his neck lifted and he smiled and lengthened his stride, devouring the ground. *Buddy, ol' Buddy, ol' Buddy has caught himself a prize.*

It was the third trap in, a chicken-bait trap, at the edge of a vine and briar thicket, shadowy in the murky dawn, a few stars still visible, the sky a low soiled overcast.

He stopped and squinted.

He had one.

A gray dog, maybe fifty pounds.

It was caught by the left hind leg. It had pulled back from Stokes' approach the length of the stake-chain. It stared at Stokes, unmoving. It was panting, saliva dripped from its tongue.

"Your ass is *mine!*" Stokes said.

The dog pulled against the chain.

The Browning was back at the truck, racked across the cab's rear window. He had a sharp Buck knife sheathed at his hip, but he'd take a couple of bad bites before he could do the job with that.

He knelt, primed the saw and jerked the cord. It caught right away—Buddy kept his machines and tools in fine condition. He hit the trigger, revving it up, and the roar filled the valley. The toothed chain rocketed around the edges of the bar.

The dog lunged against the trap.

Stokes advanced. He revved the saw in bursts, showing his white even teeth. Bone poked through the raw flesh of the dog's leg where the trap had bit. Unable to escape, the animal twisted back to face Stokes. Its lips wrinkled from its teeth. Stokes set his legs and pressed the trigger down. The saw screamed. In a unified motion, he threw one foot forward to take his weight, he crouched and swung the saw in an arc from left to right. The dog bit at it. Its tongue and lower jaw were ripped apart in a spray of blood and teeth. The dog went over backward. It thrashed upright to face Stokes again. Its eyes were insane. Stokes doubled the saw back. The animal threw itself away, nearly pulling its broken leg apart. Stokes went after it. The saw chewed into the back of its skull—and Stokes' neck exploded in fire. He was knocked sprawling.

The gray bitch had reached the chicken first. It squawked and beat its wings and jumped in a circle. The bitch went after it. Something erupted from the ground. It seized her leg and she fell yowling. The spotted dog leapt past her and killed the chicken. The bitch twisted around biting at the thing that held her leg. Orph charged and bit it too, but only once: it had no life. The gray whimpered. The pack gathered around her. They sniffed, they pawed at the earth, uncovering the chain. The black and the dun licked solicitously at the blood on the gray's leg. Orph frowned, tried to comfort her with his tongue on her face. The pack circled uneasily. Now and then one of them would lie down next to the bitch, or draw off looking over its shoulder barking for her to follow, returning after she'd jerked futilely at the chain, whining. They lay down with their heads between their paws and watched her. She groaned. They made little sounds of anxiousness. Orph got up and paced back and forth. He wanted to be gone. He could feel the danger in his chest. He chewed on the chain, transforming his repugnance for the taste of metal into anger at the thing. The bitch pled to him with whines.

The metal would not give. He lay close to the bitch and brooded. The black dog prowled restively. The woods tensed around them.

Orph smelled a human. He didn't understand how, but he knew the human had done this. It upset him to have been bested, and it made him apprehensive. He swiveled the cups of his ears. He scented deeply. The human came with menace.

He led the dun and the spotted and the black bellying into the brush. They waited, watching, with their ears flattened. The gray strained toward the thicket. Then she went still. Footfalls sounded. She turned to face them.

Orph winced when the great chattering noise began. The others crawled backward and shifted unhappily, wanting to flee, waiting for Orph to lead them off.

Orph sprang to his feet: the man was killing the bitch.

Orph bounded from the thicket and went up in the air. His teeth sank high, in the neck, and his weight slammed into the man's back.

Stokes fell atop his saw. It chopped into the meat of his thigh. He screamed and threw himself off. The motor died, he heard vicious snarling, there were spikes in his neck. He struggled to his knees and rammed his elbow back hard, once, twice, driving the bony point against hard flesh. The spikes jerked loose. Stokes somersaulted forward and came up on his feet, spinning to face the dog. A big shepherd, almost on him again. He kicked hard. The dog seized his boot. The pressure was great, but the heavy leather stopped the teeth. Hopping, Stokes grabbed his knife from the sheath. The shepherd took him on the shin. Stokes shouted in pain. He swung the knife blindly. He was struck on the hip by another animal and knocked

over the shepherd. The blade cut nothing but air. Black
dog on his hip. Tooth grinding on bone. Another animal
tore into his forearm. Knife, hold onto the fucking knife!
Oh God! A fourth dog slashed at his side.

"Aii-yah!" Stokes flung the spotted dog from his arm and
heaved to his feet, the teeth of the others tearing down
through his flesh.

"*Goddamn you!*" he roared. He stabbed with the knife,
hammered down with his clenched fist. His cry went rolling up the mountainsides.

The shepherd came into his side and he went down in
agony. The shepherd cracked a rib apart and bit again.
They were all over him. Stokes chopped the black with
the knife. The blade plunged into the black's neck. The
black snarled and bit Stokes' elbow. Stokes screamed. His
hand jerked open, losing the knife. The black released
him, twisted and snapped at the knife embedded in its
neck, then lunged back. Stokes' vision filled with teeth
and gaping red mouth. He threw his hands up but the
black had him, and Stokes squeezed his eyes shut in terror,
his hands bunching the black's ruff and skin. The black
tore his cheek away and split his nose, came again and
ripped scalp off. The shepherd ground through the biceps
of his left arm and the arm fell useless and the shepherd
bit into his chest. Shrieking, Stokes found the knife with
the fingers of his right hand and pulled it free. The dun
buried her teeth in his armpit and the knife fell from his
hand. He clawed in the dirt for it, throwing his head from
side to side trying to slip the black. His genitals were
savaged. He choked on vomit. He rolled over, pinning a
dog beneath him that bit into his belly. He rolled again,
madly, with a high puling, and the dogs went with him,
ripping. The spotted tore off an ear. The black vised his
face and crushed his cheekbones. The dun opened his belly.
Stokes flopped across the ground, threw off the spotted

and blindly—his mind shrunk to a functionless pea—got the black's ear and wrenched the dog from his face. He pulled to a sit, flailing with his right arm. Orph hit his throat and tore it open. Blood fountained. Orph crushed through the larynx. Stokes went up on his knees, then his torso bent forward until his forehead touched the ground, and he stayed arched that way, his lungs convulsing against the blood flooding into them and coughing it out in thick drops and explosive mists through his opened throat and his mouth and nose. Orph bit into his back. Stokes fell face down on the soddening earth. His muscles went flaccid. Orph, teeth sunk to gums, strained and lifted him a few inches from the ground. The dog shook the heavy, limp body. Lowered it back down and stood with teeth deep, rumbling low in the chest. Stokes twitched. Orph shook him again. Stokes lay still.

Orph released the body and stood several moments poised to bite again. There was no movement. Orph walked around the body, sniffing. The spotted was still worrying one of the legs, but with fading interest. Orph pressed his snout to the man, drew air and opened his cells to sense for vital force. The life was gone.

Orph walked to the gray bitch and licked at her broken head, scented. He turned away and walked off, dropped heavily to the ground. A shoulder muscle ticked. Storms of excitation still surged and collided within him. He was matted with blood. He began to lick it off with long lavings of his tongue. He became aware of a stinging line across his chest. He licked and nibbled at it. It wasn't very painful. He licked the blood from his forepaws.

The others had nosed around the gray bitch, and then left her. The dun, her dugs engorged, her belly big and low, near her time, bent backward to chew at a wound on her thigh. The spotted dog licked the hole in the black's neck, which the black couldn't reach. The black groomed the spotted gratefully with its tongue.

When they were done cleansing themselves, they looked to Orph. He was weary and wished to rest, as they did. But they could not stay here, not anywhere near, not a moment more, his cells insisted, and so he stood and took the wind, and padded off up the side of the mountain. The dun and the black and the spotted fell in behind him.

CHAPTER 9

BAUER sat in front of the television with a tumblerful of Scotch. He didn't want to see what was coming, he didn't want it to be real. He'd heard about it at school in the late afternoon.

The report was videotaped, which gave it that curious quality of suprareality inherent in the medium. First there was a view of Stokes' house. The camera zoomed slowly until the front door filled the screen. Cut to a black-and-white snapshot of a big, heavy, square-faced smiling man. Which was replaced by Stokes' widow, weeping.

Buddy Stokes, the announcer said, left for work Wednesday morning and did not return that night.

"Sometimes," Mrs. Stokes said dully into the camera, "he'd run into friends and stay out all night and just go to work the next morning. But when he didn't come home Thursday night, I made some calls, but no one had seen him. I stayed up waiting, and then in the morning"—She

bit her lip—"in the morning, I called the sheriff's department, and. . . . Oh! I was mad at him, and all the time he
was, he was. . . ." She broke down sobbing.

"This is Watson Hollow," the commentator said som-
berly, "a small valley between two rugged mountains.
Buddy Stokes was cutting timber here. His pickup truck
appears just as Sheriff's Deputy Bill Sanders found it at
ten o'clock this morning, an auto-loading highpowered
rifle still secure in its brackets. . . . Stokes walked this
trail five hundred yards to the maple stand he was working. But he didn't stop here, he went on up the rock shelv-
ing and through this brush, past this copse of trees. Buddy
Stokes had found the spoor of wild dogs back in these
woods. According to his wife, the only person in whom he
had confided, he couldn't know whether or not this was the
same pack that attacked and grievously injured young
Homer McPhee last month and he didn't want to sound
the alarm without cause. He set a line of traps, like this
one, and checked them every morning. Here, on this ridge,
he found a wild dog caught fast, and that discovery cost
him his life."

The camera dropped to a tarpaulin covering a body.
Legs moved around the edges, a state trooper knelt on one
knee in the background. Muffled voices could be heard.

"Covington Coroner James Castleman and Conservation
Officer William Burgher reconstructed the event after
careful examination of the site. The trapped dog was not
alone. There were four others—the size of the pack that
attacked McPhee. They slunk into hiding at Stokes'
approach. When he became aware of their presence, and
probably as they menaced him, Stokes fired up his chain
saw, a potent but unwieldy weapon. The pack attacked."

The camera raced from a briar thicket and came to a
jarring halt on a chain saw lying crookedly on the ground.

"Stokes must have abandoned the clumsy saw early and

resorted to his knife." A shot of a bloodcrusted knife lying atop a handkerchief in someone's hands. "It was a terrible, violent fight." The camera spun about the surrounding trees, up to the sky, down to the torn and stained earth. "A primitive battle between a lone man and a snarling pack of wild beasts. Stokes managed to kill one of them" —The camera came to rest, for an instant, on the twisted corpse of a gray dog—"and to wound others, though how many and how seriously is not known. In the end, though, he could not stand against them—it is likely that no man could—and he fell dead beneath their teeth, savaged beyond imagination.

"We spoke to Deputy Bill Sanders, who was first upon the scene and who discovered the body of Buddy Stokes. Deputy Sanders, you have seen death in many violent guises in the course of your duties. What was your reaction early this morning when you made the discovery?"

The face of a uniformed young man appeared, pale and troubled, eyes on his feet. He shook his head. He was barely audible. "I turned away. Because he hardly even looked like a man anymore. And I went and sat down until I got my stomach back, until I could force myself to look again." His eyes rose slowly to the camera. "They tore him apart," he said in awe. "They tore him to pieces. Pieces."

The camera pulled back to reveal the reporter standing near the deputy, a mike in his hand, a portable recorder slung from his shoulder, and farther back to include the tarp-covered bulk, the dead dog, and a handful of men in uniform and civilian clothes who were milling about, consulting, examining the ground.

"And so," the reporter said, "the wild dogs of Queensbridge County, with one vicious attack on an unarmed youth behind them, have now killed their first human being. This is Gerald Becker returning you to the studio."

Bauer set his glass aside. He leaned forward with his elbows on his knees and held his face in his hands.

A new voice said, "Gerald Becker's report was taped early this morning. Continuing this story, we have a series of interviews conducted this afternoon, and a summary of the operation already in progress to find and destroy the feral dogs who killed Buddy Stokes two days ago, early last Wednesday. Here now is Dr. Elizabeth Collier, Covington veterinarian and authority on canine behavior."

Elizabeth appeared on the screen, mouth tight and eyes narrowed.

"Dr. Collier," the reporter said, "it's almost certain that the same pack of dogs that attacked Homer McPhee has now killed Buddy Stokes. Is such ferocious behavior within the natural capacities of the animal that is so generally called Man's Best Friend?"

"If you mean to suggest that house dogs are killers in pets' clothing, then the answer is absolutely no. I want to emphasize that as strongly as I can. There is no cause for alarm among dog owners and their neighbors. On the other hand, if you're asking if it's *possible* for dogs to kill without being rabid or insane, the answer is yes. That's obvious, isn't it? But it's a freakish occurrence. You're much more likely to be struck by lightning than seriously injured by a dog. Last year 24,000 people were murdered by their fellow citizens in this country—and eighteen were killed by dogs. Most of those eighteen were small children who were bitten once or twice by a large dog—bites that would have required only a couple of stitches if they'd happened to adults."

"Would wild dogs hunt human beings as prey?"

Elizabeth was annoyed. "Never. We don't taste good to most predators. Some fish and reptiles will eat humans, and occasionally a tiger develops a taste for us, but we are definitely not prey to dogs."

"Why, then, do you think this pack has attacked people?"

"Most likely in self-defense. Homer McPhee stated that he attempted to drive them off the calf they'd killed. He used rocks and a club. Only then did they attack. As the media have reported, Buddy Stokes did trap one of the pack, but no one has mentioned the additional fact that, according to the evidence, he then proceeded to butcher this trapped animal with a chain saw. That was the catalyst, in all probability, for the pack's violence. Like most wild animals, feral dogs will not attack a human being without provocation—which means you have to corner them, assault them, or threaten their young. They'd much prefer to flee."

"They had every chance to run from the McPhee boy. Why didn't they?"

"They were defending their kill, their food, which is vital to any living creature. Also, and here I can only speculate, we have no concrete evidence, this pack's Alpha dog—" She paused. "In wolf or dog packs," she explained, "there is always an Alpha animal. That's the dominant member of the pack, its leader. This pack's Alpha dog is probably very bold and aggressive. It's likely he was a pet at some time in his life. He would be wary of human beings and wish to avoid them whenever possible, but far less afraid of them than a dog who had been born in the wild, if indeed he is afraid of them at all."

"Then you would say that this pack is quite dangerous, and liable to attack again."

"They will not actively seek an encounter with humans, but yes, they are still very dangerous."

"Why do you think they let the McPhee boy live but killed Buddy Stokes?"

"Even a totally berserk dog will stop its attack moments

after its victim stops moving, which usually occurs when the victim loses consciousness through shock, as was the case with McPhee, or loss of blood. Unfortunately, Stokes was a strong man, he fought hard, and he sustained mortal injuries before his body could go comatose."

"One final question, Dr. Collier. What is the best course of action for a person confronted by this pack, or any other hostile dog?"

"First, don't run. This triggers a powerful predator's instinct, which causes the animal to give pursuit. Second, do not attempt to frighten it off by menacing it or throwing things at it, which might cause it to counterreact with aggression of its own. Third, avoid direct eye contact. Among canines, eye locking is a challenge and there are only two possible responses—one animal offers submission by breaking the contact, or they fight. Last, if you're bitten, no matter how painfully, freeze, remain perfectly still. If you're not moving, the dog will release you. He might try another bite to see what will happen, but he won't continue an attack on a motionless person."

Colonel Edwin Mulcahey of the state police appeared next. He was stiff and uncomfortable before the camera. Delivering a prepared statement, he said that three spotter planes would take to the air at dawn; a combined force of state police, sheriff's deputies, and conservation officers would set out to comb Heerman's, Claypipe and the neighboring mountains; a squad of professional hunting guides was being assembled, and two teams of bloodhounds would arrive tomorrow afternoon. Citizens were requested to report sightings of unfamiliar dogs, but Mulcahey warned against civilians taking to the woods with guns. He did not want an armed horde loose on the mountains, which would only invite tragedy.

A nervous conservation department spokesman tried to

justify the failure of the first hunt, explaining the difficulty of locating animals as clever and chary as feral dogs, but pledged his department's unflagging efforts until the menace had been eliminated. The governor followed with a short statement of sympathy and reassurance. He vowed full support and promised speedy resolution. Harry Wilson flailed against a variety of officials and demanded passage of his proposed dog code not only by the city of Covington but the state legislature as well. The commentator concluded with an invitation to stay tuned for a special report on the grave problem of wild dogs across the nation.

Bauer walked out of the cabin. He looked up at the dark bulk of the mountains.

It is you, Orph.

And I spun you out of the wool of my own circumvention.

It is me.

There was no place Orph wanted to be, only the need to go far from where the killing happened. He drove them at a hard pace, and he maintained it past his strength and theirs, until his body tore free of his will, and then he would collapse, shaking, while the others dropped down around him. He wouldn't let them rest much, only long enough for the worst of the exhaustion to leach away, and then he forced them up and moving again. They neither questioned nor rebelled: he was the leader, their mind and direction. In alternation, there was climb and descent, but always motion, and mountains gave way beneath them. Their pads became swollen and bloody.

The dun bitch grew nervous and restless. She hadn't eaten in several hours, though they'd made a small kill and there had been food. She began dropping behind, sometimes she went angling away from them. Orph bullied her back, shouldering and nipping her. He smelled the strange odor from her loosening vagina. It made him anxious. A sentiment of profound gravity unfolded in his viscera, and with it, the inexplicable knowledge that they would not go on much longer, that somehow the dun was becoming their center. It simply was, as his heartbeat. But he set himself against it to squeeze whatever hours he could from her, then finally whatever minutes, and by midafternoon he could wrest nothing further, and the tide surged forth and propelled her into primacy.

She stopped. He went back to her. She growled. He nipped at her flank. She attacked him. He drew back rapidly, blood pearling on his ear where she had pierced it.

She stood panting, her head low. She whined. She turned down the side of the mountain.

Orph followed. Behind him came the spotted and the black. They remained some distance behind her; she snarled wildly whenever they came too near.

Orph did not like this direction. But to follow the bitch was what was to be done.

Her path down the mountain was erratic. She changed directions frequently. She doubled back. She circled. She stuck her snout into rock crevices. She pawed the stoney soil.

Toward evening she stopped, low on the flank of the mountain, and reconnoitered around a stream with unhappy whines. Finally, at the base of a tall stone escarpment, she began to dig.

Orph advanced, but stopped when she turned and barked at him. This, then, was the boundary. He lay down and rested his head on his paws and watched her. Unhappy.

They would be here for some time. It smelled and felt not alarming, but not satisfying either. He was disturbed by a light thread of human scent. A fair distance off, but there nonetheless. It was a limp odor, empty of hardness or danger, but he didn't trust it and wished to be gone from it, gone from human scent of any kind.

But there was nothing to be done. It was what was.

The dun scratched out a burrow nearly twice her width and length and crawled into it. She lay on her side, panting. Her abdomen began to cramp.

In the darkness, Orph crept closer to the den. He settled a dozen paces from its mouth. He lay with his ears pricked, listening to the bitch.

The first pup was squeezed from her body half an hour after the contractions began. The size of a man's hand, eyes tightly shut, face rumpled, little legs tucked against its body, it was encased in a wet sac. The dun tore the sac open and pulled it away from the twitching little form. She scissored the umbilical cord with her teeth. She ate the sac then licked the puppy carefully from head to rear. She nosed it in gentle tumbles several moments, and it began to breathe. It wriggled clumsily and laboriously up against her warmth and rooted around her belly with weak, tiny squeaks until it had one of her dugs in its mouth. The bitch laid her head down to rest. She breathed heavily.

Shortly another pup edged toward birth. She yelped as it emerged, panted when it was out, opened the sac and ate it, cleaned the pup.

At dawn, there were six pups piled against her belly and the exhausted but consummated bitch was sleeping.

Orph had not slept. He'd watched and listened to the burrow through the night. He was charged by each tiny little cry. He could bear it no longer. He went to peer into the den.

The bitch snarled out at him.

He walked away. His blood understood what he had smelled. There was sense.

A few hours after sunrise the bitch crawled into the light, relieved herself and went to the stream to drink. There was whimpering from the den. The bitch watched Orph and the other two dogs closely while she drank. She was back in the hole again in moments.

In the late afternoon Orph and the black and the spotted left to hunt.

It was dark when they returned. Orph had eaten much of the kill. He stood at the entrance of the burrow and whined. The bitch crawled out. She sniffed, licked his jaws. She opened her mouth wide. He regurgitated into it. She ate and went back down to the pups.

The next afternoon the black emptied its stomach for her.

The pack disappeared from national news in days, was relegated to minor status in state news shortly after. It remained a volatile issue in Queensbridge County and a crisis in Covington. Harry Wilson's paper and radio station drummed it daily. Civilians shot two vagabond dogs and crippled half a dozen more with clubs. Neighbors wouldn't speak to each other. There were fistfights in bars. Children threw stones at tied and fenced dogs. The city council tentatively approved a modified version of Wilson's dog proposals and Wilson announced his candidacy for the state legislature.

A few armed men were arrested in the woods, one after he'd shot at movement in a ravine and wounded a sheriff's deputy in the leg. No sign of the dogs was found. Colonel Mulcahey's confident optimism seeped from his press releases. He promised the hunt would continue until the animals were dead, but, by degrees, the costly manpower was withdrawn from the mountains. Harry Wilson's editorials condemned everyone from the governor to the American Kennel Club.

Bauer no longer wondered. The hard evidence was scanty—McPhee's description of the dog and a pinch of hair gathered from the site of the Stokes killing that Elizabeth Collier identified as German shepherd—but his apprehension solidified into conviction, and with it came an anguished guilt, a paralyzing despondency.

I did this, he thought. Through my own fecklessness, my own will-lessness. My hands are filthy with the death of a man and with the horror of my own child. He turned from himself in revulsion.

Santo DiGiovanni's letter brought him to his knees.

It was printed in pencil. The lines wavered with age.

Dear Mr. Bauer:

Today makes five years exactly that my Anthony has been in jail. My heart is broken and I have been dead all this time, but my body will not lay down and let me sleep yet. I hope you thought about Anthony this day because it would be terrible for a man to condemn another man to spend his life in prison and not even remember that he did that.

Anthony did wrong. And he must answer to the law and God for that. But you knew him before he murdered. You knew the other bad things he was doing. You knew what he might do. You could have stopped him or you could have told others who would stop him. But you didn't. You did nothing. You waited until Anthony killed, and then you came forward.

You are free now. You can make love and drink wine and please yourself with your work and go and do whatever you like. Anthony cannot. Anthony is in a little room like your closet with steel bars and my son will stay in his cage until he grows old and his teeth fall out and he makes water in his pants and can't stand up by himself and then dies.

I do not hate you. I am only an old man who waits for death and the day his soul can be with the soul of his son. But I do not forgive you either. If that can be ever done, only you can do it, and you will have to find the way how. I would not like to live with your heart. It must hurt you very bad.

I cannot wish you well, but I do not wish you evil either. I wait only to die and my pain to end. Goodbye Mr. Bauer.

Santo DiGiovanni

Bauer had no substance. He was dust in the wind. He had given way, always. He had drunk equivocation and starved his will. Renunciation had shriveled his soul.

He lay stunned in his cabin. Grayish stubble spread over his cheeks. He took a little water, watching his hand raise a glass to his mouth, an immense, slow feat of strength, and he saw signs of his passage—a hardening crust of bread scalloped by his teeth, a broken cup on the floor—but he could not recall them and could hardly understand them.

How he longed for nothingness!

No. He forced himself to shower.

He forced himself to shave his face, to clean his mouth, to dress his body in fresh clothes, to control the external and compel its order inward. He ate. In moderation, but still his stomach threw the food out. He waited a little and ate again, and this time he gagged up some of it, but most remained.

Kathy appeared at the cabin. With a tall golden boy whose name he couldn't fix. She touched him. They laughed. Their teeth were brilliantly white. They talked to him and he heard them, but couldn't speak, and Kathy thought it would be fun and wonderful if all three of them took off their clothes and went into his bedroom and made love to each other, but he didn't answer, he looked at them with a still face, and the boy frowned in gathering anger, and Kathy brought her face close to Bauer's and slipped in through the small holes of his pupils and said Hey are you tripping or something and after long moments of emptiness she grew annoyed but then she recovered her laughter because she could experience abrasive emotions only in flickers and she shrugged in silliness and went up on her toes and kissed him on the cheek and said smiling Okay we'll split I'll catch you later all right? and she left with the boy and he heard the boy say, "He's obliterated, man. Totally obliterated. Jesus."

He got his car keys off the dresser and went out. The day was ending and he turned the headlights on. He drove to Elizabeth's. The lights were on in her living room.

She opened the door and said, "Hi, Alex," puzzled.

"I need you," he said. He took her in his hands.

She tried to pull back and said, "What do you think you're doing?" but he was too strong, he hurt her, and she realized she could be hurt much worse, and that eliminated the possibility of her escaping this, and as he set to her clothes she remained resistant and unwilling but didn't struggle as if her life were at stake because she thought that it might be if she did. He spoke but wasn't coherent. She didn't recognize anything in him or the manner in which he seemed to be beating at his own body, and he couldn't penetrate even though she presented him with no impediment, he was impotent, and he got off her and raised his fists and opened his mouth, as if he would scream, as if he would wail, or hurl some great violent noise out, but he didn't, and he lowered his hands and looked down at her with an expression of unendurable grief.

She got up, pulling her abused clothing about her. "That was wrong," she said calmly. "I don't know what you destroyed, but you did destroy."

After several moments he said, "I'm sorry."

"I don't want to see you again," she said.

There was no indication he'd heard. "I'm going to find Orph," he said.

"You can't."

He nodded.

He went to the door. "I'm sorry," he said, and this time he meant it for her.

He left. She sat in a chair and hugged herself.

The pups' eyes opened on the tenth day. The bitch grew lean with their greedy suckling, but she held her strength and didn't go hungry, enough food was brought her. The pups lengthened and put on weight. They bustled one another and wobbled when they stood. Their tiny pin-pointed teeth made her nipples raw. The bitch spent a few minutes in the sunshine when she emerged to relieve herself and drink from the stream, then five minutes, then ten, a quarter hour. She lay on her side relishing her respite. She came close to playing with the males. Though they sniffed at the den mouth and stared into it, they made no attempt to enter, and she loosened into trust again and was no longer as harsh with them as she had been. The largest pup gained its legs. It explored the burrow in bold adventures of inches. The bitch grew sure enough to ignore for a while the small whines and squeaks they sent up the burrow mouth when, after a vague, uncomprehending search for her warmth and succor, they could not find her. One afternoon she went recklessly off on a run with the spotted dog, returning half an hour later, exhilarated. The pups were voicing their unhappiness. She went down to them in contentment, and lay on her side. They clambered over each other to jerk at her dugs. A few days later she carried them one by one in her mouth out of the burrow and deposited them in the sunlight on the warm earth. With proud wariness she watched Orph and the other males nose, and sniff, and turn the pups over. The pups quailed and squirted urine. They tried to scramble back down into the burrow, but she blocked them. The black dog walked into the forest to sulk. Orph wandered several paces away and dropped down to enjoy his comprehension, and the surety that they would not have to remain an endless time in this place, which offered shelter and water and adequate food, but where the occasional trace of human scent reached his nostrils, without overt threat, but still a danger simply because it was human. The spotted dog lay down close to the bitch and her brood. He stretched his neck to lick the pups. The biggest pup mastered its terror long enough to stand the licking a few moments. Then it clawed back to its mother and tried to squeeze beneath her. The bitch moved to let them at the burrow, they scrambled to its edge and went tumbling down inside. She followed, in copious happiness.

CHAPTER 10

IS intelligence, had he inquired of it, would have told him he had no chance of finding Orph. But it was a matter of knowledge, not intelligence: whatever streams of existence and time he and Orph tumbled through, they were moving toward confluence. He felt this in every fiber, knew it without question. It was a matter of harmony. Belief was irrelevant; he perceived the necessity.

He took a leave of absence from the school. Sometimes he camped with Mike and Jeff, and he had most of the equipment he'd need. He bought the rest, and a stock of freeze-dried food. He didn't own a gun. Ben Nichols was a young history professor who lived half a mile up the road. He wore his long hair tied back and dressed in jeans and sandals, but he was a mountain boy at heart. Bauer knew him well enough to ask him for a weapon. He told him why he wanted it.

"You haven't got a chance in hell," Nichols said.

Bauer shrugged. Nichols didn't press it, as Bauer had known he wouldn't. Nichols didn't let anyone tell him what to do with his life; in exchange, he never hassled anyone else.

"Do you have gear, have you ever camped?"

"Enough."

"How familiar are you with guns?"

"I'm not a buff, but I did some hunting when I was a kid, I classed 'Expert' in the Army."

Nichols took him into his study where there was a glass-fronted gun case. Nichols unlocked it, slid a panel back, and took out a rifle with a shoulder sling and telescopic sight. The checkered stock gleamed, there was a film of oil on the metal.

"See how this feels."

Bauer slid back the bolt to check that the weapon was unloaded.

"That's good," Nichols said. "I don't worry about putting one in your hands now."

Bauer butted the rifle against his shoulder and aimed it out a window to a tree. The scope's lenses were covered with leather caps. Bauer lowered the gun, then snapped it to shoulder. Lowered again, shouldered, and this time tracked smoothly across the wall.

"It fits me," he said. "And it has good balance." He read the stamp in the metal. It was a Winchester, Caliber .270.

"I don't know the cartridge," he said.

"It's hot and flat. 2900 feet per second, 1900 foot-pounds at impact. These mountains are mostly carbine terrain. You don't ordinarily get a clear field of more than fifty or sixty yards, but sometimes you do—a ridge, a spine, an open cliff." He took the caps off the sight. "The gun is accurate up to five hundred yards, but I've never had an open shot like that around here. It's sighted for two hundred. At one hundred you have an inch-and-a-half rise, at three hundred you get a two-inch drop. They don't make 'em any tighter. Anything over three hundred yards, don't shoot, you're on a highway. Have you ever used a scope?" Bauer said no and Nichols explained.

Nichols set the rifle aside and opened a drawer at the base of the cabinet. There were four handguns. He picked out the smallest, and a holster that fit it.

"You need a belt gun, too."

Bauer looked doubtful.

"Around camp you're not always going to have your rifle in hand. And close in, like it was with that guy Stokes, the rifle wouldn't be worth much anyway, too clumsy and slow. This is light. You won't even know you're carrying it. It's chambered for a .38 Special, not a cannon but punchy enough. You know pistols?"

"Not beyond .45s in the Army."

"Doesn't matter. You'd be using it at ten feet or less, and I can teach you in an hour."

They drove to a friend of Ben's, who had acreage and a target range. Bauer ran thirty rounds through the .270. The first five were scattered, but he hadn't lost the basic feel; each would have been some kind of hit. By the end he grouped three near perfectly at 200 yards, three in an area the size of a silver dollar, half an inch high at 100, and three in a two-inch circle around the bull at 300 yards.

"Those were all kills," Nichols said.

"It's a good gun."

Nichols worked with him on the Colt until he had it well enough.

They went back. Nichols persuaded him to borrow his trail bike too. "You can get up a mountain in an hour that would take you five or six of hard climb, and you don't have to carry your gear on your back. It spooks everything for a mile around, but they settle down pretty fast. You can cover ten, twenty times as much territory with it. You're going to fall flat, but you might as well give yourself all the help you can."

The machine was a front and rear wheel drive brute whose cleated low pressure tires could haul it over rocks and deadfalls like the treads of a tank. Nichols said it could climb right up the trunk of a tree. He demonstrated, slipping off the bike when it started to fall, and easing it down. The biggest problem was hitting the throttle too hard when climbing an obstacle. The surge of power tore the bike out from under you. Slow and easy was the key. Bauer wasn't really comfortable, but he could handle it well enough not to break a leg.

He was ready Thursday evening, but didn't plan to leave until Monday morning; he wanted the weekend with Jeff and Mike.

He didn't wonder what he'd do when he found Orph. There had never been alternatives, not from the moment of the dog's, or his own nativity, not even from the time of the boiling oceans. He submitted to the inexorable, he embraced his responsibility.

Agony lay before him. But he would enter it, and emerge from it. Now he experienced a deep calmness. His movements were light and had grace. He was comfortable in the silence of the cabin. He rested and listened to music, which was sufficient engagement with himself and everything that was not him. He listened attentively, and understood the music.

Friday afternoon he called Ursula to confirm the time he'd pick the children up in the morning. She wasn't in yet. They'd met in family court last week and the judge had granted him the visitation rights he'd petitioned for.

Ursula had shot him a single venomous glance of hatred, but then had composed herself. They'd exchanged a few minutes' polite conversation as they left the court. He got no answer after dinner, nor a couple hours later when he tried again. He went to bed and slept restfully.

He woke early, showered, dressed, and cooked sausages and eggs. He took a second cup of coffee outside, drank it and looked up at the sun-flooding mountains through a cigarette. He drove into town.

He found the front door locked. He rang the bell again and waited. He walked over to a living-room window and looked in. He tried to identify exactly what was askew. Then he saw; details. The brass cigarette box was gone from the coffee table, the ivory Art Nouveau dancer from the mantel, there were lighter blocks of paint on the walls where pictures had hung. He went around the back and tried the kitchen door. It was locked too. He got a rock from the yard and broke out a small pane of glass, reached through and opened the lock and went in.

The house was utterly still. He went upstairs. Most of the toys were gone from the boys' rooms, most of their clothes. The aquarium no longer stood on Jeff's dresser. Michael's joke books were missing from the shelf over his bed. Ursula's makeup and jewelry chest were not in her room. Her closet was only a quarter full, the clothes that remained had never been her favorites. There was a squeezed-out tube of toothpaste in the bathroom, a topless deodorant stick that had shrunk to a dry cracked nub. Downstairs again, he picked the receiver from the wall phone in the kitchen. He hadn't expected a dial tone and he didn't get one.

He went next door and knocked on Janie's door. She came from the living room. When she saw him she bit her lip.

"Just a second," she called.

She disappeared, returned a minute later with her husband Bill at her side. They looked unhappy. She let him in. Bill stood with his back to the refrigerator, his arms crossed over his chest.

"Where did she go?" Bauer said.

"Let's not allow ourselves to get upset," Bill said.

"I'm not upset."

"I don't know." Janie wouldn't meet his eyes.

"She must have said."

"She didn't. Not a word."

"The personal stuff is gone, but there's still a couple thousand dollars' worth of possessions in the house. She didn't just throw them away—money and things are important to Ursula."

Janie looked helplessly to her husband. He came from the refrigerator to stand beside her. "She left some money with us to have the stuff put in storage. The truck is coming next week. That's all she said." His tone grew belligerent. "Nothing more."

Bauer nodded. "When you talk to her, tell her this is senseless. It can only hurt Jeff and Michael. I don't care what she does. I'm not angry with her and I don't want to take her children away from her. I only want to see them. Tell her to call me."

"She won't," Janie said. "She—"

"She nothing," Bill said. "She just asked to see that her things got into storage. That's all. She didn't leave any messages, and we're not taking any for her."

Bauer left. He went back to his cabin. He called her parents. They were nervously cordial but wouldn't tell him anything. Her brother, whom he'd never gotten on with, refused to talk to him.

He sat for a moment, thinking. He dialed New York City Information and got the number of Gruman Security & Investigations. The receptionist said Mr. Gruman didn't come in Saturdays. His partners Mr. Charleston and Mr. Webster were there, she'd be happy to connect him. He told her to call Wallace Gruman at home and ask him to phone Alex Bauer as soon as he could. He gave the girl his number and hung up.

Gruman called back forty-five minutes later. Bauer had once written a series on Gruman and his agency. It attracted interest and was responsible for a lot of new business.

"She might have gone to California," Bauer said. "She lived in San Francisco once. She has a cousin there she's close to, some friends and an old boyfriend."

"Is she whacky, dangerous to the kids or anything?"

"No. Actually, I don't think it's all me. This town's too small for her, and I think she had a love affair that went sour. She probably wants to start everything over. That's fine, I don't care where she lives, and she'll get over hating my guts in a few months, but I want to know where my kids are. I want to talk to them. I want to work out times I can see them—school holidays if she wants to stay in California, or wherever she is, summer vacations. How long will it take to find her?"

"That depends. Since she's straight—a solid citizen—and has children with her, it won't be very hard. She'll be applying for a telephone, have to list her Social Security number on job applications, get a new driver's license, make arrangements for schooling, that kind of thing. Unless you're really going underground—and that's only for kids, crazies and fugitives—it's just not possible to keep your whereabouts unknown long in this society. With a couple of lucky phone calls, we've found people in under two hours. I'd say a week to ten days at the outside."

Bauer gave Gruman Ben Nichols' number and asked that a message be left there if Gruman couldn't get him personally.

He hung up. He didn't feel anything but a kind of firmness, a still and steady certitude. He respected the tranquillity; it seemed a rite of preparation.

He could set off now. The bulk of the day still remained. But he didn't. He'd fixed a point of beginning, Monday, and it was better to adhere to that, not to alter the rhythm of it.

He went walking in the woods, through areas he'd wandered with Orph. He was saddened, but armored by his will against despair, against the sanctuary of disengagement. He listened to music before he went to bed.

The pups were five weeks old, and the bitch had weaned them. Orph and the black and the spotted dog brought small kills and pieces of larger ones back. The pups pushed at each other over the food, dragged bones and hunks of meat off to private corners and showed their teeth, growled if one of the others came too close. They ate ravenously, they were growing round. Their hair was soft and fuzzy. Heavy and big-boned, they favored Orph. They had his broad skull and bull neck, his powerful chest and shoulders. The bitch had pulled most of their muzzles, which were longer than Orph's. One, the biggest, a male, had a head and front assembly that were replicas in miniature of his sire. Another had an upcurled tail. The bitch's dun color had washed and sported with Orph's deep black and rust, and one pup was a sable with a light tinting of red.

They were frolicsome and aggressive, happy to play outside the burrow as long as the bitch would allow. They ran after blowing leaves, and bit them. They stalked insects. They wrestled each other with mock snarls and sharp nips.

They chewed on the older dogs' tails and bit their ears. They charged their mother or one of the others, barking loudly, snapped playfully at legs. They harassed the males until one would lose patience and knock the offender to the ground and give it a harsh snarl or a low growl, which immediately caused the pup to roll over on its back and sprinkle a few drops of urine, which infantile display guaranteed its safety.

Orph liked them. They amused him and he felt good playing with them. In another week the bitch would bring them from the den a final time and then they'd begin to live and sleep in the open with the rest of the pack, and a week or two after that they'd be old enough to travel, slowly and not any great distance at a time, but Orph could lead the pack away from here, and the human scent that drifted sporadically through the woods. He was more tolerant of the pups' enthusiasm than the black, who warned them away frequently and sulked into the woods when they became too much to bear, but less than the spotted dog, who seemed nearly as proud and devoted to them as the bitch. The spotted dog rarely rebuked or withdrew from them. He licked them, he groomed them, he baited their charges with his swishing tail, he rolled on his back and let them climb on him and didn't object to their little needle teeth.

When the bitch returned them to the den after an hour's play, they squeezed together in exhaustion and went immediately to sleep, soundly, and for a long time. The bitch was then free awhile, to relax, to run. She didn't worry overmuch. If they woke, they'd call for her, growing querulous if she didn't answer, but they wouldn't brave the outside world without her. A few days ago the biggest one, the dominant pup who looked like Orph, growing daily bolder and more aggressive, had climbed the tunnel to the mouth and emerged into the sunlight blinking and immensely pleased with himself. But the bitch seized him by the scruff of his neck and lifted him off the ground and shook him furiously, growling, until he screamed in terror. Then she brought him back down and left him to cower with his littermates. He had not courted such cataclysm again.

This morning, the pups played themselves silly after they breakfasted and wearily allowed her to shepherd them back into the burrow without protest. They promptly fell asleep. The bitch padded restlessly up and down the treeline with the males, who were ready to set off hunting. She whined. She missed the tension of the stalk, the thrill of the pursuit, the heart-pounding frenzy of the kill. She had been shackled to the burrow an unendurably long time. Orph was unhappy with her distress. He circled the clearing, looking at the burrow, at the woods, nuzzling the bitch. The black and the spotted were waiting. Orph moved into the trees with them.

The bitch watched them go. She could stand it no longer. She barked. They stopped and turned. She barked again. Orph answered. She ran to them. She butted muzzles with all of them in a nervous round. The spotted dog yipped and went racing away. The bitch shot after him. They ran with flat bodies in a wide fast circle, tearing up the ground with their nails. Orph and the black joined the game. They raced, they leapt over deadfalls, plunged into the brush in a follow-the-leader game. The bitch was exhilarated. Her spirit infected them. When they finally stopped, they panted happily with long tongues hanging.

Orph began to cast for a scent. He found something of interest and angled off between a pair of dead gray trunks. The other males followed. The bitch hesitated, anxious, then launched herself after them: to hunt, to run, to be free—until the twin ties of time and distance that bound

her to the burrow stretched too taut and brought her
back to her litter again.

Bauer wrestled up from the twisted sheets sweat-
soaked and chilled, wrenching toward consciousness, hearing himself cry: "I didn't do anything. God I didn't!"

His cheeks ran with tears. His breath sobbed.

He sat in the early Sunday stillness with his arms
wrapped around himself, feeling the bewildered, annihilat-
ing agony of a child whipped for no reason it can understand.

The dream had vanished, leaving only the sickening
residue of emotion.

He closed his eyes and tried to empty himself of feeling.

He rose and went to the bathroom and splashed cold
water on his face, toweled the sweat from his torso.

Santo DiGiovanni's letter was on his dresser. He unfolded
it and read it again.

I tried to find what was right, and I failed, old man.

I tried to explain, Ursula, but I couldn't find the way.

Orph, I could not see *you*, only what I wanted in you.

Suddenly, he ripped DiGiovanni's letter to pieces and
hurled them away.

"But *I* didn't shoot those poor black bastards."

He swung his arm across the dressertop knocking off
wallet and change and crashing a lamp to fragments on the
floor.

"You bitch! *I* didn't walk out on you when you needed
me! *I* didn't condemn *you* for my own disappointments."

He spun to the window, through which the hump of a
mountain was visible. "And *you*—I didn't repay *your* love
by tearing your son's face apart."

He balled his hand into a fist. His forearm trembled. He

hammered his fist against the wall. "You bastards! . . . Bastards! . . . Bastards!" He wept in rage and grief.

He leaned his head against the wall and rested. He dressed. He made breakfast. He sat in the living room, drinking coffee. His camp gear was laid out along a wall. He looked at it.

Am I going? he thought.

He wondered if he had been enacting a hollow drama for himself.

Should I go?

For a moment, a sense of Orph loomed over him, a nearly palpable presence. He was drawn into it, felt the pull of the inevitable.

He shook it off.

The presence subsided, but would not disappear, lingered as a soft murmur in his awareness.

He smiled. That's my good boy. Yes. You were true to your own self, you were false to no man. Ahh, Orph.

Wind scraped a branch against the house.

You never sought to hurt anyone. Do I come for you, Orph, or do I wish you long life, your life, your way, with your kind?

The wind gathered strength, coming down the mountain from the north, and increased its velocity as it swept unobstructed through the channel of the valley, and struck the house like a blow, making it shudder and rattling the windows.

They skipped sunrise meditation and set right to breakfast, then most everyone piled into the van and headed off toward Wintergreen. The theater department was staging a medieval fair on campus. Ed and Billy had helped carpenter booths, Josie had sewn pennants and made costumes.

Billy was going to wander the grounds as the ascetic monk-leader of a heretical sect. Pancho would play his flute as a strolling musician. The fair had received generous attention in newspapers and on radio—even a jousting tournament with papier-mâché lances was planned—and it looked as if the turnout would be large. It promised to be great fun.

Only Harriet and her son Hero, both of whom disliked crowds and noisy bustle, and Ed and Josie remained. Josie had menstrual cramps and a headache. Ed preferred to work in the garden awhile and then just lie around in the sun.

Harriet packed sandwiches, an apple, and some rock candy into a bag and at midmorning set out with Hero to wander in the woods. They tramped aimlessly, Hero listening with interest while Harriet named trees and flowers for him and told him stories of the Indians who used to live here long ago, and how they loved the land and lived in peace with it. Eventually they began to follow the course of a small stream, walking up the gradual incline of the lower mountain shoulder along the banks, where the going was easier. Hero threw stones in the water and floated sticks on it. They snuck up on deep pools and Hero was able to catch sight of trout hanging suspended with slowly beating fins before the fish saw them and darted off.

The big pup woke up yawning. He hadn't napped long, but he wasn't tired. He lay quietly a few minutes, then tried to rouse the other pups. They groaned and rolled over. He succeeded in waking only one, a female, and she was crochety and bit him on the foot, then crawled to the other side of her littermates and promptly went to sleep again.

The big pup nosed around the burrow awhile, but he knew each part intimately and it no longer held any fascination for him. He stretched out and gnawed on an old bone. There wasn't much taste left in it and he wasn't hungry anyway and digging his new teeth in stopped pleasuring his gums shortly so he pushed the bone aside. He grew bored. He tried the other pups again but none would wake. He crawled halfway up the burrow and began to call for his mother. She didn't answer. He worked himself into a loud fit of self-pity, and close after that, indignation. He moved closer to the den mouth. And then he became excited. He could see out the hole, to an immensity of interesting things, and he was overcome with lust for the outside. He trembled, recalling the terrible punishment his first independent venture had brought him. He edged closer, stopped just short of the mouth and yelled until he reached a pitch that had him shaking all over. He poked his head out, ready to duck back instantly if his mother rushed him, and yipped inquisitively.

There was no one there.

He called to the big dogs several minutes. No one answered. A leaf skittered by on a breeze. He jumped reflexively and sank his teeth into it, tore it to shreds. Then the wind gusted over him and he stiffened. He was outside. He remained still several moments, blood racing through his vessels, breathing quickly. Gradually his apprehension subsided. His mother was not there to punish him, nothing was unusual or threatening. He became charmed with himself.

He prowled the clearing. He lay down in the sun and stretched himself like the big dogs. He got up and swaggered over to the brush line, stuck his nose into the grass. A grasshopper exploded with whizzing wings. The pup yowled and went scrabbling backward. The fear passed, and he became embarrassed. He sat and groomed himself. He found a stick and wrestled with it and bit it, picked it up and pranced around the clearing. He was deliriously filled with himself. For no reason than that he was happy, and flooded with proprietary boldness, he stood in the center of the clearing, filled his lungs and emitted a deep rolling "*Wuuufff!*" of the kind he had heard from Orph and the black. The sound was a short squeaky parody; but he heard it as the confident proclamation of the king of the woods, and even he was impressed by it.

A yellow butterfly fluttered past and came to rest on a stalk of grass in front of him. He was provoked by its effrontery. He pounced. The butterfly rose again and went bobbling off just above the earth. The pup ran after it snapping his teeth. The butterfly danced on unperturbed. The pup gave reckless chase—and fell head over heels into emptiness. He landed frightened but unhurt in a half inch of cold water. He stood and barked for his mother. Nervously, he shook off the stuff that clung to his fur, lifted his feet against the strange, unpleasant and chilly water.

He'd fallen two feet down into a basin formed by small boulders jammed tight together at the side of the stream. Had it been spring melt-off, or a period of heavy rain, the basin would have been full of swirling water and the pup would have drowned. The rock on the water side was half the height of the others and damp. The stream lapped at its top and now and then a small trickle spilled over into the basin. The pup tried to clamber out, but couldn't find any purchase on the smooth stone. He jumped, and scratched against the rock as he fell. He wore himself out. He began to whine loudly in fright.

"Mommy—what's that?"

"What's what, sweetplum?"

Hero put a finger to his lips. "Sshhh. Listen."

Faintly, above the bubbling of the stream, Harriet heard a whimper.

"Did you hear, Mom, did you hear?"

"Uh-huh. Quiet a minute, hon. Let's find out where it's coming from."

It was somewhere not far ahead, at the edge of the stream.

"It's a animal," Hero said with concentration. "Is it hurt?"

"I don't know, hon. Let's go see."

Harriet took his hand.

They found a puppy trapped at the bottom of some rocks.

Hero was excited. "What's he doing here?"

"I don't know." Harriet looked around. She didn't see anyone or any sign of a camp. She shouted *Hello!* She didn't get an answer. The puppy huddled against a wall of its trap shivering and looking up at them in fear. Harriet lowered herself and sat back on her heels. "Hi, little fella. How'd you get yourself lost way out here, huh?"

The pup whimpered.

Hero got down beside her. "He's scared."

"Sure. He's just a little baby. We're not going to hurt you, sweetheart. There, there, it's all right. Nothing bad is happening to you."

"Can we take him home, Mom? Can we? Can he be our dog, *please!*"

Hero had cried and cried as the days had gone by and it became clear that Spirit was never coming back to the Treehouse. He missed the dog awfully.

"Well, I don't know," Harriet said. "I guess we can't leave him like this all alone and helpless."

"But can we *keep* him, Mom?"

"Maybe." The last few weeks they'd been meaning to take Hero into Covington and let him pick out a puppy from the SPCA. "If his owners put an ad in the paper we'll have to give him back. I mean, maybe there's a little boy who loves him and maybe he loves that little boy just like Spirit loved you." Hero tightened his eyes against tears. "But if that happens, we'll go right into town the same afternoon and get you a brand-new puppy, okay? And just between you and me, I don't think he belongs to anyone who wants him. They'd have been more careful with him if they did."

Hero became happy.

Harriet spoke soothingly to the puppy and reached down for it. It showed its teeth as her hands neared. It snarled, and when she touched it, it bit her.

"Ouch!" Harriet jerked back. Little drops of blood glistened on her fingers. She put them in her mouth and sucked them. "You're a tough little guy, you are," she said without anger.

"Why'd he do that?"

"He's very frightened. We're big scary giants to him."

Hero leaned over the basin. "Don't be scared little doggy. I love you. It's all right. We're your friends."

Harriet tried again, and was bitten again. She laughed. "You're a regular tiger." She unbuttoned her denim shirt and shrugged out of it, her breasts swinging free. "Mommy's going to make a sack out of her shirt," she said to Hero. "I don't think we can handle him otherwise, and he'll probably feel better and calm down once he's inside."

She got the pup into the shirt at the expense of a couple more tiny punctures. She carried it carefully, trying not to bounce it much. After a while it ceased struggling and settled down. Hero crooned to the sack.

Ed got a piece of rope and Josie brought some meat scraps and a bowl of fresh goat's milk. The pup fought hysterically and lacerated Ed's hands before he got the rope around its neck. He tied the other end to a big log in the yard.

The puppy went berserk. It lunged against the rope. It twisted and jerked, got itself tangled up and thrashed about on the ground. Hero started to cry.

Ed sat down and crossed his legs. "Hero, get beside your mother. Josie, sit over there." They joined hands in a semicircle around the crazed pup. Deeply, Ed intoned: "Ohhhhhmmmmmmmmmmmmmmmmmmm."

The others joined him.

"Ohhhhhmmmmmmmmmm . . . Ohhhhhmmmmmmmmmm."

The pup struggled violently until it wore itself out, vomited, and collapsed and lay with dulled eyes and heaving sides. They maintained the chant. The pup recovered and fought the rope again. Then it began to quiet, and soon, as far from them as the rope would permit, it lay down and stared at them.

"Keep it up," Ed said.

"Ohhhhhmmmmmmmmmmmmmmmmmmm."

Josie placed the milk and the meat scraps within the pup's reach, then sat back and joined hands again.

The pup sniffed the food. Keeping its eyes on them, it lapped from the bowl of milk. It snatched a piece of meat and ran to the other side of the log, peering around the end to watch them while it ripped and swallowed the meat.

Ed stopped the chant.

"It'll be all right. By the end of the week he'll be sleeping in your bed with you, Hero, and he'll follow everyone around so that we'll hardly be able to walk without him getting underfoot."

"What's his name?" Hero said.

Ed thought a moment. "Loki."

They all knew, even Hero, that the pup was going to stay with them.

"What does that mean?" Josie said.

"He's an old Teutonic trickster god. One of his sons was a wolf."

"I love you, Loki," Hero called softly. "Do you want to be my doggy?"

The bitch's joy lessened with every passing minute. They hadn't traveled far, or been gone very long, but still she grew nervous and began to falter on the track and look back over her shoulder the way they'd come. She was cresting the moment she'd spin and hurry back when Orph gave tongue over a strong scent. The pack broke into a lope and the bitch was swept up with them. They ran the scent to ground a quarter mile later, a possum burrow. They dug the burrow out, killed the possum and her brood and ate their fill. It didn't take long. Then they turned back. Trotting, the bitch carried a piece of the possum for her pups. The spotted dog brought the carcass of one of the young ones.

The black caught the human scent first, while they were still a little distance from the clearing; he slowed and the hair on his back went up. The pack stopped and lifted their noses to the breeze. Orph growled.

The bitch made a sound of dread, dropped the meat, and went streaking forward. The pack raced after her.

They burst into the clearing. The pups were calling shrilly. Human odor was powerfully mixed with the puppies' fear. The bitch plunged into the den. She clawed back out in terrible agitation. Orph and the black were sniffing by the side of the stream. The bitch ran to them and pressed her nose to the ground. The human scent was dense. She jumped into the basin, sniffing, and smelled her lost pup, and its terror. She wailed and leapt out. She ran around the clearing barking. She rushed to the burrow, crawled halfway in and snarled insanely at her pups, to send them shrinking back in horror; they wouldn't dare to venture out until she returned.

She went back to the basin, took the scent deeply, and turned downstream. Orph and the black and the spotted went beside her.

Josie squinted. "Look," she said, pointing.

Ed and Harriet turned their heads. Hero was lying on his stomach gazing rapturously at the puppy. "What?" said Ed.

"Over there, by the big tamarack."

It was a little past noon and the sun was bright in the yard, but the treeline was shadowy. There was movement near the tamarack.

A dun-colored dog stepped from the shadows.

"I've never seen that one before," Josie said.

A second form detached itself from the gloom and came abreast of the first. It was a German shepherd, big and heavy.

Ed got slowly to his feet.

To the left of the dun, a spotted animal appeared. Then a moment later, a huge black dog moved from the forest to stand beside the others.

"Oh God," Ed whispered. "Oh my God."

Josie stood up. Harriet gathered Hero in her arms and got to her feet.

There was a .30-06 and a box of cartridges in the house. Ed began inching backward.

"Don't say anything, *don't move*," he said in a low urgent

voice. "Now . . . very gently, start making for the house. Whatever you do, keep quiet and don't panic."

"Mommy, what's the matter?" Hero said in alarm. "Who're those dogs?"

"Hush baby, don't say anything." Harriet pulled his face into her shoulder. "Everything is fine, Mommy'll take care of you, just keep still, love."

"Ed?" Josie's voice cracked.

"*Shut up*," he hissed.

The dun dog barked. The puppy answered and went running toward her. It hit the end of the rope and was jerked over on its back. It leapt frantically and screamed.

The dun bitch howled and hurtled forward. The other dogs exploded after her.

"Freeze!" Ed shouted. "Don't move! Even if you get bit —DON'T MOVE!"

The pup swung through an arc at the end of its rope, brushing close to Harriet's feet.

Hero pulled his head around. He saw the dogs rushing toward them. "Mommy! Mommy!" He fought to climb higher up her torso.

She squeezed him tight, trying to stifle his struggles.

The dun dog bit deep into her thigh. She threw her head back and cried out, but she didn't move. Straddle-legged, clutching Hero, she didn't move. The other dogs were poised around her, growling and showing their teeth. The bitch held tight.

Harriet turned her face to the sky, her eyes squeezed shut. "Oh God . . . Please . . . Please . . ."

"Hang on," Ed said desperately. "Hang on, you can do it baby, it'll let go—hang on!"

Several moments passed, in which the only sound was the low rumbling of the circling dogs.

"I can't *stand* it!" Harriet screamed.

"Harriet! Stop!"

Hero screamed. He began to fight crazily against his mother, and Harriet twisted away, dragging the dun with her, and tried to run.

The pack attacked. Harriet and Hero fell beneath them. A rolling jumble of bodies, screaming and snarling.

Josie bolted. The spotted dog went after her. It tore a piece from her buttock.

Ed spun and ran for the house.

Josie crashed into the lower branches of a cedar tree. She pushed herself into the impacted branches; twigs snapped off and the pointed stumps stabbed into her flesh. She clawed over her head for higher branches, locked her hands around them and struggled up. The spotted dog bit into her leg as she pulled herself from the ground. Josie shrieked. The dog hung suspended from her leg a moment, then dropped down. Screaming, Josie fought her way higher.

The black dog hit Ed ten yards from the house. It went up high and took him in the shoulder. The impact sent Ed crashing forward and somersaulting. The black lost its hold and came in again with a roar. Ed threw his hands over his head and pressed his arms to his sides, tucked his chin to his chest and pulled his knees up.

The black bit his hip, tore into his side. Ed clenched his eyes shut. He ground his teeth together. The agony became visible, red lines fractured the darkness of his eyelids. The black had his arm. Freeze. Freeze. Freeze. Ohhhmmmm. God, he couldn't bear it! Ohhhmmmm. Harriet and Josie were screaming. Ohhhmmmmm. Oh help me someone! For the love of God help me! Ohhhmmmm. HELP ME!

The teeth withdrew. He smelled the animal's musty breath, heard its rough breathing.

Ohhmmmm.

Guttural sounds. The screaming stopped.

Ohhmmm.

Ohhmmm.

Someone was sobbing.

Ohhmmm.

"Ed." Josie's quavering voice.

Ohhmmmm.

"Ed. They—" She choked. "They're gone."

His mind was numb.

"Ed, answer me! Please!"

Slowly, shaking, he uncoiled himself. Josie was climbing out of a tree. She was torn and bloodied.

He tried to stand. He fell down.

Josie was on her knees over Harriet and Hero. Her fists were in her mouth and she was biting on them. She rose and came unsteadily to Ed.

"Hero's dead," she said hollowly. "Harriet's still alive, but she's not conscious. She's all—" She shook her head violently.

"Get bandages," Ed rasped. "Sheets, shirts, anything." She knelt beside him.

"I'll be all right," he said. "Hurry!"

She left him. He crawled to Harriet and Hero on his hands and knees. Hero was mutilated. The back of his skull had been crushed. Blood had run from his ears and his eyes. His face was twisted in horror. Harriet lay on her back. One of her breasts had been ripped apart. Bones and gore showed in other wounds. Her eyes were closed and her breath rattled. The ground around them was soggy with blood, and blood still pumped from her flesh.

Ed vomited. He collapsed. He sobbed.

"Ed, I have the bandages. . . . Ed? . . . Ed, stop. We have to help Harriet. Ed!"

She lifted his head. She slapped him. He blinked at her. Her face was drawn and paper-white. She had an armful of bandaging. She carried the rifle in her other hand.

"Come on," she said. "We have to tear these up and stop Harriet from bleeding any more."

Josie kept the rifle close to her while they worked and she raised her head frequently to look at the treeline.

They did the best they could with Harriet, then Josie fashioned compresses and bandaging for Ed. He sat dumbly beside Harriet. Josie put the rifle in his hands. "It's loaded," she said. "Watch for them . . . do you hear me?"

"Yes," he whispered.

Josie went to the house and brought him back a jar of water. "Kathy left her keys," she said. "I'm going for help."

"What if you run into them on the way to the car?"

She held a hunting knife tight in her fist. "They won't," she said. "They're gone." She leaned and kissed him on the forehead.

He began to cry.

"Damn it, stop that! You've got to protect Harriet."

He wiped his arm across his eyes, then across his nose. He bobbed his head. "I'll be okay," he said.

Josie left.

Ed gripped the barrel of the gun with his left hand. He pushed the safety off and slipped the index finger of his right hand into the guard and rested it lightly on the trigger. He stared into the woods.

CHAPTER 11

THE telephone rang. Bauer answered.

"Do you have your radio on?" Ben Nichols asked.

"No, why?"

"Your dogs attacked again. At that commune on Sproul's Mountain."

"Oh no." Bauer closed his eyes.

"They killed a child," Nichols said quietly. "And his mother died on the way to the hospital."

The weight of these new deaths settled over Bauer. He braced against it. "When?"

"A couple of hours ago. They're calling in police from all over the state. They're mobilizing National Guard units."

"Ben, can you load the bike into your truck and get me over there, right now?"

"I don't think you should be in it now, Alex."

"Can you do it?"

"Yes."

"I'll be there in twenty minutes."

Bauer went into the bedroom and changed into Levi's and a wool shirt. He put on his climbing boots. His gear was laid out along a wall of the living room. He pulled the stuff apart, threw food for a couple of days into the pack, a change of pants and socks, compass, fire starter, rain gear and a thermal parka. He belted on a knife. He took the pack and the sleeping bag out to the car.

He caught the news on the way. Spotter planes were already up. State police, sheriff's deputies, constables from neighboring communities, and conservation officers were establishing a perimeter around the mountain's base. Acting on the request of state police Colonel Mulcahey, the governor had ordered five National Guard companies mobilized. Guardsmen were reporting to their assigned armories and trucks bearing the first detachments were expected by the late afternoon. A state police sharpshooter team, accompanied by a tracker, was at the site of the attack, but the effort of the moment was to secure the base of the mountain so that the dogs would not be able to escape it. Colonel Mulcahey had issued a terse statement: "We're going to get them this time." While there was no conclusive evidence, interrogation of the two surviving victims indicated that one of the pack had borne a litter of pups. If this was true, said a conservation department spokesman, then the animals were certain still to be on the mountain. If it was not true, and the dogs had fled the area before it could be sealed, then it was anyone's guess: hundreds of thousands of wilderness acres were accessible to the pack, and without burning half the state down to bare rock, finding them would be more a matter of improbable luck than anything else. Police warned against civilian involvement. Unauthorized persons would be arrested, their weapons confiscated, and they would be heavily fined.

Nichols was waiting in his yard. He'd run the trail bike into the bed of his pickup. A piece of the .270's stock was visible at the top of a leather scabbard strapped to the bike's frame.

Bauer transferred his gear from his car to the pickup. "Thanks, Ben. I appreciate this."

"Alex, this isn't rational. If the dogs are on the mountain, they're not going to get away, and it'll be done whether you're there or not. These people know what they're doing. You don't. They'll find them. It's not your responsibility."

"Yes, it is. I have to find them first. *I* have to find Orph, and no one else."

I loved him. I *love* him. This wasn't his fault. I can't let him be torn apart by a mob. He deserves better. I can't allow him to be debased and butchered like vermin.

"You're crazy," Nichols said.

Bauer didn't answer.

"They're sending a small army up tomorrow morning. You run a very good chance of getting your ass shot off."

"I'm going up there, and I'd like to use all the daylight I can. Can we leave now?"

"What if I said no, I'm not going to help you act like a fool and maybe get yourself killed."

"Then I'd drive into town, buy a rifle, come back and walk up that mountain."

"Okay." Nichols opened the pickup's door. "Get in."

They pulled out of Nichols' drive.

"There's a two-gallon tin of water on the bike and a one-gallon tin of gas. The tank's full. You can get sixty, seventy miles out of that."

Bauer nodded.

"The .38's in the glove compartment. There's a box of shells with it, and another one for the Winchester."

Bauer undid his belt, ran it through the loop of the holstered revolver, and closed it again.

"Here," Nichols tossed him a government Geological Survey Map without taking his eyes from the road. "Find the best side up and tell me where to go."

The elevation lines were widely spaced on the southwest face, the most gradual angle of ascent. Several draws were indicated, too, which would help.

Police cars flashed past them on the drive, sirens wailing and beacons spinning.

Nichols turned off the highway onto a country road, turned again five minutes later. The road was bumpy and densely foliaged on either side. They came upon a parked cruiser. A state trooper stood beside it sweeping his eyes up and down the road. He ignored the truck. A hundred yards ahead, a second trooper kept watch, and 150 yards beyond him they passed another cruiser and a third man.

Nichols lifted his chin toward the treed juggernaut looming on their right. "Sproul's Mountain."

They circled the mountain, passing police cars parked at intervals and officers in various uniforms carrying rifles or pump shotguns who paced slowly, watching the road and the brushline beside it. Men and cars were spaced widely, but there was little terrain that didn't fall under the scrutiny, at some distance or another, of at least one man.

Bauer looked at the map. "Left at the next fork, a quarter mile ahead. Then we go about a mile, it looks to be."

"Give it up, Alex."

"No."

As they neared the point from which Bauer wanted to start, Nichols said, "I'll pull off in the biggest gap I can find between the cops. We'll have to do it fast or they'll grab you. When I set the brake, jump out, drop the tailgate and climb into the bed. There's a two-by-ten next to the bike. Shove it out to me. I'll set it, you wheel the bike down. Toss your pack on your shoulders, you can lash it to the bike later. I'll start it—she's temperamental sometimes—then you get on and go. You'll only have a minute or two."

"Right." Bauer folded the map and slipped it in his shirt, he shoved a box of cartridges into each pocket.

They passed two more cruisers and a couple of policemen. Then a section where the officers were stretched more thinly.

"Okay?"

"Okay."

Nichols swung off the road, stood on the brake pedal and threw the emergency on.

Bauer was out the door. Nichols followed a moment later. Nichols took the bike at the bottom of the plank, straddled it and turned the key.

"Hey! You two guys. Hold it!" A cop 200 yards away was walking toward them.

Nichols stomped on the kick-start. The engine turned over. The cop was running now. Nichols revved the engine, drowning the cop's shouts. Bauer clapped Nichols on the shoulder and swung on. "Thanks!"

He drove off, careful not to hit the throttle hard.

The cop skidded to a halt beside Nichols. "God damn you, stop!" Bauer was drawing away slowly. The cop's face twisted in anger. He raised his rifle.

"You going to shoot a man for riding a motorcycle?" Nichols said.

The cop glared at him, then sprinted after Bauer. He gave it up after a hundred feet and returned to Nichols. "Okay, mother. Get your license and registration out."

"What for?"

"Your buddy might have made it, but you didn't, and you're under arrest six ways from Sunday. Get 'em out!"

Floyd Tyndall was the tracker. He was seventy years old, stoopshouldered to the approximation of a hunched back, and nearly blind in his right eye. He carried a Marlin .32 Special, his favorite deer gun, the one he'd taken the second and third largest trophy bucks in the state with. He was a right-handed shooter, and hadn't been able to switch when he'd begun to lose the use of his right eye more than a decade ago. So he'd had crazy-looking stocks made for his long guns, with wide curves setting them to the right of the barrel line, and telescopic sights mounted inches out to the left of the breech. He still butted the guns to his right shoulder but now he sighted through his left eye, and he could shoot just about as well as ever.

He'd spent an hour leading the three sharpshooters over the first quarter mile of track and they were growing impatient.

Officer Laughlin said, "Hell, they'll be in the next state before we even make the first ridge. They're going straight along the stream, why don't we just haul ass after them?"

"That's where they've gone so far," Tyndall said. "It don't mean that's the way they kept goin'."

"It's the easiest and most logical way."

"For you, but you ain't a dog. I don't think."

Half an hour later they were still edging up the stream and Laughlin's fellow officers agreed with him.

"Well, you boys just charge on up ahead," Tyndall said. "Me, I got to hang around here because I haven't seen no sign atall for a while and your mouthrunnin' don't help me one little bit."

The officers looked down. They were on stoney ground

and couldn't make anything out. Embarrassed, they went silent and followed Tyndall like subdued schoolchildren while he went into the water and across to the other bank, then came back again and shuffled in widening circles muttering to himself. After a little while he stopped and pinched something off a nettle.

He held it up for the troopers. "Ain't deer hair, nor raccoon, nor fox, nor anything you run across in the woods very much. Offhand, I'd say it's from the undercoat of a dog." He rubbed the gray, downish stuff between his thumb and forefinger and let it fall.

Minutes later he had the track again, which angled severely away from the stream.

In the early evening they came upon a clearing. There were dog droppings in the woods around it, paw prints all over, gnawed bones, pressed-down beds in the grass.

"See, this here stream," Tyndall said, "is a feeder into the one they were following at first. About the third or fourth, I'd reckon. If we'd of went bustin' on ahead we'd be standin' someplace God don't even know about scratchin' our butts and figurin' there wasn't a dog around nowhere and we'd best be headin' back before it gets dark."

"Yeah . . . well." Laughlin resented the old man for making a dummy of him. "Well we found it, sure, but I still don't see any dogs, and it *is* going to get dark soon."

Tyndall swiveled his head, looking into the brush and up the rises. "Don't know much about dogs and their habits, but they're around all right. They're watchin' us right now."

Instinctively, the officers raised their guns. They looked about. "How do you know?"

"This much sign, it means they been livin' here a spell. Now a creature like a wild dog's supposed to be, he wouldn't stay in a place this close to people unless he had to. So you got to figure that what those two kids said about a pup, it means there's a she-dog with the pack and she *has* got a litter, right close to us now, and the pack's been bedded here waitin' for 'em to get old enough to travel. And that means, with the pups still too young, the pack's got to stay with 'em, the she-dog anyway. So then you got to figure further that they smelt us and heard us comin' awhile back, and they're hidin' somewhere in these woods, maybe even up by that outcrop there watchin' to see what we're goin' to do."

"How do we find them?"

"We don't. They come to us. Now you boys just split up and stand around the edges here. Keep a sharp eye."

The policemen took positions. Tyndall began quartering the clearing. He paid special attention to the ground around stumps and half-buried boulders.

Crr-ack! A rifle spat. *Crr-ack!* "There, there! A brown dog, it was right up by that twisted spruce!"

The policeman was jabbing his arm. "There, right there! I saw it."

"Did you hit it?"

"I don't know. Jesus Christ, let's go, Tyndall."

"Calm down." Tyndall moved his eyes across the woods. "You wouldn't've seen it unless it wanted you to. It'll show itself again in a bit. But not in the same place, and only for a second. You ain't likely to get a good shot off."

"Jesus, what are you talking about?"

Tyndall was enjoying himself. He didn't like these so-called marksmen. Maybe, their rifles resting on sand-bags, they could pick off a criminal through a window at 500 yards, but they weren't worth a tinker's dam for this.

"One gets me twenty that's the she-dog. And what she's doin' is teasin' you. She wants to draw you off from the pups. She'll get you runnin' after her and she'll show you a little hide every now and then to keep you all hot and bothered, and then when she's led you a couple miles

away, she'll just disappear and you'll be left all alone with
your rifle in one hand and your pud in the other. Just
stand tight. She'll come again."

Ten minutes later she did. She drifted out of a bush
across a short, open space to a dense stand of saplings,
seventy yards up the slope. Laughlin fired three quick
sloppy shots. One of the other officers put two more into
the saplings.

"Well, this isn't going to do," Tyndall said. "You boys
just aren't snapshooters. One of you give me your flashlight." He pushed through brush to the base of a stone
escarpment. "Spotted the den before. Didn't want to do
this, but I guess we got to get you an easy shot somehow."
He lowered himself to his knees, pampering his creaky
joints. "You boys make sure nothin' comes flyin' onto my
back," he warned.

He stretched out, thumbed the light and pushed his
head into the den. Four pups huddled at the bottom. Their
ears were flat against their skulls in fear, their eyes bright
discs in the flare of the flashlight. They climbed atop each
other and showed him their teeth and snarled.

"Now don't you worry," Tyndall said, squirming in and
stretching an arm forward. "No one's goin' to hurt you.
Go easy now."

He closed his hand around one of the pups' forelegs.
The pup jerked and barked and bit at him. Pulling the
pup out, he said, "Ouch! Cut it out. Come on, stop it."
But he didn't mind, he wasn't angry at the pup.

He got a grip on the loose skin over the pup's shoulders, so it couldn't reach him to bite. It began to cater-
waul. The pups in the den raised their voices. Tyndall
hurried to the center of the clearing. "Get around me," he
said, "and watch like you never did before. I don't know
what's comin', but somethin' sure as hell is."

He didn't want to, but he pinched the pup and shook it.

It set up a great racket. Tyndall's eyes darted around the foliage. He held his breath.

At the Treehouse, the bitch had chewed through the rope, picked her pup up in her mouth and trotted into the woods. The pups in the den were wailing when she reached them. They swarmed over her. She soothed them with her tongue until they quieted. Then she brought the big one, Loki, the one who had been taken, outside again. The others tried to follow. She drove them back down. Loki had recovered most of his equilibrium; he'd inherited his sire's character.

Orph was pacing the clearing in a fire of agitation. They could not stay here. This was understood by all. A den, once discovered, was no longer a place of safety and succor to the pups. It became a trap. Orph's hackles rose and fell with the surge of his apprehension. He growled at the woods. He cast for scents with deep breaths. The black and the spotted circled with his unease.

The bitch started up the slope with Loki in her mouth. Orph went beside her, their shoulders brushing. The black and the spotted followed.

They climbed for the better part of an hour. Loki was unhappy carried thus. It was uncomfortable and affronted his dignity. He struggled. The bitch growled around him and hurt him enough to make him stop. She'd never done that before. He was frightened and took it seriously. He remained worried and subdued when she finally set him down and dug out a small burrow in the spongy earth in the center of a tangle of dead, rotted trees.

Orph stalked about while the bitch finished the burrow and pushed the pup into it. She punished the pup, to keep it there. They went back down and the bitch ferried another pup.

On the low ground, as they made their third trip down, they ran up against a wall of human scent, thick with blood hunger. They stopped abruptly and filled their lungs with it. The bitch whined. They were seized by a powerful urge to flee, but that was not possible.

Orph led them forward, into the terrible storm of that scent, crushing his unwillingness.

They approached with excruciating slowness, placing their paws with careful delicacy, bellying the last few yards until they could look over a brushy bluff, through the leaves, down into the clearing.

The men and guns were there, close to the den.

The bitch whimpered.

They waited, tongues hanging out and drops of saliva falling from them to the ground, muscles spasming.

It was hardly bearable.

The bitch moaned. She slipped away. Orph went tensely to his feet. The black and the spotted sprang up. They watched the bitch work her way down closer to the clearing. She stood a long time behind a brush growth, sides heaving. Then she lunged, was in the open for an instant, and behind cover again.

Crr-ack! Crr-ack!

Orph jerked with the shots.

He watched the bitch wait. She scented and listened for pursuit. But the men remained in the clearing. She worked her way further around, exposed herself again, and again was fired upon. Once more she waited for the men to come after her.

She went down on her stomach and lay watching in torment. She twitched. A man approached the den. She jumped to her feet. Her hair lifted. Her tail stiffened.

The pups began to wail. The bitch stepped forward. The men had a pup. The pup screamed.

The bitch pulled her lips back from her teeth and crashed out of the bushes toward the clearing.

"There!" Laughlin slammed the rifle butt to his shoulder: *Crr-ack!*

Tyndall dropped the pup and brought up his own rifle. The bitch was charging down an incline.

The other troopers had their guns up.

Crr-ack! Crr-ack! Ka-pow! Crr-ack! Ka-pow! Crr-ack!

Slugs tore up dirt around her. She came headlong into them.

A slug burned her side.

A slug hit her in the chest and hurled her around. She wobbled, and came on.

Ka-pow! Ka-pow! Crr-ack!

Her shoulder exploded and she cartwheeled.

Ka-pow! Ka-pow!

She was hit in the hip. A slug went through her body and punched out a splinter of rib when it exited.

Crr-ack! Crr-ack!

She struggled up and staggered forward.

She was hammered down.

Gunfire rattled, empty brass cartridge cases clinked against stone.

Slugs thudded into her, gouged the dirt and *pinnnnged* off stone.

She writhed. She choked on her own blood. She bit into the dirt.

Ka-pow! Ka-pow!

One cop dropped his empty rifle, grabbed his service revolver, and cut loose with it.

The bitch's muscles tightened, she humped up, belly

lifting from the ground, back toes curling under, teeth in the dirt, then toppled over on her side and didn't move again.

Several more shots sounded. The firing stopped. The reports rolled echoing up the mountains, dissipating slowly.

Tyndall walked up the incline and stood looking down at the dead, mutilated bitch. The policemen pressed in around him. They were excited and jittery.

"You boys are real good," Tyndall said.

"Goddamn. We sure rolled her."

"You better keep a watch," Tyndall said. "There's three more and they might be in the air comin' for your back right now."

The cops tightened.

Tyndall lowered himself stiffly to a squat. He reached out a veiny, liverspotted hand and rested it on the bitch's head. He patted her head gently.

The officers were reloading. Tyndall didn't have to. He hadn't fired.

Far off to the side, came a long wavering howl.

The officers spun. Two fired at nothing.

Moments later, there was a thin snapping of a branch.

"They're gone," Tyndall said.

"How do you know?"

"Because an animal understands. Not like a thought, and he couldn't put it into words even if he could talk, but he understands all the same. There isn't any reason for them to stay now."

"What about the pups?"

"They were hers. And there's nothing they can do for them now. Nothing," he challenged. "Right?"

They went back to the clearing. Laughlin dragged the bitch by her tail. One of the other officers took out his flashlight and revolver and crawled into the den so that only his buttocks and legs were visible. The shots were dull and smothered. When he tossed out the first small, ruptured carcass Tyndall turned and walked into the woods.

"Hey!" Laughlin called. "Where are you going?"

Tyndall didn't respond. The foliage closed behind him.

"It's gonna get dark soon," Laughlin shouted. "We need help getting out of here."

Tyndall didn't bother answering.

The heavy bike required strength. It collapsed a log he was going over and jammed itself in the pulp and he had to haul it out with brute force. Balance demanded muscle strain. Sometimes the angle was too steep and he had to walk alongside the bike, engine throttled low, the bike half-pulling him up, he half-wrestling it to keep it from toppling over backward. Thickets were broader and denser than they first appeared and he had to stop and bull back the way he'd come. The rugged ground jolted the butt of his spine, put sudden, painful strains on the muscles of his back and shoulders; his kidneys began to ache. Draws narrowed into crevices too steep to climb and had to be backtracked. Sheer cliff faces caused long circling. Leaf-filled holes dropped his front wheel without warning. Once he was pitched over the bars and landed hard on his back, the air rushing from his lungs. A pile of stones skittered from beneath the tires and threw the bike sideways on him, pinning his leg. Nothing broke, but his thigh was badly bruised and the leg stiffened in the next hour and was painful to move. He reached the summit as the sun came to rest on the peak of a mountain to the west. He was sweaty, grimed, and tired.

Shadows seemed to leap across the ground. The sun disappeared. He had an hour of deepening twilight before night was full. Out of the warmth of the sun, and no longer expending energy, the sweat began to dry chillingly on his skin. He changed his damp shirt for a dry one. He took the .270 from its scabbard, made sure the safety was on, and propped the rifle against the fork of a tree branch. He swung out the cylinder of the revolver to check that the chamber beneath the hammer was empty. Hurrying in the thickening darkness, he cut spruce branches to lay beneath his sleeping bag and gathered firewood.

He fixed food when the fire burned down to cooking embers, then boiled water for coffee.

The partial moon was unremarkable. Intermittent clouds obscured the moon and stars. The blackness was dense. He built the fire up, creating a small capsule of light in which he sheltered from the black void that surrounded him, that lay over the earth and mountains as far as he could see, deeper than the sky, a smothering blanket pierced with uncertain temerity by occasional house and cabin lights in the thin valleys that spread like spokes far below him.

He tried to think, but specific inquiry seemed hollow and broader reflection was not possible alone, in the night, atop such a colossus. The mountain's philosophy was mass, its existence stone. All else was fragile and transient.

Somewhere, Orph was on the mountain with him. He knew that. He felt the animal. Rationality would have called that a phantom construct of his desire. But the mountain dwarfed rationality into the meaningless frenzy of a sporing lichen. Orph was with him. They were drawing nearer.

It was time to sleep.

Orph dozed fitfully, ears erect and turning toward creaks and snaps, rustles and little scurries across the leaves, nostrils a-twitch. He opened his eyes frequently and rose to walk about in search of the flesh of the menace that stalked the night. The black and spotted raised their heads to watch him.

Orph stood on a bluff from which the mountain swooped long and unevenly down to the valley. Far, far below he saw a thin ribbon circling off to either side to disappear behind the shoulders of the mountain. Now and then little dots of greater brightness moved slowly along the ribbon. Once or twice he heard a tiny blare of sound that was a horn, and the muffled, indistinct whisper of something like a human voice that was a bullhorn. Rising from the valley on occasional drafts was a great, nearly solid cloud of human scent, streaked round and through with the fire of savagery, of bloodhunt. It was not to be fought; it was to be fled.

Colonel Mulcahey's tie was loose, his sleeves rolled up. His cheeks were stubbled and they itched. His eyes were bloodshot. He'd drunk too much coffee and his stomach was sour. But he'd done it, the big map tacked to the wall of the communications trailer, his command center, was flagged the way he wanted it. The disparate and initially disorganized elements had been welded into a single coordinated force, liaison was smooth and fast, the mobile commissaries had got hot coffee and cold breakfast to everyone, the ammunition had been issued, and platoon leaders were standing by their walkie-talkies. He'd caught his second wind, and now he felt better. It was an hour after dawn.

A trooper opened the door. "Choppers coming, Colonel."

Mulcahey went outside, blinking in the fresh air. He hadn't realized how smoke-filled the trailer had become through the night. He ordered it ventilated.

Three helicopters were floating toward them through the deep notch between a pair of mountains to the south. The sound of their rotors became audible—*whackatawhackatawhackata*—then filled his ears, and the helicopters were hovering over the treetops across the road, downdrafts whipping branches about and billowing clouds of dust and stinging pieces of grit. The men around the trailer put their hands over their faces and turned their backs.

Mulcahey went back in and spoke to the pilots over the radio. He went to the window and watched a helicopter soar off to either flank and disappear around the mountain. The one remaining passed directly overhead and moved 300 yards up the slope in front of the waiting police and guard line.

The radioman waited in his chair.

"All right," Mulcahey said, "move them out."

"Command to all units. Signal green. I repeat. Command to all units. Signal green."

Around the base of the mountain, like a noose being tightened up a cone, Mulcahey's forces stepped forward and began to climb.

The scent broke over them in heightening waves. The black and the spotted trembled, watching Orph move back and forth across the bluff.

At last he spun, unable to resist the jangling alarms of

his cells any longer, and they rushed to meet him with sweeping tails.

Orph leapt over the poles of the scrambled deadfall and thrust his head into the small mouth of the burrow. He roared at the two pups. They cowered back and mewled.

He struck into the woods with the black and the spotted.

They ran with their heads high and tails flowing back, circling to gain the far slope, where there would be the hard bulk of the mountain between them and the men, where they could flee down the side to the valley, and up other mountains, until the air was cleansed of men and their slaughter.

But the scent, which was nearly palpable now, stayed always at their side, edging them higher, and it channeled across their path, and they were unable to plunge through it, it was there, always, in front of them, and grudgingly Orph gave way to its relentlessness and turned higher, to find and top the thickness and come down its other side.

Several times, as the morning passed, a strident thing in the air approached them, and Orph led them to cover and they crouched looking upward even though they could not see and waited until the racket thinned to nothingness, and then they ran again.

By midday, Mulcahey's forces were halfway up. The ring was shrinking and thickening. Soon he'd begin ordering units to drop out at staggered intervals, so he wouldn't lose efficiency to density.

Clearing logistics problems along the way had taxed him and finally begun to drain his reserve strength, but he knew he could keep his mind clear and stay on his feet until sunset, when the circle would be closed. Not one sighting had been reported, and he couldn't prevent an infiltration of unease, but his conviction and confidence remained firm.

In the early afternoon he consented to see the reporters, consented in the service of his own morale.

The sun was falling down meridian. Bauer didn't have his watch. He guessed it to be around three-thirty, four o'clock.

Standing on a high jut of rock and looking down through the rifle's scope at its highest magnification, he could see small figures beating their way slowly upward. He reckoned they'd reach the top in two hours.

He walked back off the jut and sat at the bottom of the thirty-foot spine of bald rock that was the crest of the mountain. The ground around him was stoney and what grass grew there was tough and rasp-edged and sere. In a semicircle, at a distance of a hundred yards or less, was the end of the treeline: twisted, water-starved trees, hideous and awesome in the frantic intensity of their survival.

Bauer sat with the rifle across his knees.

His body was still, but within, he convulsed and sickened under the chaotic turbulence that flung Orph back and forth across the mountain, drawing him ever nearer.

The racketing came upon them when they were clawing up a barren ridge. Orph scrambled the last few feet and raced into cover, the black at his side. The spotted dog fell and slid halfway down the ridge. It stopped against a boulder and lunged upward again.

"Contact! Contact!" the radioman shouted.

Mulcahey threw a switch that sent the signal through the general speaker.

"—on the top, running now, into—"

"This is Mulcahey," the colonel interrupted. "Identify yourself."

"—a stand of . . . This is Abel Bird, Colonel."

"Give me your coordinates." The pilot did. Mulcahey said, "Where is he now?"

"We're coming up on brush growth, maybe fifteen hundred square feet, he made it in there, he's out of sight now."

Mulcahey paused, then said, "Get right over the top. Go down as low as you can. Hold there. Jockey back and forth if you have to. Beat him out with your downdraft and take him when he breaks. If he won't break, keep your position until the ground forces reach you, and pour some fire in there."

The pilot moved his two-man open-doored craft over the brush. The trooper seatbelted next to him carried a 12-gauge riot gun. The downdraft whipped the brush around.

Crouched in the black shadow of a layered rock ledge, Orph and the black watched the helicopter lash the brush around and raise a storm of dust and leaves. Orph pricked his ears and creased his brow. His teeth showed. The black hugged the ground, ears against his skull and eyes squinted.

The spotted dog trembled beneath the branches. Topping the ridge, it hadn't seen Orph and the black and it had run in panic from the swooping machine to a stand of brush and hurled itself within. Above it now was a deafening roar that hurt its ears and shook the organs in its belly. Branches whipped down at it. Twigs and small stones hailed into it. The world was being torn apart. It could endure no more. It sprang to its feet and bolted through the heaving brush and into the open.

"There he goes!" The gunner shouted. "Eleven o'clock!"

The spotted dog was streaking across a field of high grass and wildflowers. The pilot swung the helicopter out and around in a tight loop and went after it, gaining fast. The gunner leaned out the door, shotgun to his shoulder.

The shadow and the screaming noise of the machine fell over the dog. It couldn't escape. It whirled and snarled up at the huge thing looming over it.

The pilot slowed and tilted the helicopter over on its side to give the gunner a clear shot.

The dog stretched up, teeth snapping.

Whammm!

The blast struck the dog in the hindquarters and slammed it against the earth. The helicopter's rotors flattened a wide circle of grass around the animal. The dog twisted and bit at its wound. It jerked its head back up toward the helicopter, tried to rise, and clashed its teeth on empty air.

Whammm!

The second charge drove it into the ground and nearly decapitated it.

The pilot clapped the gunner on the shoulder. Hovering at thirty feet, he radioed in his kill.

Mulcahey acknowledged. "Did you see the other two?"

"Negative. He was all alone."

"Can you land?"

The pilot studied the ground. "Affirmative."

"Then set down and pick up the carcass. Bring it down to command center. We'll give the reporters something to photograph."

The pilot brought the helicopter to earth. The gunner unbuckled and jumped out, bent beneath the rotors and unconsciously shielding his head with an arm, he hauled the dog into the bubble and belted up with his feet on the body. The helicopter rose and went skimming down the mountain.

Orph and the black fled.

Orph was in a frenzy. He wanted to turn and charge into the human scent that beat upon him in wave after wave, into the dim shouts, and attack, plunge teeth into meat and destroy. But the primeval wisdom of his blood held him in check and forced him higher yet, away from the vast, many-headed predator whose killing-lust was acrid in his nostrils.

They circled half around the mountain again, stopping to rest with loud pants only minutes at a time, then forcing on again. This high, the mountain was greatly narrowed, and growing smaller.

A helicopter appeared in the distance while the black was collapsed on his side, eyes glassy, and came smoothly toward them. Orph rushed into a tree stand. The black groaned and struggled up. The helicopter was coming too fast for him to reach the trees. He veered and ran down a brushy ravine, squirmed beneath a fallen tree. The helicopter passed by. The black went over on his side with a groan.

He lay a long time, letting the pound of his heart subside, his vision clear. His muscles began to stiffen. He was desperately thirsty. He groaned and dragged himself out of the ravine. He didn't see Orph, he couldn't find Orph's scent.

He traveled until he found water. It was only damp

earth, but he dug out a muddy pool and then he drank from it. He heard voices, the crackling of brush. He ran from the pool, his mind empty and his body functioning without his direction.

A guardsman blinked and said, "Christ." He brought his rifle up. Eighty yards, he estimated, moving at a perfect transverse. Big and black. He'd only seen a flash. Might be a bear, but he didn't think so. Behind leaves now. Nothing to see. He swung the muzzle, matching what he guessed to be the animal's speed.

A gap. Dog! But not time enough to fire.

He flicked his eyes ahead. The dog would have to pass through an open space in ten yards. The guardsman swung his rifle, checked, waited. The dog appeared. The guardsman tracked, and squeezed off a shot.

The dog was knocked over. The guardsman fired again and missed. The dog was up and running crookedly, then out of sight.

"Dog!" The guardsman shouted. "I hit him! Over here! Hurry!"

Guardsmen converged, crackling through the brush. "Right up there in that opening." The clustered guardsmen split into three groups. One went directly up, the other two climbed the flanks.

They found a blood spoor and went jogging along it. Over rocks and deadfalls, under a low arch formed by two boulders, past a pool of blood where the animal had fallen and been unable to rise for some moments. The spoor led into a tight growth of scrub laurel. Guardsmen split to either side and took up stands. Three went in to beat the laurel.

The woods were quiet save for the cracking and snapping within the laurel.

Then the black dog burst out in a staggering run, trailing a rope of bluish intestine. Six guardsmen opened fire.

Their M-16s spun 5.56-caliber cartridge cases into the air.

The black dog fell. The hail of slugs splintered bones and shattered his jaw, ruptured organs and punched puffs of dust and gouts of blood from his flesh, tore pieces from him for half a minute after he was dead. The guardsmen swarmed up to the corpse.

Shadows were lengthening, the sunlight was a deep orangish gold.

There had been a fusillade of muffled shots a quarter hour ago. The drone of the circling helicopters was growing louder, and to his right Bauer could hear occasional indistinct sounds of men calling to one another, a crackle of static from a communications device. His hands sweated lightly on the rifle.

He rose and walked from the spine of rock to the center of the plateau. He stopped. He called Orph in his mind.

Orph gave way before the pressure; snarling, he turned and climbed straight up. His claws dug into the earth and scratched against stone. Blind, murderous rage seized him. He went growling and grinding his teeth, lungs swelling and muscles bunching, foam billowing around his jaws.

He rushed through the gnarled trees, shaking his massive head.

A roar stiffened Bauer. He jerked around.

Orph was bounding toward him, jaws gaping.

Bauer's hands locked on his rifle, but he didn't raise it. "Orph!" he shouted. "No! Down!"

A sound struck deep into Orph's brain. The rhythm of his charge faltered.

"Down!" Bauer shouted. "ORPH—*DOWN*!"

A tightly encysted capsule burst in Orph's mind. The memory erupted and came flooding out like the tonnage of water through the breached wall of a reservoir, and his legs floundered beneath him, and he missed a step, and a scream rose silently within him, filled him, and his motions became spastic, and he dropped his head, and came to a quaking halt, and he howled up into the empty sky. He whimpered.

Him! *Him!*

The memory was warmth and the ecstasy of love, transports of pleasure, a bond of textural richness, adoration, an engorgement of rapture.

Twenty yards away, the dog hung its head and shook violently.

"Good boy," Bauer said with tears filling his eyes. "Good boy, that's my *good* dog. Oh, sweet baby."

Orph cried.

Bauer set the rifle down and stepped away from it.

"Come," he said softly. "Come, Orph. Good boy."

The dog stepped forward, hesitated.

"Come," Bauer said.

Orph crouched low, his tail went between his legs. He came slinking, whining.

Bauer squatted. He held his hands out. "That's my good boy. Come, Orph, come. That's my big good puppy. That's my baby. Good boy."

The dog bellied up to him. It hung its head and peeped up shyly. It licked tentatively at Bauer's fingers. Its tail swished uncertainly.

Bauer took its head gently in his hands and stroked back

to the matted ruff. Tears spilled from his eyes. "You came home. You're my good boy, my good boy. That's my dog, it's all right now. Everything is all right, you came back to me." He forced back a sob.

The dog whined anxiously and licked the tears from Bauer's cheeks. It made a little *blurff* of a sound.

Bauer hugged the animal tightly and rubbed and petted it. Orph licked his ear and his hair. The dog's tail beat on the ground.

Bauer squeezed his eyes closed. "*Oh God!*" he said, clasping the dog. He drew a shaky breath. Orph nibbled at his chin and whined.

"Yes, I love you too. I love you, Orph. You're my good dog. You're a funny puppy. Big puppy. Good dog. Pretty baby."

The dog rolled over and splayed its legs open. Bauer rubbed its broad, hard chest. Orph groaned and wriggled in euphoria and love.

"Good dog, good boy," Bauer repeated, massaging the animal.

Orph's tail pounded wildly. His mouth was open and his tongue hung out, the corners of his lips were drawn up in bliss.

Bauer heard a man call.

Orph, ravished with Him, was oblivious.

Bauer sat back from the dog. Orph wrestled himself up and sat next to Bauer, pressing against Bauer's side and licking his face.

Another muted voice. Orph licked Bauer's mouth. Bauer laid his hand on the dog's broad skull and rubbed it.

"What's that! What is it!" he said, snapping his eyes to the treeline.

The dog swiveled its head. It cocked its ears and frowned. A tentative rumble sounded in its chest.

"Good boy," Bauer said.

He slipped the .38 from its holster and placed the muzzle an inch from the base of Orph's skull.

"That's my good boy, *my good boy*," he choked. He fired.

Orph was flung forward. His front legs lay straight back beneath his chest and belly. His jaw rested on the ground. A tiny sliver of bone protruded from the bullet's exit hole. His eyes were open. He was perfectly still.

Bauer lowered the gun. He laid his hand between the dog's shoulders and he patted gently. "You're my good dog," he whispered, "my good dog."

His head sank toward his chest and he wept.

He was empty and silent when the first guardsman stepped from the trees with a rifle at port arms. Others followed in moments, a squad of a dozen young men led by a thin corporal with a moustache and long neat sideburns. They approached Bauer, who was seated next to Orph, indecisively. They formed a circle around him. The corporal cleared his throat. "Who are you? What happened here?"

Bauer uncoiled himself and stood up. "He was my dog," he said looking down at Orph.

The corporal screwed up his face. "Your dog?"

Bauer didn't answer.

"You shot him?"

Bauer nodded.

The corporal radioed a report over walkie-talkie down to an officer lower on the slope, who relayed it to Command. Bauer stared at the dog.

The corporal received instructions. "Potter," he said.

"Get that dog up on your shoulders. We'll switch off with it on the way down."

"No," Bauer said.

"What?"

"No. He stays up here. I want him to stay here."

"That's not possible," the corporal said. "Pick him up, Potter."

The pistol was hanging from Bauer's hand. He cocked and raised it and pointed it at the corporal's chest.

Several guardsmen lifted their rifles. "Put those down," the corporal ordered, not moving his eyes from Bauer's. "Come on, Mr. Bauer," he said evenly. "This is trouble. You don't want to do it."

"I'm going to bury my dog up here."

The pistol didn't waver.

"Can I use my radio?"

Bauer said nothing.

The corporal handled the walkie-talkie with care. "Uh, I have a problem up here," he said, staring at Bauer. "The guy Bauer is holding a cocked pistol pointblank at my chest. He says we're not bringing the dog down, he's going to bury it up here. I'd like instructions, please."

The answering voice was tinny. "Is he serious?"

"Yeah, I think so."

"Do you believe he'd shoot?"

"I wouldn't want to gamble either way."

"Any chance you can disarm him?"

"Not before he could get off a shot."

"Hang on. I'll call Command."

After a short silence the voice returned. "Ask him if he'll surrender his weapon and submit peacefully to arrest if he's allowed to bury the animal."

The corporal raised his eyebrows at Bauer.

"Yes," Bauer said.

"He will."

"All right. Do it his way then. Can a chopper land there?"

The corporal gauged the terrain. "Not likely."

"Can you get down with lights in the dark?"

"No problem."

"Then start as soon as the dog is buried. Let me know when you jump off."

"Wilco. Over and out."

The pistol steady, Bauer said, "Take your men back into the trees. I'll join you when I'm done."

"Do you give me your word on that?"

"Yes."

"Okay. Try to be as fast as you can though, huh? Gene, leave Mr. Bauer your entrenching tool."

The guardsmen withdrew.

Bauer holstered the revolver and dug out a grave. The stoney soil permitted only a shallow hole. Bauer eased Orph in and laid the carcass on its stomach, crossed the paws and positioned the head resting atop them. He closed Orph's eyes. He laid his hand on top of the big head and patted it, once.

He built a cairn of stones over the grave to ensure that nothing would dig it up.

He walked into the trees, to the guardsmen.

It was late at night when they reached the foot of the mountain. He was taken to the state police barracks outside Covington and interrogated, then brought to a judge where he was formally charged and ordered to appear before the bench in two days. He was released on his own recognizance. A trooper drove him home.

Dawn was breaking. He washed, shaved and changed

into a clean shirt. He got in his car and went back to Covington.

The lights were on in Elizabeth's house, though it was early. He'd expected to wait in the car.

She answered the door in slacks and a sweater, groomed, her hair brushed.

He said, "I found Orph."

"I know, I heard it on the news last night. I thought you might come." She paused, searching his face. "I hoped you would."

"May I come in?" Bauer asked.

She stepped aside and held the door for him. "I'll make breakfast," she said. "There's coffee on."

Loki and the bitch-pup waited in the burrow until they were driven from it by thirst and hunger so great that punishment held no terror for them.

They called and whimpered in the bright sun, while the woods rustled around them, but no one answered and no one came. No one.

Loki found them water in the midafternoon. He tried to catch a frog. He couldn't, the bitch-pup circled around and drove it back, then he pounced and caught it under his paws, bit, ripped off a leg and a piece of the soft body and gobbled it down. He seized the head while the bitch-pup sank her teeth into its midsection and they tore it apart and ate it.

They slept curled together on a bed of leaves in a rock crevice that night. Loki slept lightly. Sharp sounds snapped his eyes open and he lifted his head to growl.

The sun rose and they left the crevice and sat in the light and called again, and in a while, when no answer came, they set off to find something to eat.